Saving

Angelfish

A TIN HOUSE NEW VOICE

Saving Angelfish

MICHELE MATHESON

TinHouseBooks

Published by Tin House Books, Portland, Oregon,
and New York, New York

Distributed to the trade by Publishers Group West, 1700 Fourth St.,
Berkeley, CA 94710, www.pgw.com

While portions of this novel are derived from real events, the
characters are fictional, composites drawn from several individuals
as well as the author's imagination. No reference to any person,
living or dead, is intended or should be inferred.

ISBN 0–9773127–6-3
First U.S. edition 2006

www.tinhouse.com

For my mother and father

one

MAX LIES ON the beach with one night clean. The sickness is beginning, and still, she has an odd, vaguely familiar feeling of being alive. Considering it's a typical Los Angeles winter morning, about fifty degrees, and she's down to a hundred pounds, not a lot of hair on her head, and coming off heroin, she's surprised she hasn't frozen to death. She can thank a Canadian postwoman's jacket for that. The ocean's rushing and waiting sounds put everything into perspective. It rumbles and sighs like it's lonely. She listens.

The surf is a force to be reckoned with. Sometimes it's calm. It sleeps and dreams. And underneath, the fish, the plants, they move like eyes rolling back and forth under the surface of an eyelid. Other times the sea swells like a heart. A big wave could kill me, Max thinks. She sees herself float on it. The sun is drying the salt in her eyebrows and nose. It's easy to appreciate these things when it seems you're going to die.

Max sneezes. Her eyes water and she wipes them. She holds her hands in front of the sun to block the light. The waves come at her. They come in and go out again, over and over. The ocean is either very giving or it's completely nuts.

The veins on Max's hands are green—same color as the Pacific. The idea of relief floats into her mind: sticking the needle in real fast and hard, pushing down on the plunger instead of a careful tap tap tap. That would feel good.

Then she remembers Ernest's line: "What would love do?"

Max had looked at Ernest from where she sat; on the toilet, balancing the needle and the bag of dope on her lap, holding the warm crack pipe in her hand. It wasn't a test question—his mind wasn't made up yet. His white knuckles squeezed the doorknob. The other hand he put in his pocket because he wanted to punch the door or smash the crack pipe in the tub, but he'd done that before. She knew that he was asking her to make his decision. What should she have said? Love would never leave? She watched the tentacle connecting them fall to the floor. Her cells tightened, suffocating what light was left inside her.

"I don't know," she'd said. *If he would just stop looking at me and shut the damn door, I can finish this hit.* She'd had the urge to throw a bar of soap at him so he'd get out.

Ernest, like he was sorry, like he was wrong, said, "It would save me from you." And then he left.

The sand is hard under her body. Her legs ache. Inside her chest is a pain like something belongs there.

How do people love one another? Max pretends she's the ocean reaching for the shore. No one is on the beach. She imagines it's summer. She sees kids and adults throwing themselves at the waves, diving in them, turning their backs to them. The waves just take it and come back for more.

They never stop.

Max daydreams about her parents. She guesses it's been almost two years since she's been home. Yesterday she got up the nerve to call Phyllis. Phyllis was on her way to the oral surgeon. Max's father, Eddie, was there to drive her so Phyllis really couldn't talk. Eddie wants Phyllis to cut off all communication with Max like he has. Max imagines Eddie and Phyllis driving in comfortable silence in Eddie's car. They've been divorced twenty years now.

Soon it will be high tide; the waves are louder. Maybe it's smart to know how much the heart can take, and just play it safe. It's possible to kill parts of it, the parts that want to be loved back. That's what monks probably do.

"I think I'm going to live," Max imagines Phyllis saying, her blond and gray hair sprawled on her pillow. By now, Max figures, the Vicodin will have taken the edge off Phyllis's recent dental surgery. Phyllis, a deceiver of age and time (she's sixty-five), has earned her place in her rose-covered bed, which has little clusters of rib bones (remnants left by her Wheaton terrier, Zelda), red licorice, and a Christmas catalog containing potential gifts for her grandchildren, of which Phyllis has zero. A Tupperware bowl holding the remains of her regular breakfast of figs, prunes, and raisins soaked in gin sits on a tray at the end of the bed, along with her laptop. Zelda lies on her back, her head on the pillow next to Phyllis, enjoying a lazy rub. Zelda and Phyllis have exactly the same color sandy hair.

Sitting in a white wicker rocking chair, wearing tennis shorts, striped socks over his skinny ankles, and perfect silver hair, a Buddy Rich tune stuck in his head, is Eddie. He is drumming a beat with his fingers on the arms of the chair. Thirty years ago he used to run with Buddy. He went to every one of Buddy's Los Angeles gigs. Sometimes Buddy would let Eddie sit in. Eddie sold the drum set Phyllis gave him when he moved into his own apartment up the street twenty-two years ago.

"What about Max? Do you think she'll live?" Phyllis asks. She presses the old red rubber ice pack harder onto her cheek.

Eddie keeps drumming, the tap of his foot building into a crescendo. Before he stopped contact with her ten months ago, he'd occasionally leave messages on Max's answering machine with no words, just a rapid and gleeful jazz pattern, making the most of the tonal quality of pots and pans. On one recording, he did sing to her, "I can't carry a tune in a bucket, I can't carry a tune in a bucket. I can't carry a tune, can't carry a tune, I can't carry a tune so I say fuck it." Eddie thought she had cleaned up and eventually felt the fool when he looked at Max's eyes one night when she and Ernest were over at Phyllis's for dinner. Her pupils were pinned as if the sun were beating down on her. That's when he stopped talking to her.

"Max," Phyllis repeats.

Eddie drums a slow steady beat and the rocking chair becomes a metronome. Phyllis stares out the window and picks at her cuticles. The half a pinky finger she chopped off carving a pumpkin never bends because the doctor sewed it back on wrong. In task, she always appears good mannered and dainty.

"I'm not going to sit with you all day, you know," Eddie says.

"Good," she replies. They both gaze at a vase filled with yellow roses, orange lacing the edges of the petals. The baby's breath indicates that these aren't roses from her garden. But that doesn't bother Eddie. He has no reason to be jealous.

"Have you heard anything from her?" he asks.

"None of your beeswax." Phyllis keeps staring at the flowers. She thinks they're pretty, but they change every day. If you cut the stems diagonally and change the water on a daily basis, they stay pretty longer. Phyllis is a painter of roses and she will never grow old. "Actually, no." Phyllis looks at her painting of a perfect white one preserved inside a dark blue background and finally says, "I haven't. I was making sure."

The ocean has now reached Max's sneakers. If I lie here, she thinks, and don't move, and let the water wash over me, I will stay clean today. If I can take the cold, I can be strong enough. Maybe the pill lady will be selling at the clinic. No methadone this time. Some antihistamines will help, too.

When she drove by Eddie's apartment building on the way to the beach this morning, there was a sign in front that said Sold. What the hell is he supposed to do?

The basement of Phyllis's house had been converted into an apartment. After she divorced Eddie and married a sad alcoholic, and then divorced him too a few years later, she bought a house two blocks from Eddie in hopes that he would help out with Max. Eddie wasn't too happy about the situation at first since it meant seeing Phyllis regularly, but eventually he began picking Max up from school and even coming inside their house and talking for a few minutes. Max became a teenager there, and Eddie and Phyllis became friends. Years later, when Max lived in the basement apartment, she kept things under control and neither Phyllis nor Eddie knew. But one afternoon Phyllis found Max unconscious against the tree in the front yard, and, at Eddie's insistence, she kicked Max out.

Eddie could have moved into the basement, but he's been content in his rent-controlled place for the past twenty years. Though he may no longer have a choice; the old cottage-style complex is going to be torn down and replaced with a generic condo. Eddie's probably been waiting them out. Being seventy-three with a heart condition has one advantage: it buys him time from the new owners to find another place.

The ocean has soaked Max's socks. Her feet are cramping from the cold water, but soon they'll become numb. She wills it, and concentrates.

Eddie says, "I looked at an apartment yesterday. It was dark and had a view of a dumpster. Awful. Today I'm supposed to look at a retirement complex. Could be pretty neat. There's a community kitchen and dining room. For breakfast and lunch, I can use the kitchen. At dinner they feed us, so at least I wouldn't have to cook for myself every night. I wonder what kind of slop they have."

"You're really depressing me," Phyllis says.

"Hey, stop it. It could work—I like Spam and airplane food." Ten years in the Marine Corps had cultivated Eddie's appreciation for processed food.

Max clutches the fabric inside the pockets of her coat. She's afraid that sitting around with a bunch of old farts talking about ailments and medications will kill Eddie. He doesn't like bingo or bridge. Max feels hot wax melting inside her chest. She wonders, when people get old, don't their expectations of others grow old too? Can expectations ever die?

"You are not a normal old person. You don't belong in a place like that," Phyllis tells Eddie; she drinks in the vision of her fresh roses again and falls more deeply into the Vicodin.

"I want a piece of licorice," Eddie says. He gets up from the chair. Now he is antsy. "Give me a piece of licorice. No, don't move. Rest your face." Eddie leans against the high bed and tugs a rope of licorice from the tub. He pops it in his mouth and starts chewing loudly, smacking his tongue against the roof of his mouth, exposing bits of the red stuff.

"You're disgusting and obnoxious," Phyllis says. "Are you hungry? There's leftover Chinese in the fridge."

"Are you going to eat it later?"

"Does it look like I can chew?" Phyllis decides she'd rather be watching a movie.

"I'll eat it later. I'm going to go look at this place."

"The old folk's home?" Phyllis's gin figs are mixing with the Vicodin, making thoughts hard to find.

"Jawohl. I wish you wouldn't—goddamnit, it's a place to live. Don't look at me like that. Okay, it's a fucking hippie commune for people who happen to be over sixty-five! I'm just looking around, exploring my options." Eddie never means to lose his cool, and he was supposed to be there to take care of Phyllis before she passed out.

"Edward. Edward, will you stay here a little while? I want to talk at you."

"Phil, stop it." He had intended to stay longer, but he needs to finish a crossword puzzle, or watch the news, or boil some eggs for a tuna salad.

"Don't, Eddie. I'm not saving the place for her."

"It's been empty two years. I'd think you need the money."

"But see how things work out. Now it's available for you."

"I don't need it."

"Eddie, I would like it if you stayed with me. I mean, downstairs. I finally washed her blood off the ceilings and the bathroom and cleaned the stove and the drawers. Everything. We can paint the whole place yellow. Bright yellow."

"I was going to do that."

"But you never did."

Max likes the way Eddie looks at Phyllis for just a second before he kisses her on the forehead.

"Call me if you need me." Eddie walks down the hall into the kitchen. He peeks in the fridge at the Chinese food and decides he'll let it go for a while. Two full garbage bags spread open on the floor are attracting flies. Eddie ties knots and carries the bags outside to the trash cans still on the street. He rolls the cans to the side of the house and notices the hose isn't coiled properly. He fixes it and leaves before he can notice anything else.

Phyllis lies in her bed. Perfect timing. Her television automatically turns on because she programmed *The Postman Always Rings Twice* with Lana Turner and John Garfield. Zelda gnaws at a beef bone at the foot of the bed.

Max's legs are underwater. Did she say her whole body had to be wet and she'd stay clean or are her legs enough? She wipes her leaky nose, takes deep breaths as her legs get used to the cold. The chill distracts from all the other aches.

People can go lifetimes without just stopping for a second. Max resists getting up. She thinks of Eddie and Phyllis again. Ernest. He stood still and everything stopped.

Max rolls to her side, soggy, and sits on her knees. Her heels press into the seat of her pants. In the hard sand with her finger, she writes: *I remember you. Please remember me, like I remember you. I'm alive.* She walks on her knees to touch fresh sand and finish. *I'm in here somewhere. You are everywhere. What do I do?* She is writing to no one in particular, but the ocean has always had answers. Max checks the date on her pager. She signs it: *Max Gordon. December 16, 2000.*

Still on her knees, she warms her hands in her armpits and reads the scribbled letters. The waves creep forth. Colder than she's ever been, she stands up and starts walking before she sees the ocean take another word. She'll go to Lenny's house. Hopefully he wants to be clean today, too.

two

THE OLD STREET lamp outside Phyllis's bedroom window has died and the early morning sun pushes through cracked white shutters. Most trees in Los Angeles don't surrender their leaves in winter. But the tree just outside the window has let all its leaves turn brown. They fall and scratch the sidewalk and gather in the geraniums and petunias in her window boxes.

Zelda springs onto the bed, onto Phyllis's stomach, waking her, and then jumps back to the floor. When Max was four, they had Lamb Chop. One day, Max laid her head on Lamb Chop's chest and heard that her heart didn't hold its usual hypnotic beat. She made Phyllis listen, and Lamb Chop was rushed to an animal hospital, where she immediately died. Every one of Phyllis's dogs since has resembled Lamb Chop: sad-eyed, wheat-colored.

Subscribe now and save up to 70%*

BEST DEAL

☐ 1 year WWD Print–just $149
(50 weekly + 250 digital daily issues)

☐ 6 months WWD Print–just $89
(25 weekly + 125 digital daily issues)

NAME (please print)

TITLE

COMPANY

ADDRESS

CITY

STATE

ZIP

EMAIL (required to receive WWD Daily Digital)

J5H1NCAR2

Phyllis lies still. She feels hot because the heating pad under her back is still on. Bursitis is a bitch. With her eyes stuck closed, she reaches for the morning eyedrops. During the night her eyes dry up. Insomnia has plagued her for years, and she thinks it takes all her God-given energy to sleep, so much so that it sucks the liquid right out of her. Phyllis fumbles around in the bamboo basket beside her bed, discarding hangnail clippers, pens, Primatene Mist, half-checked to-do lists, dental floss, a cordless phone, a tiny tape player, and nail polish, for the bottle she deftly unscrews. She squirts drops into the corners of her eyes. It seeps in, stinging and then burning, like it's never going to stop.

"Oh, no!" Phyllis has used the antifungal drops that are for her fingernails. "Oh, Jesus!" The phone rings. This is the third time she's done this within the month. To help her, Phyllis's friend had painted the eyedrop bottle with red nail polish. "How can I see that?" Phyllis shouts now. She lets the phone ring while she rinses her eyes. During a particularly rough patch when she was smoking a lot of pot, she punctured a cornea with her mascara brush. Another time, squeezing an eyelash curler tightly around her lashes, she sneezed. It took fourteen months to grow a new set. Phyllis has learned patience from having to be patient with herself and her frequent calamities.

She hears her daughter's voice on the machine down the hall. "Hello? Ma, you awake? Sorry if I woke you. I know I'm not supposed to call, but I'm going to wait. I'll wait here on the phone." Phyllis knows she shouldn't pick it up, but it was so nice to hear Max's voice last week. Eddie will be angry. On Max's birthday, she did well when she resisted calling.

Phyllis hangs her head over the sink, reaches for her pink towel without looking. When she presses the towel against her eyelids it feels like potato chip crumbs are stuck under there. She runs to the cordless phone next to her bed.

"Max."

"Mama," Max pants. "How's your tooth?"

At the sound of Max's voice, Phyllis decides she must stay close to the surface of things. "I just poured a gallon of my fungus drops in my eyes again, almost broke my neck getting into the bathroom. It all really fucking hurts."

"When your eyes get fucked up, it probably means there's something you don't want to see," Max says.

"Funny you should tell me that."

She hears Max sigh.

Then Phyllis says, "You're all I see."

"I just wanted to see if you are okay, and tell you I'm good. And it's good what you and Dad are doing. But—"

Phyllis squeezes her eyes shut. "But what?"

"Maybe I can come home for Christmas."

Phyllis wants to ask her where she is. "You know the conditions, honey."

The tears burn.

"How's Dad? How's his heart?"

"He's doing fine."

"I broke it."

"No, you didn't." Phyllis feels the urge to hurl the phone against the mirrored closets and it makes her disappointed with herself. She has analyzed these moments of anger in the past and described them as "displaced." Her Al-Anon group told her she was experiencing sheer powerlessness. Phyllis hates weakness; it's unattractive.

"What he's got is a clogged carotid artery, Max. He's got three stents now, so don't worry about it." She rips a tissue from the box next to her bed.

"How?" Max sniffles. "Well, you might want to stop seeing your faults in everything."

"What?"

"So you stop getting the eye problems. Just see things for what they are." Max coughs and says, "Anyway, sorry they sting, sorry if—Sorry."

"No, it's okay." Phyllis resists rubbing her eyes and blows her nose instead. "I'm going. Got to clean my eyes."

Max doesn't say anything.

"I'll never stop seeing you," Phyllis says, trying to sound cheerful. She presses the phone harder against her ear and holds her breath so she can hear Max breathe.

"Bye, Mama."

"Max?" Max has already hung up. The phone beeps when Phyllis presses the off button. She sits on her bed, holding the phone, caressing the numbers with her thumb, and thinks about calling Eddie. The pain in her tooth that had the abscess reminds her to take a Vicodin, and she does. Phyllis presses Play on her tape player and lies there listening to Deepak Chopra, waiting to float.

@

Max is sitting in front of a coffee table in her friend Lenny's apartment, thankful she's safe from the sky dogs and the cops. Lenny works for the airlines so he's out buying urine from one of his neighbors because he has to give a sample today. He lets Max stay with him when she needs to as long as she straightens up after herself. He has a nice set-up in Mar Vista next to the park. It must remain tidy, he says, because sometimes he watches his neighbor's son. Max saw the boy once, and he told her that he loved Lenny because Lenny always had dough-nuts, which is true.

At the moment, Max owes her dealer money, and he knows where she lives because he manages her building. Max gets up from the couch, goes into the kitchen, and turns one of the gas burners on the stove to low. She opens a drawer and gets out a spoon; black on the bottom, sticky on the top. She opens a cab-inet, gets out a glass, fills the glass with water and grabs a Q-tip. She drops the little piece of tar from Lenny's stash into the spoon, squirts in maybe forty cc's of water, and holds the spoon over the flame on the stove. When it starts to bubble, she pulls the spoon away. She's probably cooked it too long, but she wants to make sure she's killed all the bacteria. She heard about a flesh-eating bacteria afflicting local heroin users from dope coming over the border in the bodies of dead babies. Max saw a girl at the methadone clinic with her left arm gone. "Flesh-eating bacteria," the girl told her. The clinic provided flyers with a detailed description of the symptoms. Probably because she saw the girl without her arm, Max actually read about it, so if her skin bubbled she'd know the difference between missing her vein and the flesh-eating bacteria.

She pulls the cotton off the Q-tip and rolls it into a nice little ball. Sometimes she uses cigarette filters, but she heard that
the fibers in them can really mess up your lungs. She drops the
cotton into the spoon. Her needle is old and dull. The plunger
sticks against the sides when she tries to pull back. It doesn't
draw up any of the stuff. She removes the plunger, rinses the
aperture a few times, and puts the rig back together. She places
the point of the needle into the cotton ball, pulls slowly on the
plunger, and the dark brown liquid fills the aperture. When she
pushes down on the plunger to get out any air, nothing comes
out. That's another problem; an air bubble to the lung could be
fatal. This might not be true, but she believes it anyway. The
needle is clogged. Maybe she should have put some more water
in the spoon to make the heroin thinner. She takes out the
plunger and dumps the heroin back into the spoon, careful not
to spill. She goes to the sink, turns on the water and waits for it
to get hot. She holds the point of the needle over a lighter's flame
until she hears the crackling sound that means it's unclogged.
Then she holds the syringe under the water. It scalds her hands,
but she doesn't take them away. She fills the aperture with
water this time to see if the damn thing will work, and pushes
the plunger again. No water squirts out the point.

"Oh, I can't believe it! Yes, I can." Max jams her hand inside
the drawer, feeling nothing but emergency cottons. Heroin
residue can be pounded out of them when no dope is around,
making the difference between an incapacitating sickness and
a bad day. And she can't find the spare rig she keeps in her
backpack for emergencies, like other people keep an extra bat-

tery for their pagers or a spare tire in the trunk. Gigi must have taken it. Every time something illicit is missing, Max thinks the spirit of her grandma, Gigi, has hidden it from her. She gets down on her knees, opens the clean white cabinet door and looks under the sink.

The Sand and Sea Motel in Daytona Beach is where Gigi lived. A few years ago, when Phyllis and Max had gone for a visit, she welcomed them wearing her passionflower swimsuit with matching coral nail polish and lipstick. That day Gigi had held Max's hands. "Your little hands are so cold," Gigi said. "Here, I have the sun in my skin." She rubbed Max's hands till they were warm, and even then she kept squeezing them in little pulses. The age spots moved over her tendons and bones as she put some heat into Max's hands. They sat watching the sun shine through a crystal hummingbird, making rainbows on the walls. All was quiet except for Gigi's favorite radio station that played only the soft hits, and the clinking of the charms on her bracelet.

"This is my favorite moment, Gigi," Max had said.

Gigi kissed Max's hands. "Mine, too." The hummingbird spun slowly in the window and the rainbows jumped.

Two years after Gigi's funeral, Max and Phyllis stayed at the Sand and Sea, each in her own room. It would be the last time before the motel was sold. Max spent the night shooting up all the stuff she'd brought that was supposed to get her through the entire trip. The next day, she passed out in Phyllis's room. Phyllis didn't want to wake her so she went to Max's room to use the phone. She suspected Max was high; the Benadryl she'd said she was taking couldn't make her that sleepy. Phyllis found the needle and spoon under the sink. In the pocket of Max's spiral notebook, she found some crystal meth, which Max had planned to use to help kick the heroin, to push the kick through faster. When Max went back to her room, the meth was no longer there, and then she found that everything under the sink, her works and the cottons, was also gone. She had sat and stared for a while at the rusty water spots on the old pipe, feeling creepy and ashamed, and thought Gigi must know, that she must be responsible.

"Got it!" Lenny shouts as he kicks the door shut. "Thank God, Max. Guess what, he gave me free pee, so I took my profits to Cisco."

"Did you get an outfit?" Max asks, banging the back of her head as she crawls out from under the sink.

"I went to the needle exchange yesterday. Look in the drawer, the top of the dresser with all my panties. I told you yesterday. You have the worst memory."

"Thank God!" Max runs into Lenny's bedroom, opens his underwear drawer, watches her hands picking through and disappearing under crumpled cotton paisleys, reindeers, and ducks. She tosses some briefs out of the drawer, and finally finds the lunch-size paper bag.

⑨

Phyllis wakes when the Deepak Chopra tape clicks off. Refreshed and ready to restart her day, she ambles from her bedroom down the hall, past the old movie posters—some of them featuring her—to the refrigerator. She takes a fork and eats her gin-prune stew out of the fridge. She notices her tulip bulbs resting on the bottom shelf and decides to plant them. She doesn't bother to change out of the flowered slip she slept in. It looks like a dress anyway. She puts on her straw hat and tosses the bulbs in the basket containing her trowel, her gloves, and plant food. Outside, she straps on her aerator shoes with the Velcro and long metal spikes. She runs in place, stomping on the plot of dirt she's chosen for the bulbs. Exhausted and delighted, she falls to her knees, breathes in the air of her roses and sticks her fingers in the earth. Her hands disappear beneath the soil and then break the surface. She rolls little clumps over her fingers. The dirt is still cool; the sun hasn't hit this side of the garden yet. It's a little dry, though. Phyllis takes her trowel and starts digging. There is an old root invading her spot and she pulls on it. It won't budge. Yank, yank, and then a long steady pull, but no extraction. She squishes her hands in the soil again to loosen it. Staring at her hands digging in the earth, she doesn't think about putting her gloves on. A gold charm bracelet flashes on her wrist, coral polish colors her nails, age spots stain her skin. Phyllis feels her rib cage open from the back and warmth rush in. She feels Gigi holding her soft as feathers, wrapped snugly around her like a blanket. Phyllis sits on her knees, still seeing her hands though her eyes are closed and her arms are crossed, holding her sides.

three

R ITE A ID IS an occasional stop between two and three in
the morning. Sometimes Max will steal a lipstick or necessities
that are too expensive to buy, like razors. Though shaving isn't
a priority these days, and neither is lipstick. Phyllis used to say,
"Never let what you do with your looks be inspired only by
men." And Max would answer, "What the hell are you talking
about? I'm just putting on lipstick." "Oh, honey," Phyllis would
continue, "don't let him break your heart." Ernest let Max put
lipstick on him once so she could feel what it was like when he
kissed her.

This night, the dark-bellied sky has swallowed the bright-
est stars, making the world look doomed, but Rite Aid is illuminated, inviting and haunted, like a lone rest stop on a long
strip of highway. Max pulls into the familiar parking lot,

permanent home to a few beat-up cars. She parks and swings her legs out of her creaky pickup. Growing up, kids called her Chicken Legs because of her skinny legs and knobby knees. In high school, when she went on the birth control pill (not because she was a sexual dynamo, but because Phyllis was worried), Max gained weight, felt her inner thighs rub together, and enjoyed it. It was like having an extra layer of protection. Not now.

She stuffs her keys in the pocket of her saggy jeans. As she spots the entrance and aligns her body with her destination, a shaft of light from the Rite Aid sign shines down on her. Her big feet jerk to a wobbly stop. Her head falls back and her shoulders settle into a natural ease. She looks into the light. On her skin is the fuzz of one hundred peaches. Blackheads sprinkle her crooked nose, and the sheen of waxy residue from heroin-and-cocaine-filled sweat sucks in the light for a second, then spits it out. She feels the light melting her, creeping through the cracks. She even smiles, feeling her skin flowing over her mercury bones. Between her two front teeth is a space she likes to spit saliva and other liquids through. The teeth are just beginning to turn gray, and a blister from the slow burn of a pipe kisses her lips. This is the first time she's let the Rite Aid light hit her. It's always been there. She just never looked up.

George, the Rite Aid greeter, stands out front next to his shopping cart, a bottle of Thunderbird in a bag in his hand, drops of it on his beard and brand-new shirt. George has a good strong cheap heroin connection and usually a stash of needles he'll sell for three bucks, but they're always dirty. No matter how paranoid Max gets from dopesickness, George never seems like a monster. He's safe. He panhandles all day for two twenty-dollar bags and a bottle of Thunderbird.

"Hey, George. Nice shirt."

"Yeah, I made out tonight, eh?" George takes a swig from his bottle. "Hey, Max, you should wear clean clothes. Take a little pride." With his bottle he points to her dirty, oversized clothes.

"Shut up," Max grabs the bottle from his hand and takes a drink.

George nods and grins. "So what are you going to give me?"

Max clears her throat. "Johnny Thunders."

"Not another goddamned one about Ernest," George moans.

She takes a deep breath. "He wrote it for his dead friend."

George runs his hand down his beard and tugs on it. He smiles with his eyes before he closes them.

Max closes her eyes too and pretends she is looking right into George. She sways to the world moving beneath her eyelids. To keep from falling she puts her legs in a wide stance as if she were surfing. "I'm sorry I didn't have more to say / Maybe I, I could have changed your fate / You were so misunderstood"—the next line makes her angry but she still tries to sing it soft like a lullaby—"You could have been anything you wanted to / Because it's a sad vacation, oh, what can I say / It's a sad vacation, oh, you knew how to play / I'm sorry, I'm sorry, I'm so sorry."

"Jesus," George says, "that's a real feel-good."

She enters the Rite Aid. It's quiet, with the respectful hush of a place of worship. Max hears the lights glow. One bored checkout lady saws her nails with a long file. At the twenty-four-hour pharmacy, there's a line of unhappy, impatient people who stare at the backs of the heads of the people in front of them. Max decides to browse in the Christmas gift aisle. She plays with a Santa and his reindeer encased in a glass bubble, shaking it up and watching the snow fall and shimmer. She sees her reflection in the mirrored backdrop. The image reflects her upside down, though all she really notices is that her pupils are still pinned, even though she's done lots of coke and crack. Amazing, she thinks. The trinket is twenty bucks. What a rip. It's too awkward to fit in her pocket, but if she gets two of them and sticks one in each back pocket of her Levi's under her long shirt, it might look like she's got a ripe plum of an ass. She picks a Christmas tree globe and the Santa and friends. Phyllis likes Snow Babies, but Max doesn't see any. It occurs to her then that she's Christmas shopping.

Max continues up the holiday row listening to the snow globes swish in her jeans. She shakes her ass from side to side a bit extra for the effect as she looks at some angels, little porcelain angels lined up, ready to battle evil. Max crosses her arms, quickly uncrosses them, and then shoves her hands in her front pockets. She stares back at the angels and tries to move the uncomfortable feeling out of her body. It's hard to let them look at her. Her shoulders start to twist to the left and then to the right in a steady motion while her weight shifts from hip to hip.

Most of the angels have blond hair and blue eyes, but some of them have warm chocolate skin; they look happier.

"I'm God's daughter," one of the black angels says to Max. She wears two braids set high on her head and a crown of daisies. Her tiny hands are outstretched. The big white sleeves of her gown cascade down.

Max feels her eyes pop open wide. "Give me a break," she says. She tries to focus because it looks as if a breeze is blowing on the angel. Then Max hears someone and she turns toward the footsteps. Max watches a young woman with dreadlocks and lots of beads around her neck, probably stoned, saunter up the gift aisle. She stops when she sees Max and turns around. "You're God's daughter, too," the angel says to Max.

None of this phases Max. She's woken up in some strange places: under bars, sinks, against mailboxes, in post office and grocery lines, all the while listening to herself talking to no one.

"You're God's daughter, too," the angel says again.

Max drops her gaze to the shining floor. Her frayed kung fu slipper presses out a spot of sparkle. She sucks back the saliva that had been collecting between her bottom teeth and lazy lower lip. "You're freaking me out," she says.

"What I'm saying," the angel drops her hands and heaves her chest with an important sigh, "is you are still and always will be in grace. Look, the only difference between you and me is that I can fly."

"Oh, man, I could fly, a long time ago. I was a bird. You couldn't see my wings, though." Max starts to slowly flap her long arms up and down, but stops. She tries to catch her words up with her brain. Cracked-out times like these, she just can't help talking.

"I would beat my arms up and down like this, and I would just float up and then it was like butter." Max lets her hands float to the top of her newly cropped hair, and she is still surprised her long, blond hair is gone. She feels like she's petting a baby's head. It tingles. "I just chopped it off a couple days ago."

The angel smiles with one side of her face. "Looks like you missed some pieces."

Max's hands search for the long pieces. "I used to have this dream that I would fly to the top of this watchtower. I could see other kids, too, resting their arms, and playing on rooftops. I painted a picture of the tower after the first night I dreamt it. But later, I saw the tower on the hill by the freeway when they took me to the emergency room because I couldn't breathe, and then I knew it wasn't a dream. It looked huge seeing it from the ground. It was actually the steeple of an old church."

"How old were you?" the angel asks.

"Four or something. Then I did a test run to see if I could really fly. I put my pillows on the floor. I stood on my top bunk, waved my arms up and down really fast, and stepped off the edge of the bed. Floated down like a genie on a magic carpet."

"Weird." The angel looks at Max's arms and squeezes the tips of the bottom feathers of her wings.

Max waits until a violently coughing woman in a wheelchair with large gold hoops swinging from her ears rolls past them. "Are you like a homing pigeon? If I tell you my wish, you think you could fulfill it?"

"Of course! I am so ready for a mission, I can't even tell you." The angel glows.

"My dad, Eddie. It's awful." Max thinks she sees the angel's wings droop. "Listen, sorry I got no Cupid crap for you. Sorry if it's a little heavy. It's just—it's because of me. I need you to make him feel better."

"Oh, I can do that. You'll see. Don't you worry," the angel laughs.

Max feels her throat tighten. This is no light matter. She peers into the angel's eyes. "Just tell him what you told me. That I'm still God's daughter."

"Yes," the angel says, "I will tell him."

Max scratches vigorously at her nose because the heroin makes it itch.

"He thinks I'm useless, and it's making him sick."

"Right. That's tough. I'll sing for him. That'll get him. All he's got to do is wind me up."

"Okay." Max picks up the black angel. "Let's get out of here."

Max holds her messenger under one of her sleeves, which are five inches too long, and they walk out of Rite Aid. George is gone, and she's afraid that he finally died. She unclips her car keys from her belt loop and opens the door to her pickup. She places the angel on the passenger seat. Max hoists herself up, holding onto the steering wheel, swinging the door shut after her. Just as her right ass cheek hits the seat she remembers. She pulls the uninjured scene of Santa and his reindeer from her left pocket and the Christmas tree from her right.

"Hey," Max says, "what's the song you're going to sing for him?"

"It's a surprise, okay? Just got to wind me up!" The angel smiles, and Max wonders how long it's been since this angel has been wound up. Has she ever even been used?

Max throws the truck into gear, and they head toward Eddie's place.

The streets are almost empty of cars, but the sky dogs are out in full force. Their eyes are drops of yellow light against the dark. Ever since Ernest read her that Anne Sexton poem, "The Death Baby"—"I was at the dogs' party. / I was their bone"— there is no avoiding them. It's usually at night, while she's driving, that she sees these dogs in the road, staring at her, her headlights shining in their eyes. They like crossing the paths of speeding cars in hopes of causing a crash and taking some souls back to the sky. The thing is they want masters who they can be loyal to and trust. They want people they can belong to and love. Heroes. They want a purpose. She knows they mean to take her back to the sky with them, where she can be free of herself, where the angels are, the dogs, and the redeemed. Max knows all this, and she isn't ready. But the sky dogs keep showing up and someday she might have to do what they want.

Max cuts the steering wheel to the right, swerving around another one.

"Man, see that? Are they fucking with me or what?" Max leans forward, her nose just above the top of the wheel.

"They don't pick people. It's random." The angel is looking up at Max.

"Guess I'm fucking lucky then," Max sees a shadowy one with neon eyes coming at her, and at once locks one elbow and pushes herself against the back of the seat. With her other arm, she shields the angel as she stomps on the brakes with the balls of her feet.

"Jesus Christ." It sounds like a question. They are sitting in the middle of the highway.

"Put on your hazards," the angel says quietly.

"Oh." And Max turns the hazards on. A few cars whiz by. A Toyota Tercel slows down just enough to peer into Max's truck.

"Maybe we should take side streets," the angel says.

"Good idea." Max checks behind her, and, with the hazards still on, creeps off the highway at the next exit. They drive undisturbed for a while. A few blocks from Eddie's apartment, Max asks the angel her name.

"Frances."

"Frances," Max says.

There are electric stars hanging from wires over Santa Monica Boulevard, and red ribbons tied in bows around some of the stoplights. They stop behind an SUV at a stoplight under a fat Santa being pulled by his reindeer. Max looks at the SUV's side mirror to check out the driver. She sees a face of gray smoke with black eyes and an empty hole for a mouth. Her eyelids get heavy. She tries to make sense of the face. The crack has run its course and is no defense against her body's exhaustion and the heroin in it. She nods off.

The first time she and Ernest spoke was at the needle exchange. He was working behind the counter. His eyes were big, brown, and wounded, like a baby orangutan's. He wouldn't look her in the face, but that way she could watch the pink surface on his cheeks when the girl working next to him told him he looked cute that day. He brought out the tray of different sized needles and put it on the counter for her. Max had been through this before—she knew what she wanted—but she let him do it. Then, she handed him her bag of dull needles and asked for all twenty-eight gauge. He gave her a bag of ten. She went to a table where there were care packages containing cookers, bleach, purified water, tiny ziplock bags of cottons that looked like they were picked off the tops of Q-tips, packages of alcohol swabs, and rubber ties. She grabbed a couple and watched

Ernest pushing his shiny brown hair from his eyes, and joking with a man with white hair, an old hype. A lifer. Ernest seemed intense but unimposing, kind and awkward. Two street punks, a young girl and boy, held on to each other and floated on a beanbag in the corner like it was a scrap of wood from a shipwreck, and they were the only ones left.

The next time Max saw Ernest she waited to see if he remembered her from the exchange. He didn't, or he acted like he didn't. The bar had pickled eggs and a slanted pool table, but the jukebox was good, filled with everything from Johnny Cash to Nina Simone. He ate an egg in two bites while he picked out songs. Like he knew she was watching him, he turned around and looked at her, and her face got hot. He didn't smile, just turned back to flipping through the songs in the jukebox. "Jigsaw Puzzle" by the Stones came on and she walked up behind him. She slipped his wallet out of his back pocket. When she went for the lighter in his front pocket, he turned to her and smiled. Warm and sad, his orangutan eyes looked down at her and found a place.

"Are you some kind of thief?"

She could see the blood in his cheeks again. "Yes," she said.

Max hears a crash and something break in the bed of her truck. She watches a wine cooler bottle fly over the hood. It misses the windshield and cracks up in the back. Max wipes the drool off her chin as a yellow convertible full of young ravers speeds down Santa Monica Boulevard. Her foot comes off the brakes and presses the accelerator.

Max parks behind Eddie's car. Frances is still lying on the seat.

"You ready, Frances?" Max asks.

"No. I want to stay with you," Frances whispers.

Max drops her forehead to the steering wheel. Her heart beats in her temples. Things need to happen a little faster now before a new day's sickness begins, before sunlight exposes too many details.

"You can handle it."

Max holds Frances against her sternum, concentrating on saying "I love you" through her heart, as she carefully and quickly walks them past the old-fashioned street lamp and the gardenia bush to Eddie's door. Light filtering into the sky changes the black into blueberry blue. The lamp above Eddie's door is still on. Moths warm their bodies against it. Max holds Frances in front of her face real close. "Thank you," she says out loud. She bends down and places Frances next to Eddie's newspaper. Her heart is beating quickly, and as she begins to stand straight up she feels something slide off her shoulders, like a bag of sand has been slashed and is emptying fast off her shoulder blades. She thinks she feels someone put an arm around her, and Max takes a swipe at the air. She feels lighter as she walks past the loquat tree she used to climb when she was a kid. She would break the branches now, or maybe not.

"Max!"

Max was going to keep walking, but she turns back to Frances. She looks so little. Max can see Frances's hands clasped under her chin. Her dress is glowing white next to the pavement and the newspaper in the gray light.

"What about you?" Frances says. "I mean, what do you wish for—for you?"

Max thinks for a minute and kicks at a couple of loquats smashed on the ground. She looks up to the tree sagging with bruised fruit. She walks back to it, reaches up, and picks a good one like Eddie taught her. The yellow skin becomes almost orange when she wipes it on her jeans. It shines, and she pops the whole thing in her mouth, like eating a memory. It tastes sweet and sour, and because the seed is big it tastes a little like tree.

"To be—," she chews around the seed and thinks. The juice almost chokes her. She spits the slimy seed into her palm. She looks at it. "Useful."

four

Now she is driving toward the 110 freeway on the downtown streets, looking for the gas station with the cheap smokes, after scoring just enough heroin and not enough coke, and then fixing in the truck. She did just the heroin so she can rest a little. It's around four in the morning. Eddie and Phyllis will be up at dawn, reading in separate beds, in different homes. She wants to lie down somewhere.

Her pager signals 911, then Voicemail, then 911. She pulls into the gas station with the $2.50 smokes and listens to the message at the pay phone. It's Wolf. Sometimes they would joke that he was one of the Nephilim—the fallen angels—not just because of his height and his way with women, but because his fall was so great. Time with him in the depths was sacred when he had enough drugs. He could make using drugs, withdrawing from drugs, and scoring drugs feel like some beautiful penance that wasn't sanctimonious but rather a valiant way of life. It's been a couple weeks since she's seen him and a couple years since they were in treatment together. Their relationship has been built on a mutual admiration, not for each other as much as for heroin. Last she heard, he was kicking dope at his rich wife's house while she was out of town. In his message, he says he's at the Chevron at the corner of Melrose and Normandie and has just gotten jumped. Max takes the 110 to the Holly-wood Freeway and exits at Melrose. At first, she doesn't see him. He's six feet six inches tall, legs thin as his biceps, usually an easy find, but at this moment he's on his knees under the pay phone, picking up all the cards that have fallen out of his wallet. His tight navy blazer tears at the backs of his shoulders.

There's a sharp ringing in Max's left ear, as if the altitude has suddenly changed. She feels time adjust to Wolf. The air leaves her chest as the concrete softens under her buckled knees. Now they are knee to knee, under the phone booth on the cor-ner illuminated by the graffitied Chevron sign. Max thinks if all the world's questions could inhabit a body, they would live in Wolf's and the answers would be just outside of him, but never within reach.

Wolf's jaw is beginning to swell and bruise, and gravel sticks to his raw cheek. Max reaches to his face and flicks some off.

"They took all my money. I was going to Mom's to pay her back. I had fifty bucks in my pocket—in my pocket! I was walking from the bus stop and three little transvestite hookers got me." Wolf wipes his eyes. It's not that cold, but the wind is coming up a notch.

"If I wasn't all sucked up I could have beaten all their asses to a pulp. God, isn't this perfect? Just gorgeous. See what happens when I have money?" Scared, Wolf looks around for more of them.

"Do you want to call your mom?" Max's knees hurt, so she rocks back onto her bottom.

"I did."

"What'd she say?"

"She told me to leave her alone until I'm clean and to go fuck myself." With his head close to the pavement, he moans, "I'm clean, Max." He raises his eyes to hers as if to show it's the truth.

"How long?"

"Four days."

"Good for you."

Wolf rolls to his side and grunts, making as if to sleep on the sidewalk. Max imagines him taking sleeping shades from his pocket, putting them on, and being perfectly content to sleep there till morning.

"Why don't I take you home to the good wife, huh?"

Wolf covers his eyes. "Can't go there," he says.

"Want to go to the park?" Max asks. "We can sleep for a few hours, then guess what? I somehow booked a commercial for contact lenses. We're down to my eyeballs now. Not that I could remember any lines. Got to be there at six."

The first morning bus roars by. The wind collects sounds from Crack Alley under the freeway and whistles to the skittish shadows, rattling the shopping carts full of bottles and brushing dust over the faces of their slumbering owners. Max thinks about trying out some of their crack, but she promised Wolf she wouldn't do any more coke around him. The times she'd done it in his presence, he'd been shocked by her "grotesque lack of graciousness." He said it made her incomprehensible and cruel. She'll leave it alone. Besides, Wolf is clean now. Four days, so he claims.

Max drags him to her truck, shoves him in, and they make their way to Griffith Park. Wolf kicks at the snow globes rolling around at his feet. He picks up the Christmas tree and shakes it up. Then he throws it out the window.

"Hey!" Max says. "That was twenty bucks!"

Wolf lays his head back and shuts his eyes. Max watches his big Adam's apple roll down his long neck as he swallows.

Just as she parks, before she turns off her headlights, they see squirrels chasing each other on a path. Then they find a spot behind some trees where they climb, knees and elbows, into the sleeping bag she's had since seventh grade—always in her truck for times like this. Max doesn't sleep. Wolf shivers and gives off heat and a stink while his body tries to cleanse itself. She listens to cans cracking open, and laughter, and is thankful Wolf is kind of sleeping and not begging for something like he does when he's awake.

At last her pager reads 5:20 am. Wolf's wound looks like maggots.

"Wait here while I do this thing real quick?" Max says, though she already knows what's going to happen. Why didn't she sleep in the car? Why didn't she just take him home? She wipes her nose and massages her tormented stomach.

"What? What thing?" he croaks.

"The eye commercial."

Wolf's eyes, bloodshot and crusty, look sadly at her. "But I'm sick and it's cold." She feels his pointy knees poking her as he rubs them together like a grasshopper making music.

"Yeah, I am too." Max says. Four days—he's through the worst of it, but Wolf has already got the fix in his mind. "But you could—"

Then Wolf puts his entire hand over her face. "My story's already been written."

They drive to Vermont and Adams and score eight six-dollar balloons fast. The stuff is cut with procaine and really burns when a vein is missed, making a rash, but it gives a prickly kind of rush when it's done right. Procaine can also cause a temporary form of lupus, but it works and it's cheap. Usually, like earlier, Max would fix in her truck and wind up doing it all and then have to score again. To avoid this, she leaves immediately and a couple blocks from the studio they fix in the car.

Max pulls up to the security gate, interrupting the old guard's first sip of coffee. He steadies the full cup and wipes the coffee off his moustache.

The guard steps closer.

"Morning," she says and immediately starts looking inside her backpack for her driver's license. Out of her side vision, she can see him looking at Wolf. A protective feeling comes over her. "That's my manager. Rough night. He's supposed to be dropping me off." Max rolls her eyes and smiles.

The guard looks at them as he blows on his coffee and takes a sip. He goes inside his booth, puts down the coffee, and takes the list of names.

Max finds her license and gives it to him. "Maxella Gordon, going to work on Acuvue."

He studies it.

"I just cut my hair."

"Well, okay. You're at the wrong gate. Go on through to Gate 5."

Max finds Gate 5 and is allowed entrance into the lot. She parks by the stage. Her shot was just enough to get her well, but Wolf is floored.

She takes the last drag off her Maverick cigarette and checks for the coke in her backpack. It's there. Wolf's face has a yellowish hue, his neck is dark pink, and his lips are slightly purple.

"Just wait in the car, okay? It'll be quick, they just need my eyes."

Wolf's eyes are closed and his head hangs forward, suspended by an invisible force field that prevents his face from smashing into the dashboard.

"Okay?" she asks.

No response. Max opens his door, pulls him out, and walks him around the truck a couple times.

Wolf leans all his weight on her. His eyelids are closing, and then suddenly they snap open as if he's been participating in a spirited discussion. He says, "Did you know you're my atom? You're half the molecule we were in the beginning. But Holy Mother of Pearl, I found you!" His head twitches as if he were avoiding some object flying by. This kind of heroin always does a number on his nervous system.

Wolf waves at her as she enters the studio.

Late, Max opens the door to a small stage. She politely says hello to everyone and goes directly to the bathroom to slam the balloon she hid from Wolf. No one is in the makeup room, so she sits on the sofa just outside it and passes out, enjoying the warmth spreading over her. The makeup artist leans over Max with her long bleached hair and wakes her to get her cleaned up. She smells like cocoa butter and her chest is tanned and crinkled. Max sits in the high chair and tries to keep her head up and not drool. The woman's feet are incredibly dark, too, flip-flops in the winter and Barbie-pink painted toes. Max catches the corners of her mouth drooping and then wipes some drool. The makeup artist firmly places her hand under Max's chin to keep her head straight. Max sees her rolling her eyes at the production assistant, who is watching from the doorway. She pops the top lids off Max's eyeballs and drops Visine in one and then the other. She dabs concealer around the dark purple circles beneath Max's eyes. She wears a short-sleeved shirt that shows off her toned biceps. Max considers explaining how sick she's been lately. Fuck 'em, she thinks and shuts her eye just before some powder is brushed over it.

The makeup lady whispers, "You've got to open your eyes, sweetie," and combs black mascara through Max's lashes.

"She ready?" the stocky PA asks. He taps his clipboard against the door frame.

The makeup artist raises one eyebrow as if to say "ready as she'll ever be" but instead she replies, "She's all yours."

"Come on, bright eyes," he says and smirks.

Max is positioned on a stool in front of the camera in a dark room. A bright light shines on her. She searches for something to focus on to avoid the light. On the floor there is some yellow duct tape forming Xs and arrows. She hears a voice telling her to look at the camera. A director who looks about twenty years old in a ski cap emerges from behind it.

"I want her pupils bigger. Angle the light, Geo," he says. Geo takes the light meter from around his neck and clicks it in front of Max's face. His potbelly grazes against her knee.

"Is this how you're going to sit on the stool?" Geo asks. Max straightens her back and closes her legs. Geo goes to the light stand and adjusts it. "Okay, look here, directly into it." Max looks at her reflection in the lens. She feels awkward and ugly like she did when she was a little girl being asked to smile for the camera.

"Wait a second, Max. Close your eyes, then open them slowly." She does.

"Her pupils aren't changing size; they're too small. What the fuck is wrong with her eyes?" The director talks to the PA as if Max can't hear, with a tone that indicates he knows exactly what's wrong.

"Can I use the restroom? Sorry, two minutes." Max slides like jelly off the stool, grabs her backpack at her feet, and sways around the corner to the restroom. It's a one-woman room with the sink and the toilet in one space and no crack under the door, perfect for shooting dope. Max gets out her makeup bag with her works in it and empties a dime bag of coke into her water bottle cap. With her syringe, she draws up some of the water. The last Q-tip has just enough cotton on it to ball up and drop into the yellow-tinted solution. She presses the tip hard into the cotton and sucks the liquid into the needle. Her apathetic pupils stare back at her from the mirror. Things seem easier when her pupils are small like this. Nothing can get in or out.

She rolls up her sleeve and ties the rubber tie Lenny got from the needle exchange around her left arm, pumping her hand into a fist. Her heart starts pounding before the vein pops and then it's in. Max licks the blood off her arm, squats to the floor, and steadies her breath and her heart, her blood pushing every hair follicle another inch out of her scalp. She tastes the tang on her tongue and feels the wetness in her panties. Max stands up, feeling for the space between her head and the ceiling, and looks for her eyes in the mirror, but she sees the television static and hears the panicked cry of the tube lights about to blow. Sweat beads above her upper lip.

"Breathe." Her heart clamors against her neck. The static disperses and her eyes become clear in the mirror. Her pupils haven't dilated. "Great," Max says to her eyeballs. Someone knocks at the door. She pats her face, almost hitting it dry, sucks at her arm again, and hits it dry too. "Just a minute."

More knocking. "They told me you were in here. Let me in."

Max cracks the door and Wolf slides in.

"Who told you? What are you doing here? I told you to wait in the fucking truck. Do you have any idea what you look like?"

Wolf leans into the mirror and extracts some leaves from his hair. "You need to check in the looking glass here, sweetheart. My God, you're wound tighter than a drum—your eyes look like they're about to pop their sockets."

"Good. Get out."

"Crackhead."

"Get out and go sit in the goddamned truck."

"Not until you flush the coke."

"I just did it all."

"Bullshit."

"C'mon, man, they're waiting for me. Don't blow this one for me. We'll deal with this later, please. Please," Max says and starts to open the door with her hand behind her back. Wolf lunges forward and slams the door shut. Max swings her back-pack, crunching it under Wolf's chin and causing him to bite his tongue. He yelps and disintegrates to the floor. Max turns the lock on the door, locks it from the inside and slips out.

The bright light and the crew are waiting as she walks in and takes her place on the stool.

"All better," she says and wipes the sweat off her neck. She looks at the moving shadows behind the lights and feels like a sitting duck. A shining bullet could come at her from out of the darkness. They all hate her and want her dead.

The director is behind the camera again. "Look into the cam-era," he says. Max finds the lens in the bright light. She closes her eyes and purposefully pictures Betty Boop and butterflies.

"Okay, relax your forehead, your eyebrows. Good."

Max notices she's choking the stool beneath her. "Open your eyes, Max."

Max slowly opens them.

The director pulls up his sagging jeans and steps around to the front of the camera. He cocks his head and walks to Max. Max's heart is beating too fast, and she's afraid he might hit her. He gets about two inches from her face and looks into her eyes.

"Shit," he says. Max smells coffee and cigarettes on his breath and tries to isolate the paranoia attacking her high. He walks back to the camera.

"We can't use her?" asks Geo.

The director stands in front of the monitor that shows the close-up of Max's eyes. He crosses his arms. "Just shoot her for a couple minutes."

Max tries not to blink and sweat as her mind flips through

its junk, taking her away from the whispering shapes and the cables on the floor moving like snakes.

There is Wolf passed out on the floor, locked in the women's room. She is grateful that he's so high all it took was one good slap to take him down. She thinks about leaving him in there, and wishes it could be so easy. If only she could redo the last twelve hours. Wouldn't a good person have driven him to a detox? Max holds on tightly to the stool because it's a good idea to have something to hold on to. If everything is cause and effect, how do you do the right thing when you don't know what it is? All you know is how to feel bad about doing the wrong thing.

"Close and open slowly, Max."

A good person would get off this stool and go check on him. From further and further away, Max hears the director telling her over and over again to close her eyes and open them slowly.

Max's reflection inside the lens looks like a hologram. She doesn't know what's worse—the images behind her eyes or looking at herself. She does what she's told even though she knows nothing about her eyes is going to change, and if she pretends everything is okay, maybe it will be.

When Max was ten, Phyllis left her second husband, Nicholas, because of his drinking. The first morning on their own, Max and Phyllis go on an exorbitant grocery shopping trip because they're hungry and they want to fill the fridge of their new place. That will make things seem normal, they think. Phyllis still wears her Rolex and diamond rings from Nicholas. Max gets to push the cart. She can barely see above Phyllis's enormous Louis Vuitton bag. A man with bullet eyes, a red silk shirt, and a black fedora crashes into the cart Max is pushing down the cereal aisle.

"Sorry, my fault," Max says and pulls the loaded cart to the side as best she can. His cart is empty. Phyllis has told her to pick two of her favorite cereals, and Max has picked Peanut Butter Captain Crunch and Frosted Mini Wheats. The man smiles at her. She smiles back. Max continues up the aisle to Phyllis, who is grabbing peanut butter and jelly. Later, in the parking lot, Max sees the man, again pushing his empty cart to his car. He waves at her. She hits their rental with the cart.

"Pay attention, honey," Phyllis says. She looks very thin. Her sweatpants have stains on them from the drinks she had on the plane the night before. But different parts of her sparkle, like her long red nails, and her thick hair, and her gold jewelry, and her big white teeth. She smiles at Max now. "You're my strong girl, let's load them."

On the way home, they listen to Patsy Cline and Phyllis takes Max's hand. "It's good to have food for our adventure, huh?"

Max looks at her mother's perfect profile, the sunlight making her even more golden. Max hopes she made the right decision. The night before, Nicholas was really acting like a jerk, throwing things at Phyllis again. And Phyllis had finally had it. Phyllis and Max met downstairs in the guest bedroom and shut the door. They lay down on the bed.

"Max, do you think we should leave here?"

Max looked at her mother's face, red from crying and drinking. Nicholas's face was always red, too, but just from drinking. Phyllis had Max's hands in hers, tucked under her chin where her tears were gathering. Max's hands were getting all wet, but she didn't mind. Phyllis didn't let go of Max's hands, and she wiped her nose on the pillow a few times. Then she looked back to Max again. One eye, then the other. One eye, then the other. Like that, over and over again, while she rubbed Max's thumbs, waiting for her to say it was okay and that she hadn't failed them. That she wasn't a bad mother.

For weeks, all Phyllis had been eating was iceberg lettuce. Max knew about the Quaaludes, knew they were what made Phyllis strange—she had flushed them several times. She knew the reason they were there in the first place because Phyllis had told her. It was so she could go to private schools, have nice things, not be around the bad stuff that happens to kids in big cities. Max wanted to say, "You didn't mess up, and you don't have to worry about me. I'll be good. I'll protect you." She wanted to ask where they were going to go. She wanted to ask if this meant Phyllis was going to get back together with Eddie, but she didn't.

And at the same time Max felt ashamed because she was angry and didn't know why. Max let go of her mother's hands and wiped her cheeks. "Yes, Mama. We should leave."

Phyllis hugged her. "We'll take the red eye. Pack what you really need. We'll get the rest later."

So the following day, in their rental sports car, Max listens to Phyllis sing along to Patsy. "I go out walkin' after midnight . . ." It feels lonely to be back in the city. Max wants to see her Dad. At the stoplight, she looks out her window. The man from the grocery store is in the car next to them. He nods, winks. He looks a little agitated. The light changes.

They arrive at the apartment. The street has old cottage-style duplexes with fancy alcove entrances. Their apartment has cracked glass in the windows. They're subletting it from Phyllis's friend who always wears a smile because if you smile you will become happy, she used to say. Phyllis's key won't open the front door, but the key to the back door, up the stairs, works.

"We can't carry all these up those stairs." Phyllis leans against the car and looks around for someone.

"I can do it, Mama."

"Don't be silly. Do you want to wait here with the bags or go see if the manager's home?"

Max thinks for a moment. If she goes next door to the manager's, then surely her mother will try to carry the bags herself. "I'll stay here."

"Watch my purse," Phyllis says and walks to the house next door, where the manager lives. Max sees the man from the grocery store parked in front of their duplex. She takes her mother's purse and one grocery bag and carries it to the top of the outside stairs leading to the back door. She wants to surprise Phyllis by carrying them all up before Phyllis gets back, so she skips down the stairs quickly. She hustles to grab another bag. The man from the store tips his fedora at her as he steps in front of his blue VW bug. She waves to him. Max counts. There are sixteen bags. Eight in the trunk and eight in the backseat. Some are heavier than others. She starts with the heavy ones in case she loses steam. That way when Phyllis returns, light ones will be all that is left.

When she's finished, Max sits on the bottom step, waiting for her mother. She sees a construction worker from across the street carrying her mother from the end of the driveway. Max can tell Phyllis doesn't want him to touch her. She pushes at his arms, which hold her underneath her legs and arms, and turns her head away from his. "I heard her screaming," he says to Max. Phyllis's face is covered with blood. Max wonders how she didn't hear Phyllis screaming. The bearded construction worker lets Phyllis go by the car because she's kicking at him. She wants Max; she calls to Max. She has to hold her sweatpants up; they're covered with urine and blood. Phyllis curls into a ball on the grass by the sidewalk, and Max wipes her tears and strokes her long hair, which is matted with blood and sweat. Phyllis, her back to the street, has buried her head in Max's stomach. She squeezes Max's T-shirt into her fists, which are also bleeding. Max feels Phyllis's sobs go into her gut. When she hears a car door open, she raises her eyes from her mother's blood and sees the man get into his blue beat-up VW bug. He pauses before he ducks inside his car. Max is scared of him now. She knows that he has hurt Phyllis, and she remembers how just a little earlier she had smiled and waved to him.

⚲

"That's it. You're wrapped," says the director.

Max doesn't move. The director looks at his assistant.

"You can go," the assistant says.

Max lets go of the stool. "No problem," she says. She picks up her purse and exits, avoiding eyes and conversation. She hurries to the bathroom to check on Wolf, to see if the purple on his lips has spread over his body and turned to blue.

five

ACCORDING TO MAX'S pager, it is the same day around
9:30 AM. She and Wolf are sitting in her truck in front of Phyllis's house. Max is staring past Wolf, who picks at the scab on his
chin. The white roses have taken over the garden, and a wreath
of red berries and pinecones Phyllis made during the year of
projects, the year Zooey the dog died, hangs on the front door.
Instead of one rocking chair on the porch, there are two, and she
has more wind chimes and a pinwheel. Max would be happy
just to watch Phyllis sleep for a while, but she wonders how long
it will take for Wolf to find an excuse to come inside and dis-
turb her.

"Why don't you turn on the heater, love?" he says.

"Broken."

Wolf turns the rearview mirror toward him and examines

the scab, but then the blackheads on his nose distract him. He scrapes his nail over the skin on his nose. He squeezes a black-head hard, and his hands shake as they press down.

Max turns off the engine. "Why don't you—" She was going to suggest he stop picking but instead she says, "Wait here."

Max reaches for her backpack, but leaves it and walks down the path by the garage that leads to the backyard. She stretches over the splintery gate and unlatches it from the inside. Zelda droppings sit in smelly piles. Max steps around the poop and remembers it was always her job to clean it up, scrape it off, and hose it down. Max stops at the extra refrigerator propped against the side of the house. She and Phyllis used to practice painting sea horses on it. She opens the fridge, touches the boxes of prunes and bags of grapefruit, and then opens the freezer, finding bags of frozen peas, corn, and carrots, and Zelda's meat. At the other end of the pool is Phyllis's studio. It's built under the porch alongside the trunks of the lemon, fig, and orange trees. She never calls it a studio; it's where she goes to paint. When people tell her she should show her work, she says then it wouldn't be fun anymore because it would have to be perfect. Inside the room, the wood is painted white, and hanging from every beam in the low ceiling are baskets and small paintings— some Phyllis's, some Max's—and empty gilded antique frames that Phyllis has collected from flea markets.

The pool is dirty with leaves and dead moths. Max walks alongside it to the glass room. She opens the door and glances past her own paintings, which she thinks always end up looking like mud. She used to start with a squiggle line and then try to make it into something, but she never knew when to stop adding and mixing color and it would all blend into a gooey brown mess. In a frame above the sink is one that became Billie Holiday's face with gardenias in her hair. That one turned out all right. Shelves are stacked with old green-glass vases and an assortment of jars. Some jars are empty. Others are filled with linseed oil, brushes, or turpentine. A blue flowered couch stained with paint and mud from Zelda is positioned in the corner behind a coffee table that holds a small easel, Phyllis's paint box, and a radio. This way Phyllis can look out the glass doors to her pool filled with leaves and the purple bougainvilleas. She can keep the door open if she wants to let in a breeze. A window behind the couch lets in light over her shoulder in the morning.

This is Max's favorite room. Once she even managed to kick heroin for two days here with just Klonopin, pot, and Tums. During the day she would go to the laundromat because it was warm and the smell of freshly dried clothes was comforting. At night she would try to sleep on the small couch in the studio, kicking her legs against the pillows and vomiting in the planters outside. It was a safe place. Phyllis never knew, but when Eddie came over to scrape up the poop early one morning, he saw her squirming on the couch through the glass door. Maybe if they had talked and he had known how hard she was trying he might have been supportive, but no words were spoken except for when he was shaking his head and looking in at her from the other side of the glass. "Not here," she thinks he said.

Max walks to the easel. Phyllis is painting another red barn. That's her thing, barns. Roses and barns. Max likes the smell of the paint, but today it makes her a little nauseated. She finds the stairs to the upstairs patio, which smells like dog pee no matter how much Phyllis hoses it off. The umbrella is upside down in the corner, blown over by the wind. It's heavy, but Max picks it up and slides it into its stand and cranks it closed. The pooper-scooper hangs from a nail at the railing and she removes some of Zelda's poop that is by the lounge chairs and tomato plant. She holds her breath when she opens the garbage can and dumps it. Then she goes to the back door. It's locked. Max reaches through the doggie door to the inside and feels for the lock. She turns the bolt and the lock on the doorknob, stands back up, and opens the door. The house is quiet and the kitchen is clean except for an empty pint of coffee ice cream on the counter. No dishes in the sink. Max walks down the hall to Phyllis's room and pushes her door all the way open. The television at the end of the bed is off and Phyllis is sleeping on her back, breathing with her mouth open, her face loose, no lines, and a book on her chest. Sleep has taken her as if she has been working hard. Max knows it's difficult for Phyllis to sleep, so when she does, it's deep and sanctified. She always looks beautiful, as if in her slumber Phyllis's past floats above her, giving her the appearance of someone who has endured, and done well. Zelda sees Max and skips to the edge of the bed, her tail propelling her.

"Shhh." Max leans against the bed and pets her. She lets Zelda kiss her face and neck even though dog saliva sometimes gives her hives. She walks around to the other side of the bed and climbs in. The pillows smell like Dove soap and Eternity perfume. Zelda won't stop jumping on Max and licking her, so Max doesn't get to watch Phyllis sleep.

"Stop it, Zelda," Phyllis says, pulling Zelda down onto her. Phyllis's skin is the color of sand, but her cheeks are pink from sleep: seashells.

"Sorry to wake you, Mama." Max lies on her side, facing Phyllis.

Phyllis rubs her eyes and then squeezes them shut again, stretching her arms out to Max.

Max makes herself small and scoots over and lets Phyllis hold her. She listens to Phyllis breathing her in and Zelda's tail thumping on the yellow comforter.

"I can't open them yet," Phyllis says.

"You want your drops?" Max starts to get up, but Phyllis pulls her back down.

"Not yet," Phyllis says. Max moves her head from under Phyllis's chin so she can see her. Phyllis knows she's looking at her, so she smiles, which makes Max uncomfortable. She doesn't want to hurt her more. It's not good to pick at a wound. It's better to leave it alone and let it heal.

"Are you home now?" Phyllis says.

Max cups her mother's hollow cheek with her hand and then wipes the sleep from her eye.

The doorbell rings.

"Who could that be?"

"Here, let me give you your drops—not the fungus ones!" Max forces a laugh, pulls Phyllis's hands from her, and rolls off the bed. She finds the eyedrops in the basket on the bedside table, takes off the cap, and places the bottle in Phyllis's hand.

"It's this one, Ma."

Max runs down the hall to the door and opens it. Wolf

stands with the top of his head pressed against the screen door and his hands in prayer position. Max can see the gray roots in his dyed black hair. He looks like a cross between a British rocker and a traveling salesman. Or a worn-out "walker" from a cruise ship, those charming, elegant men who give the older ladies their exercise. Even clean, he reminds Max of junk because he's so bony, but also because his eyes have shadows. They can fool you, the way they seem sad, but always want something. His navy blazer with two gold buttons (there are supposed to be three) is pulling at his shoulders as he bends his pointed elbows. He turns in his white patent leather shoes, then pushes his knees together and bends his legs.

"So sorry, I have to pee."

"You never have to pee," she whispers.

Wolf opens the screen door and pushes past her. "Where's the bathroom?" His voice is way too loud. He starts walking toward the hall.

"Right there on the left."

Wolf lifts his knees and his hands real high to indicate that he's purposely moving with stealth as he creeps to the door and opens it.

Max stands in front of the bathroom and listens to Wolf pee and to Phyllis moving around in her room. She makes fists and hits her cheeks a few times, then she leans up against the door. "I forgot to tell you not to flush. Don't flush," she hisses.

"What?"

"A lot of toilet paper in the bowl, you can flush! If not, don't! She likes to save water!" As Max is talking, Wolf flushes and opens the door.

Phyllis turns on the hall light just as Wolf comes out of the bathroom.

When he sees the panic on Max's face, Wolf says, "What?" He looks at her as if she's like all the other friends, employers, and lovers who always misunderstand him. Wolf shrugs. "There was lots of toilet paper," he says. "You're losing it."

Max shakes her head. He's ruined it already anyway. "I know there wasn't any, but you need me to believe your lies all the time. Only you can lie straight to my face and then try to make me feel bad for not believing you."

"Are you crazy?" Wolf tries to get around Max, but she blocks him in the entrance to the bathroom. He grabs her shoulders and hushes her. She feels his long fingers hook in under her bone. "Take it down a notch. You're behaving like a paranoid freak."

Phyllis wears an off-white cashmere robe with holes in it. She has pulled her hair into a ponytail. Her eye is pink and swollen. She slides toward them in socks. "Be nice, Max."

Wolf holds out his hand. "And this must be your incandescently beautiful mother." Max quickly puts her hand over Wolf's purple track marks and scabs that etch a path down the back of his hand to his knuckles. But it doesn't matter. Phyllis knows. Max can tell by the way Phyllis raises her chin and forces a smile. Her dimples are so deep it looks like they've been pushed in by someone's thumbs. Phyllis gives Wolf's fingers a polite shake as she hurries past them to her kitchen, to her space.

"Mom, this is Wolf. He's just . . ." Wolf tails Phyllis into the kitchen.

"Max was kind enough to get me out of a jam. I was attacked

late last night, and I paged her." Wolf reaches out and touches Max's shoulder; she bats his hand away. "Who else could I call?"

Phyllis takes her gin prunes and grapefruit juice from the fridge and sets them on the counter. Then she takes out some eggs and cheese, milk and bread, and tulip bulbs.

"Oh, that's terrible." She goes to the cupboard. "Or do you want crepes?"

"Oh, Mom you don't have to . . ."

"You can help me plant some bulbs later!" Phyllis puts the pancake mix next to the eggs.

"I would love some crepes." Wolf sits down at the kitchen table and pushes the sleeves of his jacket up, disregarding his tracks.

"I'll do both." Phyllis points a spatula at Max. "You need the protein."

Max sits at the table and watches Phyllis open drawer after drawer, and then all the cabinets, pulling out pots and pans in search of the crêpe maker. The bangs of glass and metal sound like cymbals crashing together and falling, like her mother's true feelings. She wants to shout at Phyllis to cut it out. They don't need any fucking crêpes, but she knows Phyllis won't listen because now she needs to find the crêpe maker. Lids that belong with particular pots are never to be found. The cheese grater always goes missing. The can opener only works if you angle the can by millimeters to a very specific position that only Phyllis seems to know. Now she pulls out a mixing bowl, a Christmas tree platter, a plate Max made for Gigi years ago, a teapot, and, finally, the crêpe maker. She leaves everything else on the floor.

"Thank you so much, Max's Mom." Wolf blanches when he notices his track marks and pulls down the sleeves. He turns his body at an angle away from the table so he can watch Phyllis and cross his legs. He crosses them as if a string were pulling his leg up by the knee, his toe pointing slightly, and he tugs at his crumpled pants to straighten a seam that isn't there. Max thinks Wolf might have been graceful at one time. After he's crossed his legs, he slouches nonchalantly, crosses one arm over the other and lets his hands dangle like his nails are freshly polished. The sleeves pull and it's clear this bothers him. Then Max hears the tear in the back of the shoulder rip some more.

"You can call me Phyllis." She washes her hands.

"Phyllis," he says and tries a smile.

Phyllis slurps down a spoonful of the gin stuff and slows herself down. "You know I was attacked too, once, when Max was a little girl."

"Mom," Max watches Phyllis wipe some gin off her chin and chomp on the raisins.

Wolf smiles at Max. He has many surprisingly white and some yellow teeth, but it's like they don't want to be there in his mouth. The white stuff around his gums and the smell of rotting gut floating off his cream-coated tongue make Max want to give him a Waterpik. White sticky saliva gathers in the corners of his mouth.

Phyllis puts two thermal glasses of grapefruit juice in front of Wolf and Max. Max's stomach already has too much acid in it. Wolf makes a sick face.

"I think Max feels the worst about it," Phyllis says.

"I'm right here, Mom."

"I know."

"So don't talk about me like I'm not here!"

"Max has a lot of hate in her." Wolf takes a sip of the juice.

Phyllis leans against the wall, facing Wolf. "Well, maybe she was angry as a child. Maybe she thought she hated me, but her hate isn't what made the bad things happen."

Max lowers her forehead to the greasy vinyl placemat.

"I'm going to go put my slippers on. My socks are sticking to the floor. I hate that!" Phyllis hums a slow tune over her internal rattling as she goes to the bedroom.

Max doesn't really want to do it but she lifts her forehead from the mat and looks at Wolf.

"I like it here," he says.

Max leans forward and tries to speak so Phyllis doesn't hear. "Wolf, just so you know, my mom knows we're fucked up, but she just wants me here. She doesn't know what to do. You get that, right?"

"Well, what are we doing here? Just dicking around? Don't tell me all that time you didn't take anything?"

Max stares into her glass of grapefruit juice. The color reminds her of the pink when you peel back the first layer of skin and how she would like to do that to the rest of that fucking scab on Wolf's chin. Instead, she picks up the glass and throws the juice in his face.

"Hey! Vile heathen!" He pushes himself back from the table and shakes out his hair, squeezing his eyes shut. "See how wretched you are on blow?"

Wolf takes some napkins from the pig napkin holder, dries his eyes, and sops up some of the juice from the table, but most of it runs down onto the floor. "That's not how we used to take care of each other."

"The only thing you understand is how you can get people to do what you want," Max says. She throws some napkins on the floor and stomps on them with her foot. "You really think I believe all this 'Oh Max you're my friend' shit? I get to not be alone for a little while is all. We don't know how to be a friend. But I can't keep—you make me feel like worse of a person than I already am."

Wolf slaps his forehead. "Well, I'm sorry. I didn't realize. You can just ask her. It's easy! You don't have to take anything! Ask her for God's sake!"

Max nods and squeezes her nose. A few drops of blood fall onto the yellow place mat. They stop to look at it.

"Look, you actually bleed." Wolf throws a soggy napkin at her.

"That's not why I hate you."

She goes to the freezer drawer and tries to find a bag of peas to hold to her nose. "I hate how old you are. That you've wasted half your life, and that you have a home and someone in it, still waiting for you, and you just keep fucking it up."

Wolf uncrosses his legs. "Full of hate you are." He stands up, reaches back, and slaps her cheek. It stings, and she's glad he did it. Wolf's gray skin is flushed. He stands there panting, waiting.

She brings the frozen peas to her nose, covering the bottom half of her face. Max feels the blood vessels working hard in her cheek and ear as she stares just below his eye at the tiny blue vein in the hollow underneath. It's that place that reminds her he's human, not the irises that have choked his pupils. So she looks at the vein and says, "I'm no better than you." The water from the melting bag of peas turns the blood pink, but it's not dark like it was before. That means it's ending. "Follow me," Max says, and Wolf looks at her as if she has just asked him to give her his last hit.

Max watches Wolf over her shoulder as they walk to the front door just in case he is planning to push or trip her. They stand outside in Phyllis's garden. Max cleans her nose and mouth with the sleeves of her sweatshirt.

"Well, your mom will be sad to see me go. I think she was in there putting on a bit of makeup, a little freshy freshy, getting herself ready for a good morning—"

Max lunges toward Wolf.

Then the screen door slams shut. Phyllis, wearing a visor and her aerators, comes and positions herself next to Max.

"Did you want some peas? You're all red. Oh, honey." She reaches up to touch Max's mouth, but Max flinches. Phyllis tries to flatten the hair on Max's head and smooth it in one direction. Max lets her for a second, then throws the bag of peas in the air and catches it.

"I'll take them with me. Sorry about the mess, Ma."

Wolf pulls down the sleeves of his blazer and fastens the top button. "Not even a ride?"

"Take the bus," Max says.

He looks to Phyllis and then to Max, combing his fingers through his clumpy hair. "Is this how you treat all your friends?"

"I don't have any friends."

Phyllis puts her head on Max's shoulder and Max lets her. They watch Wolf fumble with the latch on the gate and then walk up the block. He stops in front of a house and steps onto the lawn. Max worries that he's going to bother one of Phyllis's neighbors, but then she notices the house. It looks like a little cottage with an English garden in the front. Wolf picks a red flower and tucks it in his lapel, then walks toward Santa Monica Boulevard, where he'll most likely catch the bus or hitchhike to Hollywood. Maybe he'll go back home to his house, to his rich wife, if she'll have him again.

Max turns to her mom and gives her a quick hug. "I better go."

"You're not hungry?"

"I got some stuff I got to do."

"Sure you don't want to plant some tulips?"

Max is on the other side of the picket fence now, and Phyllis runs to her, pulling some money from her pocket like she had planned for it. Because Max does need it, because otherwise she'll be sick tomorrow, she takes the eighty-five dollars. Phyllis doesn't dance, blow kisses, or wave good-bye like she used to. She turns around and gets on her knees in the dirt, her back to Max, pretending to prepare the ground for the tulips. When Max sees Phyllis's shoulders start to shake, she drives away. She's tempted to go by Eddie's and see if he took Frances, but she doesn't want him to see her yet. On her way home, she has the discipline to score just heroin, no coke. It'll be nice to finally go back to her apartment now that she has a little bit of money to hold off the building manager.

six

EDDIE HAS MADE his coffee and is on his way to the front steps to get the morning paper and his crossword puzzle when he opens the door and sees the angel. He tightens his velour robe and walks past the angel to the street to see if Max is still sitting in her truck, the engine sputtering. Usually, she waves, blows him a quick kiss, and drives off before he can tell her to leave. But this time she isn't there.

He returns to find the angel lying down on its back, facing the sky. Eddie picks up the doll and the paper and closes the door. He puts the doll on the oak table in the kitchen. When Max and he played Boggle or gin rummy or Scrabble, they sat at this table, but that was years ago. He dumps one Sweet'n Low into black coffee and pours shredded wheat into a bowl.

As he takes the milk from the refrigerator, he looks at all the crude black ink drawings Max has left under the doormat over the past two years. He has stuck them on the freezer door with fruit-shaped magnets. He's managed to uphold his vow of silence so far, but he hasn't been able to part with the drawings. One is of him playing the drums with Max when she was small enough to sit on the bass drum, waving a drumstick. In another one they are at a piano. It's titled "Got my bags, got my reservation!" The one he likes the best is of her, again as a small child, in the moment just after he has thrown her in the air but before he catches her. This one isn't as detailed as the others, more like stick figures, but he likes their outstretched arms and funny expressions. Other times she has left him sugar-free chocolate and low-sodium salt.

Eddie sets the milk on the table and from the AM section of his pill organizer he takes a multivitamin, a vitamin C, an E, B6, B12, and a folic acid for his circulation. Then he takes a Toprol for his arteries, 81 mg of coated aspirin for his heart, Atacand for high blood pressure, and a Prilosec for acid reflux. He's already put his nitroglycerin patch on his chest. He swallows the pills with water, not orange juice, because he is still at risk of becoming diabetic. He pours the lactose-free milk on his cereal. *Imus in the Morning* is on the radio, talking trash as Eddie eats. Out of the corner of one eye he watches the angel and thinks this is definitely not a present he wants to keep. She looks cheap and overly cheerful with a know-it-all smirk on her face. He considers putting her in the trash.

He puts on his crisply seamed gray pants and a matching gray wrinkle-free T-shirt, his usual uniform. It only varies in color. Eddie feels it displays the kind of self-respect one acquires in the Marine Corps. He laces up his black walking shoes, grabs his keys off their hook next to the door, and glances back at the angel. Something makes him take a look around his apartment, the walls are stripped of his pictures and paintings, which lean against the back of his beige couch. Everything in the apartment is either brown or orange or somewhere in between. After he heard the building had been sold, he took the pictures down to start taking himself out of the place and to remind himself it was over. He isn't going to put them back up even though he plans to stay until the last minute.

On his way to the library, where the lady librarians all know him and always ask about Phyllis, Eddie stops by Phyllis's house to pick up a book that's due. As he pulls up he sees Phyllis kneeling amid her roses, behind the white picket fence. Her head, with her straw hat on it, is tucked into her chest and she is hugging herself.

"Whoney," he calls softly, to let her know he's there. It sounds like "honey" with a "W." It's a call they would use to find one another when they got separated in the grocery store or if they needed something urgently.

"Whoney," Phyllis answers, not lifting her head.

"You 'kay?" He is talking baby talk.

"My legs have fallen asleep."

Eddie helps Phyllis up and she shakes out her legs as they creak toward the house. Eddie hasn't let go of her hand. He pulls her to him and holds her for a second.

"I want the library book," he says.

Phyllis slaps him on the arm. She enjoys the sound of it. She slaps him again.

"Hey!" he says as he follows Phyllis into her house. "That's going to bruise!"

Phyllis has decided she is not going to tell Eddie about the visit from Max.

"Have you heard from Max?" Eddie asks.

"Why, have you?"

"I'm pretty sure she left me an angel doll on my doorstep."

"An angel," Phyllis says.

"That's why I wanted to know if you'd talked to her. I don't think it means she's going to kill herself. I think she'd leave a note, you know?"

Phyllis doesn't say anything.

"I think she's just letting me know she's okay in her own way. She's so fucking out of her mind. Remember that birthday present she sent me from New York a few years ago? That piece of wood she painted and glued pictures of me and Zelda on, and that horrible poem. She should have just written, 'Hi Daddy, want to let you know I'm crazier than a shithouse rat.'"

"Edward."

"Phyl, if she calls you, you're not supposed to talk to her. Or tell her she's dead to you. Tell her you absolutely don't want to talk to her."

"I think she's reaching out for help. I think she's done."

"How do you know that? You spoke to her? You're killing her."

"Mother's intuition," Phyllis says. "Because she left you that angel. When are you going to make up your mind about living downstairs?"

Eddie picks up a bag of sugar-free candy Phyllis bought for him off the table. "She doesn't care. If she was smart she'd leave us alone."

Phyllis starts to search for the library book. Her dining room table is covered with mail, dog leashes, and bags of clothes to be returned to Ross Dress for Less. Of course, Eddie immediately finds the book under a lace doily and leaves.

That night, after he takes his Coumadin, the blood thinner, Zocor and Zetia for cholesterol, and another Prilosec, Eddie sits at the edge of his bed in his pajamas. On his bedside table there is a picture of his mom he had blown up to eight by ten inches. He winds up the angel, and as she begins to sing he remembers one Christmas when he was a boy, watching his mom and her sisters get smashed while they decorated the tree. How funny it was to them when the tree teetered and crashed down, his mom straddling the top with the star in her raised hand. After a few notes, he says, "Oh Christ," and crawls under the covers. Just as he did the night before, and the night before that, he places a pillow next to him, like a warm body. The angel keeps singing. Eddie turns the dial on Frances's back in the opposite direction, trying to turn her off, but Frances won't quit. He places her under the pillow next to his chest to muffle her song. He curls up to the pillow and lets go of days and nights to the faint and relentless whine of Frances's last few clinked-out notes.

seven

IN MAX'S DREAM, she kneels over Eddie and pushes his cheeks toward the center of his face like she is scooping him up to splash onto her own face. His eyes look past her, their blond lashes curling at the corners and touching the long silver hairs of his low brows. Her hands are cupped and tingling at the tips, almost burning. Then they touch his shirt. A singed hole appears in the cotton and she presses her hands deeper into his skin, through bone and lung. When they hit his heart, her fingers spread like tentacles and wrap around it. Eddie takes her hand and says, "It's not my heart, Max! It's the arteries. My heart is fine, but nothing can get to it."

Siren screams bring Max back to the world. Blood swells her hands and her temples feel constricted. She scratches at the damp mat of hair at the back of her head. She stretches, sucking in air and arching her back. White-turned-gray sheets stick to her legs and she throws them off. Her bed is against the window, two flights up in a brick building. She gets on her knees and jimmies the window open. It has no screen and beneath it is a fire escape landing that she likes to perch on while she smokes cigarettes and people-watches. The corner store across the street is guarded by an old man with a shiny head, round belly, and lightly tinted square glasses. From morning till noon, he sits on a milk crate and nods to his community. They call him Grandpops. He manages the building Max lives in and he deals heroin.

The sirens have stopped. It's warm for winter, but not for Los Angeles. Max leans out the window and feels heat scorch her face. She looks to the right. Flames lick the air like they are shooting from a dragon's mouth, multiplying from the window of the next building over. An Indian woman in a purple sari reaches for the fireman. The flames almost lap up her sari as she gracefully extends her bare foot, her face calm and open, and steps onto the platform, into the arms of the fireman who saves her. The fire truck's crane cranks the pair to the ground.

Grandpops claps for the fireman and motions for his minion to bring him a soda. A very muscular teenage boy comes out of the store with a grape soda and gives it to the fireman. Grandpops nods, takes a sip of his coffee, and raises his face to Max's window.

Max silently curses herself for being in the windowsill. She hugs her knees, hides her face, and rocks.

"Mission accomplished," says Frances. She's resting on the railing of the fire escape, shaking some ash from her pigtails. She coughs and dusts off her gown. "Good balance, huh?"

The sounds of people shouting at each other down on the

street make Max feel more tired and defeated as her body endures the withdrawals. There are no more favors from Grandpops. Max studies Frances, who appears quite proud of herself, and leans back, patting the sheets for her pack of Mavericks. She lights one. "He's all right?"

"Whaddya mean? Didn't you see him? He just threw me up here."

"How does he know where I live?"

"Fathers know things."

"Huh." Max has an urge to flick Frances off the ledge and watch her fly. She pulls her knees tighter to her cramping stomach. The cigarette is not helping.

"He put me under his pillow," Frances declares. Max takes a big drag and blows the smoke in Frances's face. "He wound me up and he listened for a second right before I really got going. Then he put me under the pillow. I could still breathe, though, so I kept singing." Max drops the stale cigarette down to the sidewalk and puts her head between her knees.

Frances watches a cop on a bike below. Grandpops waves at the cop and looks up toward Max's window.

Max starts to suck on her left knee. It tastes like vanilla, and she blinks away some wetness from her eyes. Maybe Grandpops didn't see her. Her right knee bears pink hickies. Her nose feels like it's swelling. She sniffles and wipes it.

"What are you doing?" Frances asks.

"This is how I quit sucking my thumb when I was five. This knee is vanilla and the other one is chocolate. I'm sick of chocolate."

Max shuts her eyes. It feels like tiny hands are tugging her eyeballs toward the back of her skull. She continues to suck on vanilla. The strong breeze becomes unbearable, but she feels too weak to move. She gives the outsides of her calf muscles little punches. Time is running out before she really gets bad. Frances jumps down from the railing and lands lightly on the knee Max isn't sucking on.

Frances takes Max's hand.

Max holds her and looks at her sideways. "I missed it."

"Missed what?"

"How you fly."

"Oh nothin'," Frances says. "I hopped."

Max puts her on the bed. "I got to get out of here, Frances."

Air hurts her skin. Fear and withdrawal make her legs spasm. Adrenaline moves her now and she picks sweaty underwear out of her ass. She sneezes, wipes her nose and eyes with the bottom of her T-shirt, and tears through her blankets for her jeans. A knock at the door. Two hard knocks.

"Damn it!" The knocking starts again without the courtesy of waiting for a reply.

Max opens the door. Grandpops leans in the doorway, huffing and puffing from the climb up the stairs. He holds his chest while he catches his breath.

"Got it?" he grunts. His round hard belly pushes his white undershirt through the holes of his brown polyester button-down.

"Yeah, yeah. Let me get it."

Grandpops walks inside and catches his breath in the kitchenette. Max leaves him by the sink, runs into her bedroom, and shuts the door.

"I knew it, I knew it." She shuffles through her backpack. She spent all the money Phyllis gave her, but there should be

$120 left over from the unemployment check she cashed at Nix Check Cashing. She paws through the bag again and again, empties it onto the bed next to Frances, who watches her.

"Wolf, that bastard." Serves her right for leaving her backpack unattended. She squeezes her nose to keep the mucus from falling out and collapses onto the bed. She should have known better. Wolf is on a run again.

"That's the last time I help him."

"Wasn't he clean?" Frances asks.

Max's guts are beginning to push themselves to her ass, and at the same time she could almost throw up. "Yes," she says. "It's my fault."

"You shouldn't have gotten him high. You didn't really help him, did you?"

"I know!" With that Max sticks Frances in her sneaker next to the bed.

Under the covers, she curls herself into a ball, stretching her T-shirt over her legs. It's still too cold but her breath is hot. Her breathing is all she hears for a moment, before Grandpops opens the door. She hears him take a few steps and then feels her bed almost collapse to one side. Then the air hurts her skin again, and what was black in front of her eyelids lightens to gray. She keeps them shut.

"I'm too sick," she whispers.

"Say what?" His neck hovers above her mouth, and for a second she thinks she could rip out his jugular. His breath comes out in long raspy sighs in her ear. Then her underwear is being pulled off. She kicks but that just helps him pull them off her legs and feet.

He smells like oily skin, and like tobacco and potato chips, and like the friend who raped her when she was fifteen. That guy had a long silky blond ponytail, and a smell that kept coming out of his neck, light at first, then stronger and thicker. It was like all the sour parts of him released in that one part of his body. Or maybe the sex smell escaped from every pore on him, but his neck was where she came to. Everybody's evil must smell different, she thinks, but do all rapists smell the same?

"No, no! I'm going to throw up!" This apparently upsets Grandpops because he slaps her across the face. The slap pushes Max deeper inside herself. All she has the strength to do is curl up and squeeze her eyes shut. Her knees are pushed open by his. She hears him unzip his fly and spit. He struggles and grunts for a moment. Something cuts her, maybe it's his penis tearing her, but the pain distracts her from being dopesick. She could almost become unconscious. That would be good. The smell is fierce like a rotten tooth. If she opens her eyes she thinks she could see it. And then Max's belly is smashed by Grandpops's belly, and he is definitely moving inside her. She turns her head and vomits. He slaps her again, and takes the pillow she vomited on and covers her face with it. The pillow separates her body into two halves. Under the pillow she smells her bile, thankfully. It stings her eyes some. But she can control her brain, just like when she was a little girl, and she would burn herself with cigarettes in front of her parents to make the point that they were bad for them. The fact that she was hurting herself alarmed them to no end, though it didn't make them quit smoking. It did give her a feeling of power. "I don't let it hurt me," she'd told them as they puffed, concerned.

She lets the pillow suffocate her. "My body is nothing," she says, but the pillow muffles it. "My body is nothing. I am nothing. I am nothing." She hears her words come out slow against the creaking coils of her mattress.

Suddenly he stops. Max hears him wheezing.

"You still owe," he gasps. The bed springs back and Max, free of his weight, takes a deep breath. The lower half of her body is numb. She holds the pillow a little above her face so she can see. Grandpops has pulled up his pants and is rotating his left arm and massaging it. He leaves the room. Max hears water running.

She pushes herself up and looks into the front room, where the kitchen and living room are. She sees Grandpops wobble in circles and then stop to look at the picture on the wall of her grandma in her sheriff's uniform. Max could get dressed and go out the fire escape.

And then, strangely, Grandpops stumbles back toward the kitchen area, clutching at his heart. Sweat pours from his shiny head. Max forgets that she is half-naked, that her vagina burns. She rushes to him, grabbing him by the shoulders.

"Here, sit down." She tries to put him down on her plastic classroom chair; she is so weak they miss. His rear slams down on the floor. Still holding him by the shoulders, she slides his upper body down as softly as she can. His head drops back and hits the mustard linoleum. She straddles him. She can give him CPR. Grandpops's eyes lock into Max's, panicked and helpless, and then they look through her. It's as if he asks her for something, but then he seems to spot someone behind her he recognizes and even likes. She turns to look. But then she hears him sigh, and she looks back to his face. His body lets go. Empty.

Max pounds on his chest. She squeezes his nose and breathes

hard into his loose rubbery mouth and then spits. She pounds on his wide doughy chest again.

"Tell me what you saw!" She slaps his oily cheek and his head bobbles.

Max makes it to the window to see if any firemen are left, but they're gone. Her phone has been shut off, but it will still call 911, so she dials it and kneels again beside Grandpops. She pounds on his chest weakly.

Wetness touches her toes, which prop her forward as she leans on him. It's the release of all his fluids mixing with the excrement from her own body, which has begun to give up without the heroin. She smells the poison and rolls away from their puddle of blood and shit. She wants to make it to the bathroom to wash herself so no one finds her like this, but she can only crawl so far. She rolls over onto her back. At least she is a few feet from Grandpops, and the linoleum feels nice and cool against her feverish skin. She looks at the picture of her grandma Grace on the wall. One of her duties as deputy sheriff was taking the female prisoners from their cells and sitting with them in front of the judge while they got sentenced.

"I sat with murderers, honey, and held their hands. They wouldn't want me to let go, they were so scared. Fear, or death, evens the field. You remember that. Sometimes it's not our job to judge, honey. You just have to be love."

On the ceiling there are little dots of brown heroin and blood from the times when Max plunged the rest of her blood through the needle. Some dots are stuck together from the times she wrote with her blood. "I luv u, anyway" is up there written in blood. The last part of "anyway" is barely visible.

Maybe it doesn't say "anyway." Did Ernest draw his own blood with one of her needles and write it? He wouldn't use her needles. When could he have done this? She tries to figure out why she is seeing it now. She doesn't move from Grandpops's side. But she's got to get up. Got to. She has to get well. Then she squeezes her hand under Grandpops's ass and pulls his wallet out. She takes out five hundred and twenty-five dollars and leaves forty. In the inside pocket of his coat, she finds two bindles of heroin. It's packaged differently. It must be stuff he hasn't cut yet.

Max starts to cry, thanks God, and rocks herself to her feet. Knowing that relief is coming soon, she climbs the winding stairwell to the top floor after she gets a spoon, a needle, a water bottle, cotton, and a lighter. This way the paramedics won't find her, and she doesn't figure that anyone is going to be too worried about what happened to Grandpops except for other junkies. One of the best things about the building is the view from the roof, but the emergency exit alarm always goes off when the door opens. She opts to sit on the top step and fix there. No one comes up here. She remembers she doesn't have underwear on beneath the T-shirt when she feels her ass on the cold metal step. She's weak and the needle shakes, but she gets it in. Finally. There's more than enough.

The sweetest feeling blooms inside Max, turning her inside out. This feeling makes being that dope-sick worth it. It's the best thing about heroin, the first shot to get you well, and if there's plenty, to get you off. Like a first kiss should be, worth waiting for.

Like Max and Ernest sitting on a quilt on top of the hill in Elysian Park overlooking Dodger Stadium. It's the Fourth of July. The fireworks are flashing on his face and couples around them cuddle, sigh, and sip beers. By now Max knows that Ernest's hands are big and soft. He has tufts of hair on his knuckles that she tugs on when he spaces out. It makes him a little mad, but it's worth it to have him back with her in the present. His nails are bitten down to nubs. She's held them and kissed them in movies, at parks, over meals.

Max takes a drink of her beer, and Ernest looks toward the exploding sky, but his expression shows no reaction. Max resists pulling his knuckle hair.

"Why do you keep working at the needle exchange when it makes you so sad?"

"Because it helps. How come you keep going on auditions?"

"Because I don't know what else to do."

They watch the fireworks.

"Dahlias," Max says.

They are aware of the stillness of their bodies as they look at the fireworks. "Sea urchins," Ernest says.

Max finishes her beer, lays it on its side and rolls it back and forth.

"How come you haven't kissed me? Are you waiting for me to kiss you first?"

Ernest hugs his knees and smiles kind of pissed off-like, like he knew this was coming.

"We don't have to," Max says. "Do you not think of me that way?"

Ernest takes a long, long drink, and then looks at Max. Suddenly, it feels like he just wrapped a blanket around the neon sky, the stars, and them. "I'm HIV positive."

Max sees Ernest is prepared for it all to be over. He holds his breath with his eyes. "That sucks," she says.

"My viral load is undetectable. I'm really healthy."

Max leans into him and rests her head on his shoulder.

"Ernest?"

"Yeah."

"Promise me this won't be an issue."

His big brown eyes look at her as if maybe she should just kill him now and spare him. She touches his face, feeling the stubble, and pulls his lips toward hers and puts her tongue on his teeth and then he opens his mouth and kisses her back.

Into her mouth she feels him say, "I promise."

eight

MAX IS BENT over so far her chin rests against the riser of the step where she sits. It's a wonder she didn't tumble down the stairs. Hours have passed. She feels her brain bobbing in liquid against the soft walls of her skull as the blood collects in her head. A collage of dead moths and flies gathers at her heels on the step below, but she can't feel her feet. Every piece of dirt should remain as it is, and the drugs are working like they should. That's why she can't smell the vomit that's dried in her hair, or Grandpops's shit on her T-shirt, or her own, for that matter. No right or wrong, but it might be a little too quiet. Her drool yo-yos, and then drips to the step below, falling into a small oval puddle and then another one, like two shining eyes. Here are the eyes again, she thinks. Every piece of crap has eyes. For example, in those wood panels she's seen on the walls in twelve-step rooms, there are many eyes. But after too much cocaine, the eyes judge. Eyes are supposed to be portholes to what? What's in there? What a weird way to not be alone, she thinks, giving inanimate objects eyes. And when was the last time she really looked a person in the eye?

"Hey, you're stealing my breath," Max would say, but every time she would open her mouth, Ernest would cover it with his and gently suck. "Hush, I'm finding your soul." He was very serious about this.

For a second, while Ernest was on top of her, she saw herself in his eyes. She was ancient, beautiful. And she thought maybe she could feel her heart soften. She liked how his eyes looked dewy and dazed as he looked into hers, and then he'd close them slowly and breathe in. She had wanted to ask if he loved her, if they would be together even after death.

"Stop it," she pushed him off her. "You're sucking the life out of me."

☞

Now Max imagines Frances's eyes, dark and glistening, inside pools of saliva on the step below her. Blood balloons the veins in her forehead. "Hey, move me. Put me somewhere. Anywhere. There's got to be . . ." She tries her legs again. She heard about this guy who was paralyzed for a couple weeks because he nodded out in a chair for the evening and slumped forward onto his lap, cutting off his circulation. Her legs are stiff and tingling. Thank goodness she can move them a little bit and there are no signs on her arms of flesh-eating bacteria. She wonders if there are any lepers left in the world. Was Mother Teresa once heartbroken? Was that how she found God? Max pulls herself up by the handrail, her legs not quite stable. One step at a time, she descends. Her front door is off the hinges and propped on an angle against its frame. She slides through the opening. Inside, on the kitchen floor, is a puddle that looks like watery tar. She unspools half the roll of paper towels, gets down on the linoleum, holds her breath, and begins to wipe up the crap.

She drifts to her bedroom and climbs over the vomit pillow and scrunched-up sheets to look out the window. Already, flowers and burning candles adorn the green crate Grandpops used to sit on in front of the corner store, holding court and selling, every day from seven to noon. There are no signs of Grandpops's family and no one is on the pay phone next to the store.

"I'm going to make a phone call."

Her Chucks are next to the bed. She grabs hold of Frances, taking her out of the left one. Lucidity is coming like a waltz. She takes tiny steps around her room. If she stops moving, she might not make it. Chances are tomorrow will be better.

"I nearly died in there," Frances says.

Maybe because she's scared since she stole so much heroin, which means overdoses and developing a heavier habit, or because she was raped, or because Grandpops died, or because getting clean always sounds achievable when you're high, or whatever the reason, Max knows she needs to make the phone call. It really doesn't matter why.

The goal is not to think—about anything. She winds up places, and that's fine. She meets people, not knowing if they're attracted to her because she's good or because she's bad, but it really doesn't matter after a while. She's tried to make a family out of the people in her life, to create a safe place because the people who knew her before don't want to know her anymore.

But it was bullshit anyway. They didn't get it. And the people who know her now, well—

"And the people I have now," Max says to herself. The pager is vibrating on the table next to her bed. Three missed pages. Wolf has punched in his code three times. She picks up her underwear from the floor by the bed and puts them on, then a pair of jeans, enjoying the calm isolation of thought and focus in her mind, just doing the next thing in front of her. But she is tender between her legs even with the heroin. Frances remains in her hand as she picks up some change shining on the floor. She crushes the backs of her Chucks as she slides her feet in.

Max doesn't give a thought to the cash and heroin she abandons in the apartment. The front door is heavy and awkward but she lifts it enough to slide through, leaving it open, and she marches, clutching her change and Frances and the walls, down the stairs and across the street to the pay phone. She sets Frances on top of the phone and dials.

The sun feels like it's exposing her and everything bad inside. It reflects off the phone's metal casing. Outside of her apartment, she thinks the brightness could melt a layer of her ugliness. She feels the sedation of her senses and the journey of her fingers to the slippery numbers on the phone.

"Actor's Fund." She squints in the sun, looks up the street. "Los Angeles, I guess."

The cashier lady has put a red rose in her feathered hair and stands just outside the store by Grandpops's crate with her hands on her hips. She yells at Max, "*Que verguenza!*"

Max waits for the recording to repeat the number. The lady yells and shakes her head. Her hair moves as one unit. "*Que pena! Que verguenza!*" She spits at Max.

"Damn it!" Max missed the number again.

"You better walk," Frances says. Max looks behind her.

"Walk away."

"Frances, this is it. This never happens on my own, I have to call . . ." She bangs her forehead in time with her words on the metal ledge that Frances is standing on. Frances hops back a couple inches.

"Stop it! Stop banging your head. Make the call later." Max peers up the street.

"Why do you think I can do that? They'll pay for my detox as long as I go away; shouldn't you already know this? Oh, no, I'm going." Max grips the receiver and falls away from the pay phone. She hangs, tilting backward by the cord.

"Let go of the phone and walk!" Frances yells.

Max pulls her body up, grabs Frances and shoves her in the front pocket of her baggy jeans, then releases her grip on the phone and drops smack on her butt. She feels no pain. She's just incapable of moving her limbs.

Max tries to get up but her head is too heavy, and her arms, and her stomach muscles aren't strong enough to lift her.

She rolls back onto the pavement and her head hangs off the curb, her arms spread to the street. The cool cement sucks on her. She hears Frances screaming at her to get up, but there really doesn't seem to be any reason.

"I feel like a starfish," someone says.

A few cars cruise by.

Did Frances say that?

Then she sees a well-kept old Lincoln pass by slowly, give her the eye, and pull over.

nine

"YOU JUST GOT to look at you cause you ain't lookin' too good. Takes a lot of effort to keep all that evil tucked inside, and now it's just oozing out of you, just spilling out all over the place, like beet juice, 'cept you can't clean it up, can you? You've gone and stained everything, huh? Just letting your natural self out like a accident, ain't you, sweetheart? Yeah, it feels better that way though, now don't it?"

The old Lincoln is a cave and the big woman its lioness. The big woman sighs and sinks into the velour backseat, her belly hanging halfway between her crotch and her knees. Blood has dried in streaks on Max's arms over the tracks. She licks her fingers and tries to rub off some of the caked blood, but what she really needs is to lie on the big woman's lap, on her pillow belly.

She puts her head on the woman's thigh and smells rose oil. The woman strokes Max's hair. All four windows are tinted. The car idles in front of the pay phone, the corner store, Grandpops's funeral crate. An upbeat version of "White Christmas" in Spanish plays on the radio, making Max think of the Chipmunks.

"Give her some stuff, Albert," the big woman says to the man in the front seat. Air vibrates the loose skin under her neck. "You need some coke, baby."

"Sure," Max swoons.

"Albert, you got someone to go to her place and get the shit she stole?"

"I didn't steal anything," Max says.

"Oh please, don't play me, bitch."

Max tries to sit up but the woman holds her down. Her gold bangle bracelets jingle while she forces Max's head onto her thigh.

The man in the driver's seat has a shaved head. It shines. From her spot on the woman's thigh, Max watches his profile. His collar is stiff and buttoned to the top. He has a hammer mustache, a look acquired in the prison system. Some call this style of facial hair "prison pussy." He pulls out a little silver bullet containing powder and begins to twist it open. He's about twenty years old.

"No, that ain't gonna do much for this one. Break off a big piece a candy for her." The man takes out a glass pipe and places a huge piece of crack on it, reaches toward the backseat to put it up to Max's mouth.

"Get outta here with your damn shaky hands, Albert. Here, baby." She cradles Max's head while she gives the pipe to her puckered lips. Max stares at the man with the shaved head, his right arm hanging over the back of his seat. His mustache makes him look older. He lights the pipe for her and she sucks in slowly. Max holds in the hit. The pores in her scalp open a little, like a flower blooming in sped-up time, and she feels her hair grow half a centimeter. Her heart jumps to attention as she exhales, and then her respiratory system kicks in and she just breathes.

She sits up. "Thanks."

"Have another," the woman says.

"Wait," Max says, "okay." She lets the pipe cool off for a second and then it goes to her numb lips. She watches the fire burn up the moisture in the little yellow-tinged ball. Tiny sparks crackle and pop. The bald man expertly monitors the degree of heat reaching the pipe as he flicks his Zippo. She holds the smoke in and then releases. "This is special stuff," Max says, handing him the pipe and wiping her hands down her jeans and then wiping them a few more times.

She looks at the big woman's pores soaking in wet air. The man is lighting a cigarette. Don't, Max thinks, we'll blow up. Gasoline air. She can only chew rabidly on her lower lip. The man offers her a Camel straight.

No thanks, she says, but her voice remains inside her head. She just stares at him and chews. The man shakes the straight back into the pack, shrugs, and slides his smokes into his shirt pocket.

Max listens to the blood beating in her ears and watches the molecules fight for space in the closeness of the car. She is holding her breath and grinding her jaw now.

"Don't forget to breathe, baby. The vein in your neck is about to pop," the big woman says.

Max blows out as her hand whips up to press on her jugular, checking her pulse. "I need some air," she says.

"Oh no you don't." The big woman rubs Max's thigh. "Now, a few facts about me you should know. One thing that pisses me off more than anything is someone denying their true nature, pretending to be something they not. Oh, and look at you. Little miss innocent, thinking you can get away with shit just cuz you look cute and stupid. And I know that you could give a fuck, I mean really give a fuck about nothing at all. You wish you had guts. Evil is as evil does, baby. I see you."

Max just bounces her heel. "So, I guess you're not into the 'We're all children of God' theory."

"Lucifer is a child of God, too, missy."

"Oh, Jesus," Max sighs. The big woman slaps Max across her cheek.

They sit in silence for a few moments. The blood in Max's cheek prickles her skin.

"You ever been baptized?" Big Woman says, looking at the gold rings constricting her swollen fingers.

"No." Max rubs the cramp out of her calf and bounces her heel some more.

"Well, that explains it. Look, I am telling you that you don't have to fake it with me. It seems I should also tell you that if you do fake it with me, you going to get a hot shot. You may think I'm helping you out. You might be so sick you forget this conversation. You won't even know when it's coming. Is that the kind of language you understand, princess?"

"Yeah." Max shrugs.

"Well, shit, I don't think you mind dying. So we gonna find ways to motivate you. Don't be looking at me like that, baby. Someday you gonna thank me."

Max stares back at the bald man/boy's eyes in the rearview mirror. He looks away when he begins to drive.

"I just want you to work for us for a while. You might like it."

"Sell heroin?"

"Yeah!"

"I don't think so. I was on my way to getting clean before we . . . met."

"Right now you have my protection. But as soon as I lift it, and the neighborhood thinks you killed Grandpops, your life could become very difficult. You could die."

"I could go to the—"

"You think playing it like that works? Like you're in a game of freeze tag!" Big Woman thinks this is funny. "Little rat!"

Max turns her gaze to the bald man as he takes a short comb out of his shirt pocket and strokes his thick mustache with it. Max wonders if he's ever lost any crack in that thing.

"My son is driving us to a doctor friend of ours. He's going to give you something that will keep you off the junk. You see how perfect? Oh and everybody says you have to have four days clean to get it put in you, but it ain't true. I mean you'll be sick, but it won't last and he got some Librium to help smooth things out." She pats Max on the head. "You gonna thank me, baby, and," she cocks her ear and smiles, "oh, Max," a creepy silly giggle escapes her. "Can't you hear him?"

"Who?" Max asks.

"Grandpops, child. He's crying, crying so hard."

After driving for about fifteen minutes, the son pulls to a stop in a spot for the disabled and hangs a blue tag from the rearview mirror. That's when Max notices that Big Woman has no legs. The man gets out and opens the door next to Big Woman.

"I'll wait here," she says. "You go on with Albert. You'll be okay with the doctor. Go on—we'll give you some pills to get you through."

Max, thankful for some air, opens the door on her side. "Jesus Christ." She looks back at Big Woman. "I can't breathe."

Big Woman slaps her across the face again.

Albert leads Max by the elbow to the door of what must be the doctor's house. It's a one-story with a front porch. A row of shoes sits to the right of the door.

Max has driven through this neighborhood many times on her way to her main spot to cop. They are in Chinatown. "Make sure you don't tell him that you've taken opiates in the last eleven days," Albert says, releasing Max's arm to ring the doorbell, encased in a homemade stained-glass heart.

"I thought she said four days."

Albert glances over his shoulder toward the Lincoln. "They want eleven."

"Okay." Max sees Big Woman staring at them from the backseat. "Why shouldn't I say?"

Albert looks at Max like he feels incredibly sorry for her because she's an idiot. He shakes his head and looks at the row of shoes. "Just keep your mouth shut. And don't try to get out of this. You don't want to disappoint my mom. Her punishment will be way worse than this." He slips out of his old-school Nikes, white with the red stripe, and Max kicks off her Chucks.

A little man with a plaid shirt of purple and green opens the door and welcomes them, patting Albert's shoulder and shaking his hand. Max is much taller than he is, and his movements are hurried and humble. He signals a thumbs-up when he notices they've already taken off their sneakers. The first things Max notices are a Buddha shrine adorned with oranges and passionflowers and the sound of the miniature fountain beside the Buddha. A woman with beautiful black hair and a tired face is drying dishes in the kitchen, just off the living room. She smiles at the strangers in her house. The doctor says something to the woman in what might be Chinese and she pulls a small Tupperware container out of the refrigerator. She follows them to the bedroom. Max passes pictures of Elvis in the hall and photos of what must be the doctor's family at the gates of Graceland. They enter the bedroom. The woman puts a hand behind Max's back and with a big smile and a nod guides her onto the bed, which is covered in blue paper.

"Lie down," she says. "It's okay."

Max lies back, her head resting on her hands. The doctor opens a dresser drawer and extracts a long syringe and a bottle of Novocain. Albert stands by the window and peeks out every couple minutes.

The doctor approaches Max with the syringe. Seemingly out of nowhere, the nice Chinese lady unbuttons and lowers Max's jeans, exposing her pubic hair. She swabs the pelvic area with alcohol and the doctor says something to her as he slips the needle under Max's skin. The lady rolls her eyes and shakes the bottle of rubbing alcohol at him as she marches away. Just as the doctor is leaving the room, a nurse—Max thinks nurse only because she wears white—enters with a razor.

"It's okay," the nurse says and shaves the top border of Max's pubic hair. The lines between her eyebrows crease and disappear, crease and disappear. The smell of the rubbing alcohol is clean and hopeful. Max looks up at the spiderweb of wrinkles lacing the nurse's face and wonders if she is a grandmother. The gentle way the old woman scrapes the razor against Max's skin makes her feel too vulnerable; an ache lies so close to the surface. She wants to cry and then be taken care of, all of this inspired by someone Max has deemed good and simple. A nurse because she wears white, kind because she is old, loving because she didn't cut her with the razor.

"How long you off for?"

Max looks at Albert at the window with his back toward them. She sees him stiffen. "How long do you have to be clean?" Max asks.

"Oh, you must have four day. You have four?"

"Well, I'm all good then. Eleven, I have eleven days clean," Max reports, suffering the lie because of the way the grandmother nurse cleaned her.

The old woman puts her hands on her hips, laughing, "I test you. You have to have eleven day."

The doctor zips back into the room. He retrieves a scalpel out of the dresser and slices into Max's skin to the upper right of the pubic bone. The area is numb where he gave her the shot. The nurse hands him a white pellet from the Tupperware container and he sticks it under Max's skin, deep into the incision. He sews up the two-inch wound. Max watches him tug the clear thread through her skin. The old woman gives Max two pills and some water, then she gives Albert the bottle. They exchange a nod.

Max starts to sit up. The blue paper sticks to her clammy back. Trickles of sweat release from beneath her breasts.

"I can't move my legs," she says, looking at the V of her pale, cold feet.

"You're just weak." Albert approaches her from the window. "Close up your pants." Max lies back down, buttoning her Levi's over the bandaged wound. Then she just lies there and blows air out of what sound like horse's lips.

"Come on, man. Get up, we don't got all day," Albert says.

Max rolls to her side and slides off the bed to the floor and starts to crawl on her hands and knees out of the bedroom.

"What are you doing?"

"Gee, I don't know, Albert. I am making do. I'm fucking crawling."

Max makes it to the door of the bedroom and Albert can't get around her.

"Have some self-respect, man." He hooks each of his hands under her arms and hoists her to her feet. "You got to walk outta here like you ain't sick." Max's head rolls back and rests on his chest. He pushes her forward. He takes his black bandana out of his back pocket and wipes her forehead.

He feels good, like a warm wall. She shivers and looks down the hall, which seems narrower now. "I'm so cold."

"Oh, please, bitch. Just move." Saliva starts to pool in Max's mouth. The bile in her stomach swells to the lump in her throat, and her stomach rolls over. The doctor appears in the darkening hall.

"You say she clean off drugs."

"She is. She just ain't eaten nothing for a few days."

Albert lifts her up, placing the rag over her mouth. It smells like fabric softener.

"Excuse me, doc." He looks down at the small man as he squeezes by him. Max looks down at him, too.

"I could have been a frog in formaldehyde to you." Max's voice is muddled under the scarf.

Albert takes huge steps, getting them outside in no time at all. He deposits her in front of the row of shoes at the front door.

"Put 'em on."

"Oh, Albert, you're not going to put them on for me?" She bends over to pick up one blue Chuck and attempts to swallow the lump down. Instead, she vomits on Albert's white Nikes. Some of the bright lime-green liquid splashes on the sharp crease of his khakis. Max dry heaves and laughs, looking at the face of a young girl who resembles Albert tattooed on the top of his hand. A full withdrawal has begun. His fingers curl up and make a fist. "You got a tattoo of yourself as a girl?" she asks, trying to distract herself.

He grabs her neck and pushes her down. Max freezes. "Eat it. It's my sister, idiot."

Max stares at her vomit and thinks about her mother's dogs. How they would always puke up the chicken or lamb bones that Phyllis gave them and then gobble the mess up, how Zooey died because a bone got lodged in her lung and her blood turned septic and neither Max nor the doctors could save her. Zooey loved her. Zooey would lick away her tears before they were even shed. She only knows she is crying now because of the drop that falls smack in the middle of her puddle of bright green puke.

"Albert!" Big Woman hollers. "*Vamonos*!" The curtains are being closed on Max's vision. She hears Albert call the big woman Carlotta and then say, "Fuck it," and feels him reach under her knees and around her back. It hurts everywhere he touches. Every nerve ending in her body is crying for comfort.

"I wouldn't have made you do it." But Max doesn't really hear him. The pain thumps her out and she closes her eyes, sinking into dark's shining as he carries her to the car.

Carlotta is still in the backseat. "Where your shoes at?" she cackles.

"She puked on 'em." Albert's voice is in her ear as he lowers her into the backseat. Max's head falls onto Carlotta's lap, and she looks up at her.

Carlotta lets out a whooping laugh. "We got a sick dog here, Al. And you know," she says, patting her slicked-back ponytail, shaking her hands like hallelujahs, jingling her bracelets, "when you get a sick dog, well, they are the most loyal. The most loyal, Al."

⟨᠑⟩

Max floats across golden water. She can't kick her legs. Yet she floats. Frances's wings reflect the gold shimmer of the water.

"You're dying." Frances says. Her wings wave, hovering her tiny body above Max's head. "You're supposed to be reflecting on your life. Letting everything wash away while you float."

"Why is it all gold?"

"You're going back. 'Nature's first green is gold.' You're on your way to being the most magnificent green a tree has ever seen."

Max lets her ears fill up with the shining liquid. She squeezes her eyes shut and manages to kick a bit to make herself sink deeper under the thick armored surface, but it won't let her, and the bright golden gleam is beginning to make her queasy. She blows all the air out of her body and then she starts to sink. She follows the little bubbles up and the arms of the sun reach for her and pull her through the blurry surface. A cold sensation spreads into her ass and she smells the old sweat stink of her bed quilt. She's about to tell Frances she's not a tree when she feels fingers and something cold and hard entering what must be her anus and icy water running between her legs. She opens her eyes to see Albert's stained khakis.

"Hey, get out of there!" she musters up a yell.

He takes his hands away fast and exits the room. Max hears him turn on both faucets and wash his hands for a long while. She rolls over and pulls her heavy wet jeans up. The Novocain has worn off and her jeans tear at the bandage protecting the fresh implant. She leaves them undone. Her body aches like she has the flu. If she could chop off her legs, she would. She lies there for a minute and just breathes.

"Fucking mess," Albert says from the kitchen/living room.

He brings her a Gatorade. A paper bag is in his other hand, and he drops it on the floor next to the bed. He doesn't avoid her eyes.

"I had you in a tub of ice. Didn't work," Albert says. He sits next to her and props her up so she can take a swig. Max's head falls back, and he holds it for her.

It's hard for her to swallow. The Gatorade tastes like syrup. "Well, that was disturbing—helpful, I guess, but Jesus." Max tilts the bottle higher to finish off the drink. The ceiling fan is still and covered with dirt. Albert takes the bottle from her. Max lets her head lay heavy in his hands as he puts it on the pillow. Then he places the vomit-stained pillow on the floor, pulls the quilt over her, and pats it down around her body. The sun is setting and dust sparkles in the streams of light coming through the window. Albert stares at the wall like it's a horizon. They listen to the motor of the refrigerator and a car horn.

Max shivers and feels a lurch inside her. She throws the blanket off, runs into the bathroom, and hurls the Gatorade into the tub, turning the ice into blue diamonds. She sits on the toilet. Complete stomach corruption has kicked in, and she can't remember the last time she peed.

When she returns to bed, Albert has stood up and a different part of him inhabits his body—the part that is responsible and does what it's told. He picks up the paper bag with all the dope in it and puts it on Max's bed with her.

Max pulls the quilt over her. She looks for some tenderness in his eyes, or sympathy, and sees none.

"What does this mean? What's going to happen?"

Albert walks to the door on his way to go do more things he doesn't want to do. The quilt feels heavy. Her skin hurts like what she thinks shingles would feel like, like every cell has spikes on it and vibrates just under the last layer of flesh.

"Albert."

He turns around and smiles at her. "Nothing."

Next to the bag of bindles, Albert has left a black cell phone and a bottle of Librium. Under her damp quilt, Max squirms out of the wet Levi's and pulls the cold shirt over her head. She pulls just her face through the neck of the T-shirt and breathes heavily. Her hand finds the Librium and the phone. She holds both in front of her face. She sets the phone on the goose-bumped skin of her stomach and holds the pills in front of her eyes. She starts to collect saliva as she picks the cap off with her thumbnail. The bottle taps on her lower teeth and she swallows all ten capsules.

Max lets the bottle roll to the floor and cups the phone to her chest. She closes her eyes. The phone sits heavy on her, and part of her starts to lift. Maybe it's the part that cannot be destroyed, or maybe it's just the pills. At first, she sees seaweed waving slowly. The light shifts through the leaves, making the green dark, and then glow. Her shadow falls on the coral, seashells, a starfish. She sees the blue turn into black when she looks out. She looks up to where the light is coming from, through the surface of the water, and sinks back down to the ocean floor. Gliding just above the seaweed and the coral, the shells, and Frances swimming through the water, Max looks out into the blue, and then back up to the light.

ten

MAX DREAMS SHE is balancing on the lip of a chimney, looking at the stars. The endless sky looks more real, more tangible to her than the city below, and she flaps her arms to fly. Just then, heat and smoke rise up from the mouth of the chimney, and she stumbles, falling in and down.

She opens her eyes and hears herself panting.

"You have four missed calls." Carlotta lies propped up against a pillow next to Max, who is looking at her stumps. Today Carlotta wears shorts.

Max sucks in air and curls her legs up to her chest. Her incision throbs. A detox doctor told her once that wounds have a hard time healing with stimulants in the body. She hears pages turning like someone is reading a newspaper. She pulls her T-shirt down over her chest.

"Who's here?" Max asks.

Carlotta holds the phone in one hand and the prescription bottle in the other. "It's just Albert," she says. Her forehead is pulled tight by her ponytail. Her olive skin shines and looks freshly scrubbed. Heavy gold hoop earrings hang in the stretched holes of her droopy lobes. Carlotta asks, "Where's your Mama?"

"Probably in her gard—"

"Don't tell me. Right now, I'm your Mama."

Max feels strangely comfortable.

"I see you took all the Librium."

Max stares at her and unfolds her legs on the mattress.

"Did you want to die?"

"I didn't really think about it." Max is surprised at the sound of her voice because it has been in her head for so many hours. She figures it would take more than ten of the pills to really do it.

Carlotta sets the phone and pill bottle between her breasts, which have spread to her sides like arms. She turns toward Max, and Max can't look away. Carlotta has dark roots of hair edging her face, fading into orange-blond, and the little baby hairs are smoothed down with V05 pomade on her tight forehead. Her eyelashes are long.

"You got any faith, of any kind?" Carlotta asks.

"No," Max whispers.

Carlotta whoops out a triumphant laugh, startling Max. "Child, I know you know faith! Blind faith. Every time you handed your money over to Grandpops, weren't you banking on it being some good shit? You fill up a rig with some nasty dope, don't you believe in your heart of hearts that you're going to get high, every time? When you hit the lick you know it's going to taste sweet. You got to have gotten some bad shit before.

Haven't you ever gone to the rock man and bought a piece of soap and kept breaking off pieces of it, putting it on the pipe, and you light it over and over again just knowing you going to get a hit? Child, I'm going to tell you a story about blind faith. I used to have a blue moped. Nothing fancy, just something to get me around. You know about mopeds, do you?"

"No." Max is looking at Carlotta's mouth now. Bubblegum lips with brown liner. She is all hard edges and lines, yellows and pinks, and everything she's saying is true.

"That's okay. Well, on one particular day I needed to get to my brother's house. Know why?"

"More dope to sell?"

"No, sweetie, I needed to get some dope for me. I'd spent the morning shooting speedballs in a vein in one of my abscesses on my leg. Pick the scab off and find a vein. Can find lots of them there because all the blood is there, pumping, trying to clean out the infection. And then I ran out of coke. And that wasn't a good thing. So I got on that little moped of mine, and I headed to my brother's place. I was passing L.A. College. Lot of traffic from the freeway, so I'm driving along on the outside next to the parked cars—not too fast, but driving. Imagine my surprise when a wimp of a boy gets out just after he opens his door in front of me. I swerved the bike into a car, went down, and the next car ran over my legs. I looked that kid straight in the eye, cussing him out, and I was trying to push myself up. I was going to kick his ass. Then I saw my legs, crushed like salsa, my Carolina boots pointing sorrily at each other. I truly believed I could get at that motherfucker, scratch his eyes out, take something from him. When the ambulance came I was still dragging my ass across the concrete. Didn't get very far, but you should've seen his face—shell-shocked and freeze-dried. See, child, that's my nature. I got blind faith. Funny thing is, I was going to lose one of my legs anyway from that abscess. But you never know. Those doctors don't know shit."

Carlotta's brown lip liner stretches into a smile and she reaches her hand toward Max's cheek.

"You believe me?"

Max doesn't flinch, even though Carlotta seems to be in the habit of slapping her. "Why not?"

Her hand is warm and dry, almost callused, on Max's damp face. Her thumb slides to the furrow between Max's eyebrows, and she rubs it in a circle. Max's forehead relaxes and she lets her eyes close. Then she feels Carlotta's thumb move in a line down from the top of her forehead to almost the tip of her nose, so hard it hurts. Max squeezes her eyes tighter and breathes deeply to absorb the pressure, because she thinks that sometimes pain can be good.

Carlotta breathes loudly too, slightly snorting, and digs her thumb now across Max's brow bone, crossing the pink line she just made in the skin. "There," she whispers as she kisses her finger and presses it on the point where the two lines cross.

"You can borrow my faith, till you get your own. I just gave you your wings, Mami. You don't feel 'em?" Carlotta smiles and her eyes and gums gleam.

Max reaches to scratch, but Carlotta pushes Max's hand away and blows on her forehead. Then she says, "I'd like to take that fucking shrine for Grandpops down."

"Yeah," Max says, not knowing why. Everything Carlotta

says makes sense. Max looks at the place where Carlotta's legs would be.

Carlotta pets Max's head and tickles her eyebrows. "Oh, child, I am so tired from carrying all this hate and sadness. You know what I'm talking about? I need God's energy, His endurance. So listen, listen to what you're going to do. You," Carlotta's breath smells like bananas, "you're going to give me back my legs."

eleven

THE CHIRPING OF the new cell phone wakes Max up. On the pillow next to her are long strands of orange hair where Carlotta's head had rested. Frances lies in the ditch Carlotta's head made in the pillow. She stretches her arms and pets the tops of her wings, which are splayed out beneath her.

Max presses Send on the phone.

Her throat squeezes. "Hello?"

"Who's this?" A series of urgent sniffles from a girl.

"You called me." Max looks to Frances and Frances rolls her eyes and shrugs.

"Who is this supposed to be?" the girl asks.

"I work for Carlotta."

"Bullshit," the forlorn voice whines. "Aww, man?"

"Listen, I'm for real. How'd you get this number?" Silence. "How sick are you?"

"Fuck you, pig." The cell phone reads "Call ended."

"This is ridiculous," Max says out loud.

Max turns on her side to face Frances. Her sigh ruffles the feathers of Frances's wings and Frances smoothes them again.

Someone is banging on the front door. Max pushes herself out of bed, as a pregnant woman would, trying not to bend, to avoid pressure on her cut. It's been two, maybe three days, but it won't heal. She takes Frances with her. Wolf is yelling her name. He worms his rubberlike body around the broken door and enters the apartment.

He is high, and delighted with himself. "I brought you a present!"

Max looks at the wilted red flower in his lapel and his scuffed white patent leather shoes and reminds herself again how many days have gone by. "Too late. Did you go home?" She takes deep breaths as she walks to the couch.

"She changed the locks." He looks at her stretched out in a T-shirt and boxers and sees the bloody slice just above her panty line. "What happened there?"

Max covers it with her hand. "I got an opiate blocker."

"A what?"

"A nothing."

Wolf, who had been sure-footed a second before, now looks toward the door and drags a foot in its direction. "What happened while I was gone?"

"I had sex with Grandpops. Unwillingly. Then he died."

Wolf stops staring at Max, looks at the ceiling, and tiptoes to the couch to sit beside her. Max scoots her legs in to make room for him. She tucks her feet under his leg.

"Well, we all know you're one hell of a good time."

"Shut up." Max lets Frances lie down on her chest. Her hands hold her there.

"And then I was kidnapped. They put something in me."

"Who kidnapped you?"

"Did I ever tell you about Ernest?"

"Yes." Wolf stares at the ceiling and sighs. "In the beginning..."

"I tried not to do any drugs at first, just here and there, weekends. But it was the only way I could handle it. Maybe it didn't even happen. You don't think he's dead, do you? He vanished."

Wolf picks his bag up off the floor and sticks his hands in it. "And so it was."

"No. He was too good for me. He didn't do the drugs, you know."

"I know."

"And I don't think he knew I did when we first got together, but I don't know. What do you think?"

"He knew."

"So what do you got? Any Klonopin?" Max asks, thinking he'd better have some.

Wolf gives her his superior-junky look, squinting his eyes. His skin bears a red strip over the bridge of his nose, and he's managed not to pick off the scab on his chin. "What do you want with Klonopin, a mere benzodiazepine? Do you want no opiates? What are you, kicking? Because, dear heart, I must tell you, due to my guilt complex and the fact that I took a few days to get back to you . . ."

"And you stole the last of my money—hence my damaged Suzy and a horrible turn of events, but really, don't worry about it." Max looks at Wolf's mouth for him to say something, but except for bits of sparkling yellow saliva, it's disappeared into the looseness of his skin.

Then his hand covers his mouth, and he shoos away his guilt or disgust, the palm of his hand waving the air. "I have decided in the spirit of culpability to overlook my aversion to your irrational relationship with cocaine. I brought you the makings of a speedball."

Max is stunned. The torture. She wants to cry. There is always the chance the thing they put in her didn't take, she thinks. Max sets Frances on the coffee table. Wolf rustles in his army bag.

"Oh, that's right, I put it in my sock. I have one all ready to go for you. I knew you would probably be hurting." He tilts his head like a dumb golden retriever and holds up the loaded rig. "Am I forgiven?"

Max sits forward, grabs the outfit. "I'm not sure how to be angry at you. What do you think, Frances?"

"I think you're both sickos," Frances says, backing away from the edge of the coffee table and Max's pumping fist.

Hopefully, there is more coke than heroin in the shot. Max's heart is already beating fast. "Do you have a tie?"

Wolf dives back in his bag and flings out a bloody athletic sock, which he ties roughly around her left arm. He looks around the room. "You talking to your little dolly?"

"You can't hear her?"

Wolf looks at Max as if he is waiting for the rest of a joke. "No."

Max figures the coke should work at least, if the heroin doesn't override the Naltrexone pellet. She looks at the vein popping in her forearm.

Max ignores Frances's dark wet eyes and blinks away some sweat from her own. She resists flinging Frances against the wall, and focuses on her arm.

"What did the kidnappers give you, Max?" Wolf says.

Max slides the needle gently under the skin and feels the slight resistance when the tip hits the vein. "Don't look at me!"

She presses a little harder and pokes into the vein. Careful not to go through to the other side, she pulls back the plunger and watches the blood swirl into the mixture of coke and heroin. For a second, she becomes aware of Wolf sitting very still at attention and Frances staring her down from the coffee table.

"Stop looking at me." Then she pushes down on the plunger and feels the warmth, the sickness, and then the buzzing in her ears as her senses close down. Backlit rain falls and flashes in heavy glimmering sheets and then blackness. But only for a second, until the Naltrexone takes over. She projectile vomits all over the table.

"That's it!" Frances slips and falls in some of the bile. She wipes off a few drops that have speckled lime green on her white dress and freshly braided hair.

"I can't breathe, Frances."

Wolf's mouth hangs open. "Something is not right with you. You're really ill."

Max looks at the vomit dripping to the floor. "I'm on the wrong planet." Max feels her head tingling and her heart adjusting. "Have any Klonopin?"

"Why don't you talk to me? Why do I feel like I'm not here?" Wolf says. "You just keep asking for things."

Frances yells, "You've got to keep moving! Don't go back!"

"Do you have any Klonopin, for fuck's sake? Do you have straight coke?" Max wraps her arms around her ribs and hunches over her stomach.

"Yes, okay. Here. Here!" He fumbles in his army bag and pulls out a greasy Motrin bottle.

Max checks the pills, grateful they are twos, the strong ones, and gobbles down a handful. Wolf looks at her sideways and puts a baggie of coke on the table.

"I can't believe I didn't just do the coke." Max's chin juts out and she works up some saliva and her throat muscles push on the pills. She wipes the bile and saliva off her mouth with the bottom of her shirt. The pills lodge in her throat.

"Well, so much for pleasantry and water under the bridge." Wolf smoothes his hair, then clasps his hands. "You truly are despicable on cocaine."

She swallows, and when the pills won't go down, she coughs unsuccessfully to bring them up and then limps the fourteen feet across the linoleum, her feet sticking to what's left of Grandpops's shit that she missed with the paper towels. She leans over her empty stained kitchen sink and turns the handle to run some water. It's difficult to twist and hurts against her raw bones. She closes her eyes and finds the cold metallic water with her mouth, making audible gulps. The lump in her throat softens and slides and she feels the cooling of her throat, and around her lungs, then her stomach. She rolls her face into the sink and the water prickles as it runs over her sweaty neck, just missing the openings of her ears. She listens to the water tell everything to hush and then it hurries down into the parts we don't usually get to see, only hear. Without moving from under the faucet, her hand that remains on the cold handle shuts the water off. She shivers as the bile rises again.

"Look," she says, watching Wolf shake his head disapprovingly at her. "I don't know why the hell these people want me

to do this. They want me to sell some stuff." Wolf puts the needle back in his bag. "And you're my only access to other junkies,
so see what you can do."

"I'll tell them someone just OD'd from the stuff. That's a
very attractive selling point."

Frances stands on the bag of coke with her arms folded.
"Why are you even bothering with him?"

"What other way is there to do it? Get off my fucking coke!"
Max half slides, half falls down the cabinets in front of the sink
onto the linoleum.

"Exactly!" Wolf holds his hands up to show he isn't touching the coke. "Oh yeah, man, there's no other way." Wolf had
long hair for years, and he still puts it behind his ears when he's
excited even though it's short now. "So, you're dealing?"

"Not really."

"Where is it? Do you keep it here?" Wolf crosses his legs and
has suddenly collected himself with a sophistication that seems
preposterous next to his torn blazer and the puddle of vomit on
the coffee table.

"No," Max lies. She stretches her T-shirt over her tucked-in
legs. "I pick it up from somewhere. I'm not going to risk having it here." She rocks from one side of her ass to the other, trying to find a rhythm with the frenetic and confused body below
her. "So here's the carrot: for every customer you bring me, I
give you a bag or two."

Wolf shakes his head as if he wasn't waiting for this proposal.
"That's not called a carrot, darling, that's junky etiquette. That's
our code, love. We honor each other." He sits forward. "Max?"

The earth tilts; she falls on her side and hits the linoleum.

twelve

EDDIE SMILES AT the scale. He's down to one hundred and eighty-one pounds: four pounds below his target weight. He now has room to play. Cutting out the carbs has made all the difference. Even his legs don't cramp as much when he walks at Wompak Park. He likes that one because it's flat, but sometimes he bumps into an old actor acquaintance from the years of waiting around at commercial casting calls, and then he has to walk with him.

Traffic isn't too bad. He's been losing it lately, letting his anger get the best of him. What is it with people? Driving confirms his opinion of the human race. They're all assholes. In fact, "asshole" is his favorite word. He likes to draw out its two syllables and then release them in a cry of freedom as he tears through intersections, defying the yellow traffic signals as well as the blank stares of drivers waiting their turns. He screeches into a parking space.

With his headphones around his neck and his nitroglycerin patch on his chest, he takes the handicapped sign from the glove compartment and hooks it to the rearview mirror. He checks his full head of silver hair and pats it down a bit. He's due for a cut from Paul. Paul is finally, after all these years, starting to get it right. Phyllis yells at Eddie every time Paul cuts his hair. He would keep it in a crew cut if it weren't for her. If she had her way, he would have had a neck lift by now. Walking outside has given his skin a healthy California glow that he likes. His nylon exercise pants slide down his backside as he grunts himself out of the Lexus. Pleased with the growing looseness of his garments, he puts his index fingers under the waistline of his pants and adjusts it up around his belly button. He zips the keys and nitroglycerin pills in his side pocket, and he double-checks that the doors have locked.

It doesn't look like the actor is here. He also scans the park for dogs and children. Looks pretty empty. Perhaps he can go for forty-five minutes straight again. When he first started walking, he would stop every ten minutes because of the cramping in his calves. Forty-two years of smoking had cinched his arteries. He resists the impulse to rush his stretching exercises. Through his headphones, the radio plays an annoying commercial for Ephedra-free weight-loss pills. Ass—holes. No discipline, those pill poppers. He turns the dial to 1260 am and rejoices to hear a lively number. The crisp morning air fills his lungs and he starts out on the walk he has walked three hundred and seventy times before.

"Eddie!" It sounds like Ed McMahon on *The Tonight Show*. Eddie cringes, but doesn't stop.

Alan catches up to him. "Ate your Wheaties, did ya?"

Eddie doesn't understand why this guy's voice always carries the tone of someone talking to a young child or a very old person. Considering Alan must be just a few years younger, Eddie is insulted. To ease his anger, he imagines Alan at seventy-three. No way in hell will he have any hair left, and he certainly won't be as thin as Eddie.

"Oatmeal and a banana." Eddie glances coolly at Alan and flares his nostrils, giving Alan, who is a good six inches shorter, a perfect shot of the interior of his nose.

Alan's legs have to work harder than Eddie's, and he tilts backward, leading with his belly as if a strong wind is blowing only on his face. "Any auditions lately, Ed?"

"No. I retired."

"Went on one yesterday, as a matter of fact. For Sony. They told me to wear a suit so I go and I got on my official nine-to-five slave-to-the-man suit, with noose, of course. I get there and they tell me I should be in a bathing suit, not a business suit, and do I have something in my car. So, I dropped my trousers right there and did the skit in my jockeys. Just had to dance around pretending to listen to a Walkman. Good times."

Eddie says, "Glad I asked."

Alan shakes his hands, which are pressed together in prayer. "I think my number is next."

"I hope so."

They walk in silence for a few minutes.

Alan squints up at Eddie. "Phyllis said you got heart trouble."

By now, the offbeat of Alan's footsteps has really begun to annoy Eddie. Alan keeps missing the one that Eddie's clean left New Balance hits. It's interfering with the rhythm of his four-four inhale-exhale, too. It's because Alan has such short legs. Eddie doesn't look at him. He breathes hard out his mouth and sprays a little spit. He feels sweat breaking through the thick layer of Ban coating his armpits, and the spit remains untouched on his chin.

Jealousy isn't really an issue anymore with Phyllis. Christ, he got over that a long time ago when he was forced to—when she divorced him and married someone who had more money. He even flew two thousand miles to show good face for Max, came to their house and had a scotch and soda with the bastard and pretended he didn't see some of his own furniture around, pretended he didn't notice that Phyllis looked anorexic and zonked, and Nicholas, the new husband, was three sheets to the wind, and, sure, Max seemed fine. *Now I am no longer a husband*, he thought'd. *I am a father to my daughter, and that is my job.* And he knew Max was happy to pretend too, that day. A few years ago, long after Phyllis had divorced the guy, he had dinner with Phyllis and a new boyfriend of hers at the time. It was fine. Just fine. But for Phyllis to talk about his health with this moron feels like betrayal. They round the corner, passing the kiddie playground with the sand and the slides, Eddie on the inside and Alan jogging to keep up. Eddie has learned to stick to the facts.

"I don't have heart disease. I have coronary artery disease," he says. "If we must call it a disease."

"No, we don't have to call it anything. I'm just floored at how great you're doing."

Fuck you, Eddie thinks.

Alan cradles his belly. "I better start dealing with this disease! Well, got to jog while I'm feeling it!" And with that he labors through the tunnel of cherry blossom trees, his little feet barely lifting from the ground.

Eddie has been walking faster than usual so he stops in front of a bench and puts his hands on his hips. As he sits on the bench, he yelps. The pain in his lower back and calves bites hard, then lets go.

In the distance, by the bathrooms, he sees a skinny boyish girl in dirty baggy clothes and a petite girl on Rollerblades wearing a tutu. They're arguing. The shoulders on the tall one are broad like Max's. I never brought her to this park, he thinks. She hunches and talks with her hands. Even from here he can see the limp wrists and feathery hands that have always embarrassed Max. He knows she wants to be tough. She's chopped all her hair off. Her head, even with the cropped hair, looks too big for her body, and it wobbles and rolls on her neck. Eddie remembers that when Max was young she would ask him to straighten her hair and he would use his special blow-dryer with the brush attached and smooth out each section of her long hair. Jesus, did it shine.

I should walk away, he thinks.

Eddie knows what is happening. Before becoming an actor, and after serving in the Korean War, he was a narcotics cop in Detroit. He knows his daughter is hustling. And just to look at me, he thinks, one would see an old, handsome, well-groomed guy getting some exercise outdoors; not a former CID in the Korean War, not a former star undercover in the narcotics division in the worst crime capital of the United States, Detroit in the sixties. He gets up off the bench and starts on the cement walk that leads to the restrooms. This may be the only way to help Max. Eddie is going to make a citizen's arrest.

thirteen

"WOLF TOLD ME you would give me a good deal!"

"This is a good deal. This is a really good deal. I can't give you two for the price of one. It doesn't work that way."

"I don't know," the girl says through her nose.

"Forget it. I come all the way down here—no, now you're cut off. You just missed out on some really superior shit."

Max turns her back on the girl and heads down the path she came from, to the edge of the park, where her truck is parked. Figures that one of Wolf's friends would be a waste of time. The coke she shot before she left her apartment is wearing off, and exhaustion is setting in. Frances is in her pocket and she tells Max to take care of her body and drink some water. At this moment, the saliva glands in her mouth flex and juice, and her thirst becomes unbearable. There was no water fountain by the bathrooms. Max checks her surroundings.

She sees Eddie coming her way on the same path. Frances says "Run!" but Max thinks she wants to see Eddie up close, hug him if he'd let her. He is much thinner than he was two years ago. The sun bounces off his white hair and hides his eyes under the shadow of his heavy brow. His mouth is tight in a grimace. He's about fifty feet away from her. She's about fifty yards from her truck.

"Wait!" the tutu girl screeches. "Max, wait!"

Max turns around. The tutu girl is slightly green under her white powdered face and she pushes with gusto on her Rollerblades. Max cuts onto the grass in hopes the bumpy terrain will slow Tutu Girl down. Max looks for Eddie now. He is panting and she can see his face contort. It scares her to see him like this. She doesn't want to make him chase her because he would have a heart attack before he'd give up. He stops, his chest heaving as he pulls something out of his pocket and pops it into his mouth.

"Dad!"

"I changed my mind!" yells Tutu Girl, smashing the grass beneath her blades, keeping her eyes on Max. "Why won't you wait?"

Then her right front wheel catches on a sprinkler. The shock of it snaps her head back as if someone has made a clean connection with a sharp uppercut. Her hands barely soften her fall, her chin bouncing off the grass next to Max's Chucks.

"Hey," Max says, reaching to nudge her.

"Don't move her!" Eddie doesn't look at Max. As he kneels by the girl, he groans, startling Max. He performs all the necessary procedures to eliminate the possibility of an injury to the back.

Eddie first gently rolls Tutu Girl to her back and then squeezes her feet and hands. "Do you feel this?"

She nods groggily and looks to both Max and Eddie as if she's not sure where she is.

"She must have a mild to moderate concussion. She doesn't seem too healthy." He lifts and examines her arm as if he's looking for track marks.

"It sure is super to see you," Max says. It's probably best to say as little as possible. The green of the grass is so intense it makes her dizzy. Max feels far away, standing high above the grass, looking down at Eddie pampering a stranger.

"How'd you know I would be here?" Eddie asks her. He wipes some sweat off his forehead.

"What do you mean?" Max says. "This is the halfway park. She lives in Venice, so halfway between downtown and Venice." She wants to ask him if he's okay, but she knows better than to call attention to any form of vulnerability.

"You didn't know I walk here?" Eddie scowls at her.

"No, Dad. You can trust me." The minute she says it, Max sees her words shoot up to the frozen clouds and drip down like raw eggs onto her face.

The girl points at the sky. "I live right over there." Max and Eddie follow her finger up to the sky. "Do you know what mass lubrication means?" the girl asks, shading her eyes, first looking to Max, then to Eddie. "I'm going to lubricate the world!"

Eddie gasps like he has touched a hot pan as he comes out of his squat. He shakes a cramp out of his calf. "Why are you here, Max?"

"Everybody's got to loosen up, you catchin' me?" Tutu Girl says.

"I had to meet her."

"I'm going to remove your Rollerblades," Eddie says to the girl.

"That's weird," she sighs.

"What's your name?" No response. She continues to be mesmerized by the sky.

"Tutu, she goes by Tutu because she always wears a tutu." Max is getting weak. She made that up. The depth of the sky looks deceiving because all the tiny clouds are close and the ones in the back are giants. Eddie's face hides the lone-puppy cloud in the front. From under the grass, invisible hands pull Max deeper, while the lightest part of her begins to escape upward. No gravity is in her body. She is slipping.

"Well, take Tutu by the legs. I'll take her under the shoulders and we'll drive her to the hospital." His Marines voice.

Max's mouth is open but the words can't find it. She doesn't even know this girl. She starts to sink to the bottom, and thinks, Not now. She grabs hold of Frances in her pocket and pulls her out. Frances shakes her head. The passage between life and death is so slippery. The sun is fierce and Max closes her eyes before she begins to fall. At last the earth glides beneath her, and everything turns to darkness as she lies protected by a pregnant cloud. She can hear some birds bickering and others squawking questions. Eddie is either gone or silent. She follows one sound to the next as if in a circle. One bird in the distance sounds an alarm-clock chirp, and then she hears the whoosh of a car passing by. Someone cracks a soda, and answering, a more confident bird chirps a cheerful call. Frances whispers, "I told you to run." A child screams in delight, a car door slams, and in her ears Max can hear her blood pumping, clean. Her organs feed the earth. If only it could be this easy to detox, she thinks.

"Max?" Frances and Eddie say.

She removes her hand from her eyes. Eddie stands over her, his head blocking out the sun. His eyes are the exact color of the sky. For a second, he crumbles, his eyes full of fear before he can change them. It terrifies her.

His face stiffens. "Can you get up?"

"How's your heart?"

Eddie lets out the sun again and Max can't see him.

"I'll take her," she says, smelling dirt. "You don't have to worry about it."

"You're in no shape to drive. Besides, you'd probably leave her at the curb."

Max sits up. The blood drains from her head, and there is really nothing to explain. She waits for the strength to push herself up and looks at her hands, pink and swollen, dirty in the grass. Eddie watches her. She can feel his patience running out. Because of the sun in her eyes, she doesn't look up at him, but she can see his hand on his hip. She shoves Frances in her pocket, and Eddie shifts his weight from one very white sneaker to the other. While Max takes a few deep breaths, running her hands over the tips of the blades of glass, feeling the tickle in her palms, she thinks about raising her hand to Eddie in hopes that he will take it and help her to stand. But it doesn't seem right, so with a burst of energy she smashes her palms into the ground and pushes herself up. She squeezes the bridge of her nose to stop things from spinning. Eddie sighs heavily. She takes hold of Tutu's little legs.

"She's so light, Max, why don't you take her Rollerblades in one hand and hold her legs in the other. I have most of the weight." A strong shot of coke would give Max the strength to help.

"The heart's a funny thing," she says, picking up the blades.

"How do you mean?" Eddie puts Tutu's purple purse over his shoulder and together they lift her off the grass.

"It's kind of awkward. I mean, there's a lot of pressure on it. It never gets to rest."

"Is your truck going to be all right?"

"Yep." Her meter has surely expired by now.

fourteen

PHYLLIS IS VERY pleased with herself as she pulls out of the handicapped space at the Santa Monica Airport flea market. She mostly looked and didn't buy. In the trunk of her car is an antique quilt for the wall in the living room, and wrapped in newspaper in her purse is a soft green-glass bottle. She has a weakness for old green glass. When she gets home, she will snip one rose from her garden and place her new bottle next to her bed. The top is down, and she and Zelda enjoy the cold wind in their hair and the warmth from the seat warmers. Zelda relaxes against the car door and lets her tongue taste the air. Right now they listen to a tape, the song "September Morning" by Neil Diamond. Phyllis doesn't like talk radio anymore, especially not that psychiatrist who doesn't believe addiction is a disease, but rather a selfish choice, and who believes homosexuality is unnatural. She prefers classical music, Neil Diamond, or Deepak Chopra because they are all proactive. At a stoplight, she squeezes a tube of sunblock, slathers it on her face and neck, and rubs the extra on the backs of her hands. This morning, after a spoonful of prunes stewed in gin and some cottage cheese, she took a Vicodin for her recovering tooth and a "natural" energy pill. The sensation induced by this combination is quite euphoric, although she doesn't attribute her present feeling of invincibility to the pills. This day just happens to be a good one.

Though sometimes on sunny, unassuming days like this, she remembers the days of Vicodin. She was staying at her divorced friend's house after she was attacked. No one thought she was stable enough to be around Max. The psychiatrist had given her Valium, but her friend told her that Vicodin lasted longer, that you didn't need to take as many. Meanwhile, Max was starting fifth grade and had become an insomniac because of her recurring dream of finding Phyllis dead.

Today Zelda waited in the car while Phyllis shopped, and so the dog was rewarded with a trip to the park. Zelda loves to chase squirrels and other dogs through the trees, but she always races back to Phyllis every few minutes to check on her and get the go-ahead to continue playing and smelling. Zelda has tasted blood in her life. She likes to pursue it. She once killed a cat because Max didn't have her on the leash. Max brought the cat home, but there was nothing Phyllis or Max could do; that was long ago, and Phyllis has learned to trust Zelda.

Phyllis walks the perimeter of the field where the dogs play, carrying a plastic bag and waiting for Zelda to do her business.

She still wears a gold Rolex, a ten-year-old keepsake from her last marriage. She doesn't check the time today, but lounges under a tree, content. When Zelda is sufficiently exhausted, she cools her belly on the spongy thick grass next to Phyllis, her back legs spread out in a froglike position. Her eyes are still energetic, but she doesn't hesitate when Phyllis stands and wipes the grass from the seat of her sweatpants. Zelda scoots her hind legs underneath her; her pink tongue snaps into her mouth. On all fours, she shakes out her sand-colored fur from tail to ears and walks proudly with light feet by Phyllis's side, the car keys and pepper spray clanging a bit too loudly in her right ear.

The sky is a cerulean blue, unbearably blue.

"And why is the sky blue?" Phyllis says now to Zelda in the passenger seat, as if Zelda had asked her and Phyllis was repeating the question. This is something Phyllis knew the answer to at one time. She pulls down her yellow baseball cap and pushes her heavy tortoise prescription sunglasses up the bridge of her pink nose, then promptly replaces her hand on the wheel.

"The sun," she ignores a piece of her long blond hair that has landed in her mouth, "the heat from the sun at that high high temperature makes the sky look blue." Zelda brings her head in from the wind and shifts her attention to Phyllis. She gets a rub in the hollow of her jaw. "Yes, Zelda, that's it! Blue light from the sun! The hottest part of the flame is blue!"

Phyllis pushes the button on her garage opener just as the tires hit the driveway. Boxes of Max's memorabilia and old furniture for Phyllis's perpetually postponed garage sale crowd the garage but leave just enough space for her little convertible.

She opens the car door and it bangs against a stack of boxes.

She wiggles her body out of the car. Zelda leaps out the back and takes off running after a small animal.

Phyllis sticks two of her fingers in her mouth, producing a clear whistle, but Zelda ignores her. She opens her mouth and calls for Zelda to come home.

"Max." She stares at Zelda and yells, "Max! Max!" She is getting angry because Zelda is running away and won't come when she's called. Then she hears the name, but can't help it. "Max! Get over here! Maxella!" She keeps calling until it comes only as a whisper, and she sees Zelda zigzagging along the sidewalk toward her, her long hair covering her eyes. Phyllis watches Zelda sail over the roses tangled in the picket fence and holds the door open for her. "Good girl," she says.

fifteen

T UTU IS SPRAWLED out on the backseat; her lavender
socks softly paw at the beige felt roof of Eddie's car. She sounds
like a small animal back there. It must be the crumpling of the
taffeta. Eddie's inner censor is working at top speed right now.
He refrains from asking her to stop wiping her feet on his car.
Instead, he pats the brakes as he weaves through the stop-and-
go traffic, causing them to roll forward and back in an arrhyth-
mic, somewhat jarring motion. Then he remembers the poor
girl probably has a mild concussion and lays off the brakes. Max
smells like she hasn't bathed in weeks. They sit for a moment,
waiting for the light to change. Max is picking at the bottom of
her sneaker, mumbling. The sock she wears through the belt
loops of her jeans must be used as a tourniquet because it's covered in dried blood. Something large is in her pocket. The top

of it shows, but he can't make out what it is; probably the drugs. Her shoulder bones stick out of her kid-sized sweatshirt like the corners of a wire hanger. Her hands are swollen and black under the fingernails. She's slouched down without her seat belt on, her ankle resting high on her thigh. She's pulled almost the entire sole of her left Chuck off, and then she looks up at him.

"I need tape," she says with half a smile, to hide her embarrassment. Her teeth are stained and crooked like his were before he had them capped.

"I need cowbells," says Tutu.

"Fasten your seat belt," Eddie says.

"So you know where I live," Max says, fastening her seat belt. She pats the bulge in her front left pocket and says, "No, it's okay."

"Mmhmm," Eddie says. The wind blows. They drive down a street that only has palm trees. The palm trees bow slightly for Eddie's car.

Max absorbs herself in the growing mouth of her sneaker. She doesn't know what to say. Eddie knows shame puts her on the defensive. Something scratches inside her, and she wants to lash out.

He recalls the night he tried to smother the angel singing under his pillow because she almost made him cry. I should not be trying to associate my feelings with hers, he thinks.

"We need to get off this stuff, Max," Tutu says, kicking the back of Max's seat until Max says, "I am off it," while she looks at her dad.

"I kicked it by going to boot camp once," Tutu says. Max rips the sole of her sneaker off in its entirety.

"My parents thought I needed discipline—they didn't know

I was strung out. I have never wanted to die so badly in my life. I took one of those double-ended shotgun barrels and stuck it in my mouth during shooting drills. They put me in the mental ward and then I got to try all kinds of psych meds. That was a much better place for me. I did a fabulous piece on the experience. Picture a row of soldiers and almost to the end of the row a soldier, that'd be me, in a tutu, of course, with a shotgun almost as big as me in my mouth. My paintings almost look like photographs. It was a very therapeutic process. Can't you just see it, Mister?"

Max squeezes the place between her eyes. Eddie can't tell what she's on. Ten minutes ago she was on the verge of passing out, and now her sleepiness has turned to aggression. She must be withdrawing.

"Yes, well, I have been through boot camp. It's a—" Eddie rockets through a yellow light, "—challenge."

"What's your name, Mister? Really, Max, how rude."

Max slaps the sole of her shoe on the dashboard. "It's Eddie! Would you please, please, shut up?"

Under normal circumstances, Eddie would be inclined to reprimand Max for this sort of outburst; however, he too is becoming agitated by Tutu's ramblings. So he chooses to let silence speak for itself. As a matter of fact, he's been wondering if she really does need to go to the hospital.

"You might want to find some sort of creative outlet to work through some of this stuff, Max," Tutu says.

"You don't know a goddamned thing about me."

"Wolf told me you are a sometimes actress and that you have all kinds of unfinished projects because of your drug addiction on top of bitter laziness and resentments. You sold all your musical instruments so you don't do that anymore, not that you really could. You try to paint but you just keep going over the same canvas till it turns to poop. We were in rehab together. All he did was talk about you. It's really sad, Max. Don't you want to make something decent from this crap? Make it matter?"

Max punches the button to put her window down and puts her face in the wind as a dog would, trying to immerse herself in all the scents of the world. A laugh erupts from her gut.

Max has hardness to her that she never had before, Eddie notices. His emotions begin to shut down, as they always do when he is afraid, and logic settles in.

"Do you have insurance?" Eddie asks Tutu. He rolls up Max's window and turns the air conditioner on full blast, drying the salty sweat in the fuzz on Max's face.

"Of course," she says. "Max, we really need to get off this stuff."

"Well, you can start today. I told you, I already quit."

"It's okay, I won't be sick for a while yet, and believe me you are not my only—"

"Would you shut up!" After Max says it she watches Eddie's face as he pulls the car over and parks under a tree.

"Max, you can't do this anymore," he says.

The air blowing on her eyes keeps them dry. She shivers a little bit. Eddie knows she hates the air conditioner, but he hates the draft of the window on his neck. The air sounds like it's working too hard. Tutu curls in a ball on her side as she watches the father and daughter.

"What am I doing?" Max smiles and looks at him like she wouldn't want to be anywhere else in the world. For a second, when she closes her eyes and opens them slowly, looking at him, she is innocent. And, really, they can talk about this stuff later. Let them just enjoy being in the same car together for the first time in years.

Eddie loses it and slaps his hand on the dashboard. Tutu yelps. Max looks out the window.

"I know you have drugs on you. I'm taking you to jail," Eddie says.

Max reaches for the door handle.

Tutu shouts, "Oh my God, I can't go to jail!" She tries to get up but can't.

"If you get out of this car, Max, that's it."

Max sits with the door open and one leg out. She looks at him like he is insane. "Dad, I just need some money, and everything will be over." Max cries real tears. More tears because she isn't getting what she wants, Eddie thinks.

Eddie feels the air leave his chest and he takes a big breath. "You're asking me for money?"

"Yes! Yes! Yes!" she yells. She wipes her eyes and nose with the back of her hand and then cleans her hand on her jeans. "Then I will come home." She looks directly at Eddie as if she's challenging him. This could be a manipulation or the truth—he just can't tell. He remembers the counselor at the last treatment center asking him if he wanted to be the one to kill his own daughter because that's what he would be doing by continuing to help her while she's using.

"Are you using anything? Anything at all, Max? Just tell me the truth, and we can go from there." He sees her shrink back inside herself, under another layer of shame.

"No," she says, looking right into his eyes.

"Let me see your arms."

"Forget it." She starts laughing strangely.

"Let me see the needle in your sock! Look at yourself! Right there in that pocket."

"That's Frances!"

Eddie tries to lock the doors with the automatic switch, forgetting Max already has her door open.

Then she is out of the car, yelling through the window. "You didn't hear her sing for you? Please," her nervous laughter turns into sobbing, "just don't worry."

"You better go, Eddie," Tutu says.

Max runs alongside of the car kind of smiling and hitting the window with the rubber sole of her Chuck. He has never seen her so crazy. He shouldn't have said anything about jail. He should have taken her to the hospital and had her committed. She is worse than he imagined. Why does it always seem to be too late? There are too many things that he should have done instead of making one more wrong choice. Maybe he should turn around.

"Don't worry, Sarge," Tutu offers, "I'll check up on her. Give me your number and I'll let you know what's up. See? What goes around comes around." Eddie crawls down the residential street over the speed bumps and watches Max in the middle of the road in his rearview mirror. Her arms flail and she pounds on her chest and throws her arms out toward him again. He thinks he hears her yell, "You can take my heart! It's getting better! You take mine!"

Maybe if he had cried the other night, and if he didn't miss her so much. Maybe if his mother, Grace, hadn't died last year, and if it wasn't a Sunday, because Sundays he would talk to both of them, he wouldn't be as inclined to cry. But, with Tutu in the backseat, that's just what he does while he drives to Cedars-Sinai hospital.

sixteen

MAX WALKS AT least a couple of miles with one sole and
two shoes before she sits behind a huge garbage can in a Bev-
erly Hills alley and reaches into her sock. She didn't feel like
looking at the needle and poking it into her skin. But now she
needs the coke to keep going the next mile to her truck so she
pushes the plunger a little to get rid of any air, and without bothering to tie off or even pump her fist, because her arms are
swollen with blood from walking and she doesn't want to take
the time, she picks a vein in her forearm. Her skin shines with
sweat and a lot of blond hairs sprout from it. As the tip pierces
the skin and a little red dot appears, her eyes fill, blurring her
vision of the rig. Her forefinger rises above the butt of the
plunger and jerks. She draws it back, and her blood turns the
coke pink. Her heart has come up into her throat and beats out

any sound except the tiny exhales coming out of her nostrils. Her jaw clenches and she forces the plunger down, knowing that within an instant she will fly above her body, with ample energy to walk the rest of the way to her truck. But she misses the vein and the coke burns into the muscle of her arm. She slaps it and then pounds her hands on the pavement, rocking back and forth, scraping her hands and elbows along the asphalt.

"Very dramatic!" she hears Frances yell from deep inside the pocket.

Max scrapes and moans and scrapes, tearing her sweatshirt and skinning her hands and elbows. Even though she didn't get the rush, the coke has entered her system. She leaves the empty rig on the ground but doesn't like the looks of it there with some of her blood in it, so she picks it up, puts it in the trash, stuffs her sole in her back pocket, and starts walking again.

Now Max can see for the first time that the big maple tree on the corner is her friend and it cries for her. The roots are trying to break free from the angry pavement to help her, but they can't. The branches droop. Frances is about the size of a maple leaf. The coke numbs the soreness of her left foot, the top of the Chuck still laced up, the bottom side bare. Max steps onto the cold moist patch of grass like she is coming off a shoddy roller coaster. The shapes that take up space in the world around her move by fast. Without looking up, she puts her arms around the big tree and rests her ear and cheek close against its trunk.

"Okay," she whispers into its dusty rough skin. She breathes in hard and some mucus rattles around in her sinuses. There is no space between them, her body and the tree.

"Tired when I stop." She looks up, and hugs tighter.

Max turns her head, puts the other side of her face against the tree, and closes her eyes. It feels like she is upside down. She holds on. She sees Ernest's hairy chest. Max found comfort in the precise order of things on Ernest's chest: the hairs just beneath his collarbones growing up toward his neck and the hairs over his sternum growing down to his belly; the hairs by his nipples growing toward the center of his chest. All the hairs honoring circles. Max would rub the hair against the direction it lay and watch it quickly adjust. Ernest winced when she said she found God on his chest. That hurt her feelings.

"Good Orderly Direction, that's what your hairs have."

"Okay, okay," he'd said, and hugged her to his armpit.

"I'm just trying to figure it out," she'd said.

Soon after, he shaved her name into the hair. That night, when they got undressed, she saw her name in big bald letters on his chest. She let herself cry.

"You were supposed to laugh."

"Wait." She had squeezed her eyes shut hard and in those two seconds momentarily snuffed the part of her that was high and lying about it. She opened her eyes. He stood there, naked, and let her laugh at him.

She lets go of the tree, and steps onto a dried-out leaf. "Got to keep moving," she says as she begins to walk, adjusting her weight to favor her bare foot. She walks for a few blocks, unaware of the crotch of her baggy jeans rubbing her inner thighs raw, the blisters forming on the bottom of her foot, her sweatshirt sticking to her bleeding arms, or the heat inside the implant. The coke and the pills are doing their job. She carries Frances to give her some air. Thankfully, it's a quiet street, and she sees no one.

The end of the block runs into the busy boulevard facing the park. Max stops.

"Frances, this corner is stretching. It's afraid to bend." Her voice gets lost in the cars racing by. "This corner isn't bending." There's no traffic light at this corner, but there is a crosswalk. The sidewalk runs straight into the traffic. Max's cell phone rings, startling her. She takes it out of her back pocket. It's an unknown number.

"Yeah?" She watches the blur of cars racing over the sidewalk.

"Where are you?"

"Wolf?"

"I'm on my way." He speaks with constricted vocal cords.

"Tutu didn't work out." Max has to look at something that isn't moving, so she looks at her feet.

"Tutu? Who? But you can front me."

Talking to Wolf is going to make her pass out. "I'm not sure I have any more hands to lend." Max looks at Frances. Frances frowns and appears uncomfortable. Max loosens her grip on her.

"Forgive me. A lonely road is one with blossoms of expectations. Nobody's perfect, sweetheart."

Max wilts to the ground. "But, Wolf, what if I expect you to let me down?" She puts Frances on her knee.

"So what you're saying is you disgust yourself because you are a bad friend. Yes, that's it. You disgust yourself," he says, as would a helpful friend trying to guide you to the answer. Wolf speaks with such earnestness, it almost disguises his anger.

"Yeah, I guess you remind me of that. So maybe stay away from me."

"There you go," Frances says. She claps her little hands.

"Oh, I get it! How could I be so utterly unperceptive? You're on coke, you bitch!"

Max hears a beep in the phone. It must be another call. She presses Send.

"Yeah?"

"You wasting my time?" Carlotta sounds like her chin is tucked into her chest, like she is choking on her own neck.

Cars slow and the passengers stare at her and then one honks. The sound reverberates inside her organs. Her body feels like it's wet cement; things are getting stuck in it.

"Damn it," Max says, glad she didn't say Jesus. "I can't cross the street."

"You don't got any fight in you?"

Frances says, "Let's go look at the ocean."

Max shakes her head no, then says, "Yeah, I do."

"You been spoiled. Used to getting everything you want." Carlotta uses more words than her air will allow.

"Doesn't count if I'm being told what I want." Max grabs Frances and tries to push herself up with just her legs.

"You're a wimp and a fake." Carlotta says this so fast it echoes in Max's brain, "wimp 'n a fake, wimp 'n a fake, wimp 'n a fake." She remembers Shake 'n Bake pork chops Eddie used to cook and serve with applesauce.

"Thanks." Max finally hoists herself up. Fleets of metal, tons of it, zoom by. The crosswalk with the signal is so far away. Her truck is just past the blur.

"You figured out what you're doing yet?" Carlotta sounds like she's holding back a belch. Or holding in a hit.

"What do you mean?" Max's gaze is transfixed on the sidewalk that stretches a path across the boulevard.

"Chin up, look both ways." Carlotta coughs up something and spits. "Why don't you come over? Come on over. I'll fix you, baby."

"Where do you live?" Max focuses past the shapes and the park to her truck at a meter under a tree about a basketball court away.

Carlotta gives her directions, then hangs up, and Max sticks her chin out and steps off the sidewalk.

"I don't want to go there," Frances says. "Let's go to the beach."

"Shut up, Frances." Max puts her away in the pocket of her hooded sweatshirt this time.

No one is going to see me, she thinks, no car is going to stop. She keeps her eyes straight ahead. To her left, she hears brakes squeak and a motor droning. She walks slowly across the boulevard. To the right a car slows to a stop. The word "fix" swarms her brain. Carlotta is the one who can make her better.

seventeen

CARLOTTA'S NEIGHBORHOOD IS called Callocco Town. The buildings are tall, six stories or more, and decorated with moldings, lions, or gargoyles. Max drives slowly and looks for the tallest one and a pair of sneakers hanging from a telephone line or a power cable. Max knows that in this neighborhood, Carlotta and Albert are royalty. She looks for a place to park. Hanging by its shoelaces from the telephone cable that stretches a line from one side of the street to the other is a pair of Nikes meant to mark territory and to indicate that this is an area where drugs are sold. These must be Albert's. Carlotta told Max that Albert was almost caught by the fireman who tried to cut down his shoes from the cable; Albert had fired his gun at the crane of the fire truck. Max passes by the Lincoln parked in front of Carlotta's building. Carlotta warned her not to park there if the space was available because her car windows might get broken. People new to the neighborhood learn fast. Most everybody is on some kind of drug.

Max parks a couple blocks away. She leaves Frances, whining, in the truck on the passenger seat and walks, her foot almost raw. Carlotta said the corner boys don't bother you if you're a local, but if they haven't seen you before, they hustle you or even jump you. She spots Q-tips on the ground, probably dropped by someone fumbling in her pocket for her works because she couldn't wait and had to crouch between two cars and fix. Either that or shit on herself. A few guys on the corner stare at her and before they can say "chiva" she shakes her head "no." They sneer at her like they know her type. Like they know what girls who are strung out like she is will do. She looks at herself through their eyes and sees the oil shining on her skin, smells the rotten potato smell coming off her, the heroin rising up like an evil spirit from her pores. She feels her vagina, tender where Grandpops tore it, and just above it the burning where the implant is, stuck under a layer of pus. She looks at the stripes of the athletic sock that holds her jeans up hanging out from under her sweatshirt. How stupid. Well, none of her belts fit. She's got good veins, thank goodness, so it's not like she has to tie off every time. An unleashed Rottweiler barks at Max as if she is some kind of dangerous person. Max nods at the dog's owner, a man with a long white beard, a hefty gut stretching a Dee Dee Ramone shirt, and a wide stance. He says, "Easy, Connie," and comes off his lean against the gate of Carlotta's building.

Max says, "I'm going to Carlotta." She acts like she belongs here, like they've got something in common.

The dog owner gives her a respectful nod, not looking at her too long, and aims his puckered lips at a window behind him, creating the loudest, clearest whistle Max has ever heard. He opens the gate and Max continues to glide while her brain feels like it's disintegrating, as if it is full of slugs, slugs with salt being poured on them. She presses the top button. There is a buzz and a click. She opens the door. The elevator creaks and wobbles. She feels the walls closing in on her as it ascends like it's suspended from a shoestring. Cries from some children in the building echo in the elevator shaft. One somber wail overpowers a festive song on the radio. A well-dressed woman who's probably going to church gets on the elevator as Max gets off. Max has an urge to jump down the elevator shaft and find the source of the cry. Maybe the kids don't feel like sitting in church—that better be all it is, Max thinks. At the end of the hall, Carlotta's door is open. She sits in her wheelchair inside the door frame, very still. Max tightens the athletic sock around her pants. Her feet don't want to touch the floor. She feels like she's walking on the forbidden grass of St. Paul's church right in front of Sister Margaret, and just then Carlotta shrieks and Max jumps. Carlotta laughs and Max decides she must be high.

"Look at you, Puppy! See, I'm here." Max finds herself right in front of Carlotta in her wheelchair and Carlotta holds out her arms, her eyes bulging like she is indeed high. "Give me a hug." Max bends down and hugs her, smelling the rose oil again. Carlotta's strong hands squeeze the cords of muscle in Max's back from the top of her spine almost to the bottom. After Carlotta lets go, she spins her chair around in one fast motion. "Come in and shut the door."

Max guides the door shut like it's an old lady and is startled by an almost life-size papier mâché Jesus.

"Albert carries Him in the parade," Carlotta says as she rolls to her spot by the window. Max stands by the door because Carlotta doesn't tell her to sit or to make herself at home.

Small, intricate shrines illuminate each corner of the square living room. Burning candles surround pictures of Jesus and Mary draped with rosary beads. Daisies and carnations soak in vases of fresh water. Max looks at Carlotta; she seems to have forgotten about Max in her vigil at the window. There is a shrine just to the right of the window, behind Carlotta's wheels. Max kneels on the plush red throw rug that lies on the wood floor before the shrine. She follows the smell of banana mixed with nutmeg, cinnamon, clove, and vanilla and finds a piece of bread on a little plate nestled between candles. A picture of a young girl, maybe seven, waving from one of the paddleboats on the lake in Echo Park, is propped against a glass vase holding white carnations and one new pink rose. Another picture is of the same girl at about thirteen, staring through heavy runny black eyeliner, her dark painted lips curled right before they say, "What the fuck are you doing, Ma?" A yellow candle encased in glass reads, "La Santísma Trinidad, The Holy Trinity." Next to it is a bottle of yellow Holy Trinity oil. Pink petals from yesterday's rose gather around a picture of a young woman in an open casket. She, too, is surrounded by pink roses and a wreath of white carnations.

"Read it," Carlotta says, still looking down on the street.

Max stares at the shrine. "Read what?"

"The candle."

"La Santísma—"

"No, the back, dummy." Max, trying to steady her hands, takes the picture of the girl in the open casket from its place against the prayer candle and lays it faceup on the pink rose petals. The yellow wax is liquid toward the top and the glass is hot there. Max holds the candle at the bottom and is careful not to let anything spill out.

"'The Son may guide me, The Father may guard me, The Holy Spirit be with me. With the grace of our Lady be blessed. With the tunic of our Lord be wrapped up, so that I will not be hurt, jailed, or killed. Jesus Christ, Savior of the World, take me away from the dangers of evil, and lead me in the path of goodness, with God the Father, God the Son, and with God the Holy Spirit. Amen.'"

"Sometimes I like to hear that out loud like that." Carlotta sighs and smiles.

"Sometimes my head aches so bad I want to stick it in a meat grinder."

"I know, Puppy." She turns her wheels so her back is to the window and looks down at Max squirming on her knees.

Max wants to ask for some pills but thinks better of it. She takes the girl in the coffin off the rose petals and places the candle back on the shrine for her to rest against. Max's arms are still sore from missing the vein and scraping them raw. She carefully pushes her sleeves up to let the air dry them out.

"My mother loves roses. She paints them."

"I don't want to hear about your mother. Albert!" Carlotta hollers toward a room off the dark hall. "I'm going to give you some of my famous banana bread," she says to Max. Her gold chains disappear inside the creases of her neck. "This is the real thing, baby. No box bread here. Albert!"

His white wife beater shows first, then his skin, creamy. He stops when he sees Max in front of the shrine.

"You can sit on the couch, you know."

Max goes to the red couch, sits on it, and puts her elbows on her knees and her cheeks in her hands. She looks at the hardwood floor and out of habit tries to spot bits of crack. She reaches for a white speck on the floor and her elbow sticks to her jeans. The white speck turns out to be lint. She picks at a piece of skin hanging from her elbow.

"She came for some of my banana bread. Cut her a slice, Albert." Albert hasn't taken his eyes off Max. He shakes his head and walks into the open kitchen.

"Looks like she need something to calm her nerves, Ma."

"Piece of my bread will be fine." Albert delivers a glass of guava juice and a plate with four slices of the bread. He stands with his back to Carlotta and tilts the plate so a pill rolls out from under the bread. Then he puts the plate in Max's lap. She takes the juice. He nods at her and returns to the room off the dark hall.

Max looks for more pills under the banana bread and finds three more while Carlotta stares out the window. She presses the four pills into the corner of the squishy bread so Carlotta doesn't see and feeds herself the wad like a dog takes pills in liverwurst or hamburger. She downs it with the guava juice. Carlotta rolls to the end of the couch. Max takes another bite of the bread. It's moist and sweet, with a chewy vanilla crust. Carlotta watches her, scowling, her hands folded over her belly.

"This is the best banana bread I have ever had." Max understands this is the "fix" Carlotta meant.

"Well, go on and eat it then. What's this picking up little bits with your fingers? Take a whole piece and shove it in your mouth. Enjoy it, girl." Max doesn't want the food to absorb the effects of the pills, whatever kind they were. And how did Albert have them so available for her anyway? He must be popping these himself, she thinks. But thank goodness he shared. Suddenly, she is consumed by a hunger that feels like it will never ever be satisfied. The bread tastes so fresh and real. There are little chunks of banana that taste like they've been marinated in honey. After she swallows the last bite of the last piece of bread, she audibly gulps the rest of the guava juice.

"My daughter overdosed on October 17, just this year. She used to beg me to make it for her when she was little. She'd sit down and eat the whole loaf."

Max can't help but lie down on the couch. This is the first time she's been able to rest in a long time. "I didn't realize it hadn't been very long. I—"

"How the hell would you know? Albert!" Carlotta hollers over her shoulder and rubs her stubs. "Bring me some lotion and Neosporin!"

Albert emerges from the hall again. Max notices now that some of his hair is growing back.

"If you haven't shaved your head since the last time I saw you, then your hair represents my fresh start," Max says.

Albert looks at her with great pity as he hands the aloe Suave lotion and Neosporin to his mother.

"You were shiny, shiny bald when you took me to the doctor." Max tries to sit up.

"No, stay there, mija," Carlotta says. "Undo your pants. I want to take a look at your cut." Max unbuttons her Levi's and works them down a bit. Albert turns to leave.

"Albert," Carlotta talks to him like he's a lazy teenager. "Where are you going? Move the table so I can get close to her."

Albert moves the coffee table out a foot and Carlotta pushes the wheels so she's next to Max. The incision is swollen and full of pus.

"Did you cut at this? Try to dig it out?" She slaps her fat hand against Max's cheek.

"No!" Max rubs the sting out of Carlotta's slap.

"You know it will still work even if you cut it out."

"I didn't think of cutting it out."

Carlotta clucks her tongue. "It should look like this." She motions Albert over. He stands by her side. His Dickies are already low enough to expose everything. She lifts his tank top and he lowers his boxers. To the right of the ridge of his left hip bone is a typical scar with two lines going through it. It's next to two others just like it.

"This is his third one. All his healed up fine." She presses around Max's wound. "Hmm. No, Puppy. This don't look right." She looks up at Albert and softly says, "Bring me some alcohol and the scalpel, and fix up a pipe for poor baby to suck on." Carlotta looks at Max and smiles. "Or do you want to shoot it?"

Max remembers what Carlotta had said about a hot shot. But shooting it would be so fine.

"That'd be swell."

"No, let's be a little more social than that." She remembers something else. "Paper towels, Albert!"

Max's body is like oil on water, keeping her from sinking below the surface of the couch. And every time Carlotta pokes into her flesh just above her pelvis in the softest part of her body, she loosens a little more. Phyllis would rub Zooey's belly and say, "This is my favorite place to rub. It's her softest part." And Max would admire how trusting Zooey was, lying on her back, her tongue hanging out and smiling, tail wagging, the softest part of her exposed, letting it be touched.

Carlotta takes the lotion off the coffee table and moisturizes her stubs. Her gold bracelets jingle as she massages her skin in circles.

Albert returns, his hands full of the requested utensils.

"Let her have the pipe before I do this."

Albert stands above Max and carefully hands the pipe to her; she holds it vertical to her lips. He holds out a lighter. It looks as big as his head. His eyes, covered by dark wet lashes, watch the flame against the rock, then the smoke rolling to her mouth. He looks at her face and her eyes for a second and then looks back at the lighter. Max watches his eyes and tries to see if they're like his sister's. They tell her that no matter how hard he tries he can't stop listening to the voices. He focuses with intensity like he's trying to ignore something. Then they tell her when to stop sucking in. She inhales the smoke of the especially strong crack a little longer, and the euphoria of being exactly where she is supposed to be overwhelms her.

"Thank you. Thank you so much," Max says, and Albert watches the smoke carve its way into the air.

"My turn." Carlotta reaches for the pipe. Max passes it and Carlotta takes a small hit and hands it to Albert, who is staring at Max like she's an imposter.

"I don't feel like it, Ma."

"I don't care. Just a teeny one to complete the circle." He takes the pipe slowly, giving it time to cool, and lets the flame touch the rock just for a second because it's already hot. The smoke is thick as it rolls down the pipe into his mouth. He bends down and his gold cross hits Max on the chin and his mustache tickles her nose as he blows his hit into her mouth, down her throat. Her lungs spread like a stingray and catch the rich smoke. Her eyes are closed. She lies entangled in the giant stems of roses. Their blossoms are old but hanging on. A few thorns prick her skin and itch. She holds her breath as long as she can, and then the smoke needs to get out. Her lungs burst and the roses tower above her, tall as trees. The force of the breath and smoke shakes the petals loose and they fall unwillingly around her.

"Sorry about your sister." She opens her eyes. Albert is gone.

Carlotta cleans Max's infection with some alcohol and blows on it. Max squirms. Now she sits prone, with the scalpel just above her skin. "Shut up. Are you going to sit still?"

Max holds herself.

"You get to be anything you want to be in life. If you want to be a junky, be a junky. I used to tell her it's not up to me to judge. She wasn't low-key about it. She went after that high with all her little heart." She rests the blade on the puffy wound. Max feels the cold metal. Then Carlotta waves the scalpel excitedly. "I got to clean this out, Puppy."

"Did she ever have one of these pellets?" The blade cuts into the lump; more blood comes out than pus. Carlotta grabs the paper towel and dabs at the liquid. It feels hot, like a bee sting.

"Yeah, she had one. She didn't OD from heroin. It was

speed. Her heart exploded." She pours some alcohol on the paper towel and soaks up the ooze. It burns. Max yelps, and she thinks maybe she should ask Carlotta to clean the scrapes on her elbows and her foot, but decides not to say anything.

"I can't blame Jesus, see; it's not Jesus's fault or man's fault. If anyone is to blame, it's Mother Nature. Mother Nature is a manifestation of God's wrath, chewing up everything and spitting it out in order to survive."

Albert is by Carlotta's side again. He hands Max the pipe, and his mother some gauze and tape. "Pills?" He reaches in his pocket and pulls out two Libriums and goes to get some water for Max.

"Better make it four," Carlotta says. Max lights the pipe with her own lighter from the pocket in her jeans. She pulls in the flame too fast, but she holds it in and takes another hit.

"I think I really need a cigarette," Max says. The small of her back sticks to the red velvet couch.

"No smoking in the house. Anyway," Carlotta takes the pipe from Max, "you got to love all these freaks trying to save Mother Earth, and I say don't you worry about her. She will destroy all of us before she goes down. Respect her, but, please, don't waste your time being a fucking martyr." She takes a small hit. Albert gives Max pills and water.

"You don't have to take them all at once," he says.

Max rolls her eyes and pops all four with the water. Albert shakes his head and goes to the window to check out the street. Carlotta squirts Neosporin in Max's cut.

"In every species there are predators. Does a lioness cry or blame anything but nature when something eats her cub?

Drugs and disease are predators. Nature as it is today, as crazy and confused as it is, took my baby away from me. And that's just the way it is."

"I'm glad you don't have to be mad at anyone."

"Well, Puppy, there is one person I was mad at. But you took care of him for me. See the nature of things? I just wish Yosakwa had had the same fight in her that you do."

"Who did I take care of?"

Carlotta breaks off a piece of tape, places the gauze on Max's pink skin, and presses it on.

"Why, child, where you been?" A snort escapes her. Recovering, she whispers, "You killed Grandpops. Grandpops was always looking for other ways to get paid. Sure, I knew about that. And, for years, I know he didn't like working for me—he wanted to be the big boss man. But for him to take my Yosakwa ... I didn't know. Grandpops was lying to me about that all this time, him telling me he didn't know where she was getting her shit. I found out about all this just after the motherfucker died. Albert flat out told me. That's not what men do. It's what women do. Relieve their conscience by giving it to you. Albert has always been soft like a woman. It's my own fault, but someone's got to take care of me."

Carlotta has screwed the caps on the rubbing alcohol and Neosporin; she now scrapes the pipe. A lot of residue makes molasses streaks inside the pipe. She pushes the Chore Boy through with a pen, does it a couple times until the pipe is clean, and all the residue sits on the Chore Boy filter. "This is my favorite part," she says. She snaps her fingers. Then she wipes her eyes and forehead. Beads of sweat reappear almost immediately.

Max quickly hands Carlotta her lighter and says, "Mine too."

Carlotta drags lightly and holds it. Her hits never leave her body. Her eyes fill with pity. "I see you're useless. You're like a twelve-year-old girl. Is that how old you were when you started getting high?"

Carlotta finally hands the pipe to Max, and Max feels like everything will be all right.

"Nine when I first got drunk." Max's eyes cross as she looks down the pipe at the lighter.

"Great. You hadn't even hit puberty yet. Why don't you go help Albert bag up that shit in there? I need to think." She grabs the hot pipe from Max. "You be careful of your wound."

Max peels her back off the couch and catches her jeans before they fall to the floor. She gets her pants buttoned, sock tied, and enters the dark hall. She can hear Albert talking. Is he talking to her?

eighteen

"SOMETIMES, THE ONLY way you can know that you're real is to tell the truth. That's why I told Ma. I'd become invisible."

Max isn't in the room yet. She is still in the blurry dark of the doorway. Her eyes adjust as bits of light squeeze in between the filter of darkness. Albert's room is moving. The air is thick with the kind of heat that rises from hot concrete. It's a small room with crates of notebooks and papers pushed to the corners and edges. There are two bookshelves filled with books. Candles wave and flicker from a long black shelf nailed to the wall. Book spines shine. The dim light from the candles makes shadows on the wall. The window directly ahead lets in some light from the buzzing street lamp outside. A breeze from the open window threatens to blow out the candles. Their flames curl and stretch.

There is nothing on the walls except for a few nails and holes where there once were pictures or posters. On the shelf is a frame, picture side down, hidden. A black futon is pushed into a corner and a long black table is at the end of it. The only solid thing in here is Albert, and he sits at the edge of the black futon, scooping powder into little ziplock bags and then placing them on an electronic scale. He's wearing surgical gloves.

"Am I hearing voices?" she asks.

"I didn't say nothing."

Max continues to stand in the doorway, the last hit of crack keeping her afloat. "I'm supposed to help you bag this stuff."

Albert doesn't look up. With his head, he indicates with his head the spot next to him, which happens to be the only place to sit besides the wood floor. "Sit down."

Max sits on the low futon. The gauze tape pulls on her skin, but nothing hurts. They're almost squatting; Albert's legs arc just about in his armpits. In this room he seems calm. He reads the scale and picks up a baggie, seals it. He concentrates on what he's doing even though he's done it so many times. His arms have dark streaks down them where veins have died. She doesn't see any fresh marks. The gold cross on its long chain swings from his neck. Yosakwa must have been younger. Max wonders if they fought or if he took care of her. Probably both, she decides. Did they laugh together? It seems that Albert hasn't laughed in a long time.

"Why don't you put some gloves on?" He reaches for the box behind them.

"Why wear gloves? I'll wash my hands."

"Because you get pretty jacked from just touching this stuff."

He rolls his eyes. "Oh I forgot, that's all you care about. Don't wear the gloves. I don't give a shit."

"Jesus," she says.

They sit in silence. Max watches Albert scoop the white powder with a little plastic spoon into the approximately one-inch by one-inch baggies.

"Thanks for the pills."

"I'll hand you the bag after I've filled it, and then you ziplock it and weigh it. The scale has to say .010. Okay?"

"Do I need to wash my hands?" Max takes the tiny baggie he hands her, and he looks at her like she's crazy and shakes his head no. She presses the bag closed and some of the powder gets on her fingers. She places it on the scale.

"This one weighs too much."

"Well, dump a little out." Albert shifts in his seat a little, and rolls his head around. Max dumps some back in his pile.

"I was just thinking of that scene from that Woody Allen movie where Woody sneezes on all this coke when the tray gets passed to him." She closes the baggie and it weighs just about right. Max licks the coke off her fingers and wipes them on her jeans.

"You say some stupid things." The baggies are piling up because he works fast. Max's hands are sweating and her lips and tongue are numb, but for a short while Albert seems almost pleasant.

"You're pretty self-righteous for having three scars," she says. Another baggie completed.

"It wore off." He hands this bag directly to her.

"It wore off?" She puts it on the scale without sealing it and some coke sprinkles out.

"Yeah. Watch what you're doing."

"How do you know?" Max wipes up the spill with her index finger and rubs it on her gums.

"Because it's been like three months!"

"And you haven't shot any dope?"

"No, man." He glares at her. "Ain't those pills kicked in yet?"

"Wow."

Albert sits back and whips off his gloves.

Max wants to ask if by chance he has a needle left over so she can shoot a few lines. Or does he have any pot so she could roll a primo. Instead, she watches him walk, silhouetted by the street lamp shining in the big window. He slouches against its frame; it's missing a screen. He's got his Camel straights on the ledge, and holds them out to Max.

"A smoke," she moans and hobbles with heavy legs to the window. The pills are beginning to loosen all her fibers. Librium legs, the patients in her first detox called it.

She plops down against the other side of the window frame and takes the cigarette Albert gives her even though it's a straight. He puts one in his mouth too and takes the lighter from his deep pocket and holds it to Max's Camel first. Down on the street, a kid rides by on his bike and whistles. About forty seconds later, a cop car drives by.

"If you had some pot we could roll some crack in it and make a primo," Max suggests.

"Yeah, we could." Albert exhales his first drag and ashes out the window except there's no ash formed yet.

"Why are you being nice?" Max draws on the Camel straight. It's like sucking air.

"I'm not." He takes his comb from his back pocket.

"Do you have any pot?" But Albert keeps looking down at the boys on the street and runs the comb through his mustache. Two of the boys could be thirteen. Albert was probably younger when he started using and dealing. The boys lean and spin their skateboards. "So this thing is going to wear off after three months?"

"Not even that long."

"Two months?"

Albert chucks his smoke down on the street and heads back to the futon. "I don't know."

"You do too! It's not like I can't go to the library and look up Naltrexone on the Internet."

"It usually lasts forty-five to sixty days. It dissolves."

"Why did I think this thing was going to be in me forever?"

"Because, like a dog, you have no concept of time." He gets back into his squat position.

"There is too much time." The smoke comes out of Max's nostrils and she pushes her relief from this idea of there being an end out of her mind.

Albert picks up the plastic spoon. "There's not enough time."

The cell phone Carlotta gave Max rings unanswered. It's a familiar number. "Should I call?" she asks, disposing of her Camel. "I might have a customer."

"Go ahead. The signal is weak." He points to a phone on his bookshelf next to the door. The phone is the old kind where you have to stick the tips of your fingers in the holes and spin. It serves as a bookend for some thick art books. Large yellow stickers that say "Used Saves: Textbooks from your bookstore" are still stuck on them.

After half a ring a girl picks up the phone and says, "Yello?"

"You just called me." Max heaves some air out of her lungs.

"I want to try this again, Maxi, and I promise I won't say no if you won't say no."

"I don't think I should drive right now."

"Oh, really?" Tutu says suspiciously.

"Hang on a second." Max covers the mouthpiece. "Albert, want to give me a ride?"

"She worth it?"

"Yeah, she's strung out, and I should probably go." Max realizes she doesn't want to go. She feels better.

Max talks into the phone and picks a yellow used sticker off one of the books. "Yeah, okay, where? I'm not going back to that park."

"Just come to my house. Victoria and Lincoln."

"Fine, Lincoln and Victoria." She hangs up. The book's title is *Art Through the Ages*.

"That's too far." Albert is reading the scale. He is almost done with the bagging.

"Shoot. You're right. I'll have her meet me at my place."

Max calls Tutu back and they arrange to meet in one hour at Max's apartment, and then she sits back down next to Albert to continue her task of weighing and sealing. Albert drops a baggie on the floor and curses it. Max reaches for the pile of sealed and completed baggies and begins to put a few in her pocket, but she stops.

After Albert picks up the baggie he dropped, he reaches under the surface of the table to a cigar box and retrieves a rolled-up dollar bill and a student identification card. He chops out six lines, using up the rest of the coke. Max watches it disappear into the money. He peels off his glove and rubs at his nose and hands the dollar to Max. She hesitates.

"I'd much prefer to shoot it."

"Oh please, bitch."

"Don't talk to me like that."

"Habit." He takes off his other glove.

"Yeah, well, it's rude, and I know you have a rig here." Albert's thighs lift him gracefully up and out of the room. He returns with a glass of water, a spoon, a Q-tip, and a brand new needle. He sets them in front of her.

"Unbelievable. You are gallant."

Albert slides lightly back down onto the futon next to Max, who picks up the student ID and scrapes her three thick lines into the spoon. Before she puts the card down, she looks at it. He doesn't have a mustache in the photo. The card is from Los Angeles Community College.

"You're handsome, too."

Albert is silent. She doesn't really care what he is doing at the moment.

Max draws some water with the syringe and trickles it over the coke. She rolls the piece of cotton between her fingers.

"What's your major?" she says, still needing to talk.

"It was art history."

Max drops the cotton in the clear solution and presses the tip of the needle into it as Albert says, "Mom will be sorry to see you leave."

Max pushes up the left sleeve of her sweatshirt while holding the outfit between her teeth and examines her arm. "I'll come around. Of course." When shooting coke, she wants to make a perfect hit to avoid a painful abscess. She quickly unties the sock around her waist and reties it on her left arm, trying not to drool because of the rig in her mouth. She pumps her fist, slurps the needle from between her teeth, and eases the tip into the vein puffing up along her bicep. She hears Albert whiff up his last line. The blood runs into the syringe thick and dark. This is a strong vein. When she pushes down on the plunger, Albert warns from somewhere inside a deep hole, "Not a lot of cut." Her insides shake loose. She withdraws the needle and Albert lies back onto the futon and stretches his arms above his head, expanding his ribs. Max stands up. She bursts up, her head hitting the ceiling. She breathes out like someone is pushing her gently every few seconds between her shoulder blades. It's Ernest. His arm's around her and he pats her on the back. "Congratulations," he says, "you're not even a person anymore."

"Holy moley," she pants.

"I feel a lot better, too." With both hands, Albert wipes the sweat and sadness off his face.

In the next room, Carlotta is putting stickers on the cover of a Good News Bible, appearing not to need company. She sits in her wheelchair in front of a card table with a stack of Bibles. Stickers of angels and crosses and saints that say "Congratulations! Your First Communion" and "Feliz Navidad" are scattered in piles. She turns to the title page of the Bible.

"Thank you for everything, especially the banana bread." Some sweat soaks and stings Max's eyes. She wipes them with the sleeve of her sweatshirt and bumps into Albert, who stands in front of the door. Albert rolls his eyes, showing no effects of the lines he just snorted.

Carlotta doesn't look up from her spread of stickers. The title page is full of carefully placed stickers, but there are a few spaces left. "Where you going?"

Max takes a deep breath to try to make sense and talk. "Tutu. A customer. She called me. My apartment."

"I like that you came here." Carlotta holds out her index finger, scanning the assortment of stickers. She chooses a slender Mother Mary and presses her between two hearts.

"Me too."

"I'm going to give her a ride home," Albert says.

Carlotta's hand lifts up and waves while she pretends to concentrate on the "Feliz Navidad" Bible. She picks out some stickers of St. Michael and St. Christopher and lays them out on a fresh page before actually sticking them on. Max looks at the stack of Bibles and stickers, and Carlotta next to them.

"Take care of our girl," Carlotta says as Albert shuts the door.

nineteen

MAX AND ALBERT walk the three blocks from Albert's Lincoln to Max's apartment in silence. She wonders what really happened with Eddie and Frances, and considers giving her to Albert, but Frances is still in her truck, back in Callocco Town. The coke in Max's system doesn't alleviate the soreness at the bottom of her left foot, but the pills fight with the coke and make things pretty. The sun's shift is ending and the moon waits in a clear spot in the dappled pink sky. The smog mixes with the changing light to make something beautiful from the ugliness. They pass a dancing lady with long wavy gray hair, holding up the hem of her lace ruffle as she twirls around her changing shadow on the sidewalk. Her skirt is made of handkerchiefs sewn together with large stitches. She is round and flushed. The skin showing on her arms is shiny and tight and barely contains the life inside her.

"That's Hanky Lady. She's my favorite," Max says.

"She's beautiful." Max is not surprised he thinks so.

It's Sunday, so there is no traffic. The electricity running along the telephone wires sounds like rain, not real rain, but the kind of rain that comes out of the nature-sound machines for insomniacs or people who live in noisy neighborhoods. Around here, it's a relief when the sun goes down. Not just because you made it through another day, but also because you get a fresh start. Plus, the shadows make it easy to hide, so you feel safer. Max wonders if anyone is noticing that she's walking with Albert and if this might get her some status—in other words, safety. Grandpops's crate is still adorned with fresh flowers. Somebody has added a photo of Grandpops, which leans against it. His dewy cheeks hold up his thick square brown glasses because he is smiling, and a bollo hat with a feather defies gravity on the side of his head. It's a recent picture, but it looks as if it was taken in the sixties. They cross the street to Max's apartment.

"Do you think it's safe for me to be around here?" Max asks.

Albert's lower lip disappears into his mouth and Max can see little black hairs growing between his lip and his long chin. He clenches his fists inside the pockets of his hooded sweatshirt.

Max walks on the balls of her feet and pulls on Albert's shoulder. She whispers, "Do they all think I killed Grandpops?"

"Shut up," Albert says. He seems angry, but Max understands he's not mad at her.

When they get to the other side of the street, he stops. They face each other for a moment. Max is not trying to hide the mounting anxiety this possibility has inspired. All she hears now is her breath. What she's learned to do when she feels this panic is focus on something. If she is with a person, she will focus on the veins. Ears are good, too. Albert is in long sleeves so first she looks at his eyes and the lashes, long and straight. Albert is looking at the ground. His face has wide planes and soft angles. His thick eyebrows, and especially his mustache, are the only masculine characteristics. The rest comes from his insides: the way he moves, what he doesn't say. Max looks into his mouth and the hairs that frame it. Two big front teeth seem very far away. She can barely make out the grayness between the two front teeth, spreading from the tight space between them.

His lips purse and then he says, "Let's go see." He takes Max by the hand and drags her across the street back to Grandpops's corner, past his crate, and into the corner store. When Max first moved into the neighborhood, if she was next in line, the lady with feathered hair at the register would take everyone behind her and they would speak in Spanish and laugh and take their time. And the customers knew what was going on, too. They would walk right in front of Max to pay. She would have to wait twenty minutes for her pack of smokes and beer over and over again. It wasn't so different from waiting for the connection. When she knows what's coming, Max can wait.

All that business was before Grandpops had sussed her out. During her first week in the neighborhood, she used to walk by him sitting on his crate in front of the store. She'd say hello and he would pointedly avert his eyes. Then one day, after a month of watching Max come and go and wait while all the other patrons were rung up first, Grandpops looked up at her and nodded his head as she went in. Perhaps it was because it was a hot day and Max had on a sundress that exposed her arms, and the bruises were revealed. The next morning, when Max rolled out of bed, once again out of cigarettes, and shuffled in her tank top, boxers, and slippers across the street, she was actually greeted by Grandpops's smile, and found herself first in line, fairly paying for a pack of Camel Wides before all the other regulars. She thought she had finally earned her place.

But when she walked back out of the store and by the crate, Grandpops took her arm and drew a line down her vein over her bruises and purple scabs with his finger and said, "If you want something, you know where I am. I collect the rent." When his finger reached Max's wrist he wrapped his meaty hand around her limp fingers. "Grandpops," he said, looking up at her through his glasses, a cup of light, steaming coffee in Styrofoam in his other hand, resting on a thick thigh.

"Max," she had said, although she had a feeling she didn't need to.

Grandpops nodded. "In 202."

Max and Albert reach the store's entrance.

"Go in and buy a pack of smokes," Albert orders.

Max just stands there, staring up at Albert, her back to the door. He pushes the door and the little bells hanging from it ring. Max turns around and then he shoves her forward. The lady with the feathered hair, her neck outstretched and her breasts fighting for space inside the Lycra of her blouse, talks with a sweaty man. She stops midsentence and looks at Max. "Jingle Bells" comes from the speakers. Max looks at the door and Albert is standing right outside looking at something other than her. Max takes a deep breath and blows it out, slow and steady. Someone breaks glass in another part of the store and Max's heart skips. She stands in line behind the man at the counter and he doesn't move. She stares at the chocolate Santas and candy canes on the counter. He slowly turns around and glares at Max.

"Just need a pack of Camel Wides, please." The feathered-hair lady's upper lip curls and disappears, and she says something loud and fast in Spanish. The sweaty man takes his time sneering at Max, from her dilapidated sneakers to the greasy hair on her head. Max turns to leave as Albert comes in and puts his arm around her. He leads her right up to the counter. The sweaty man backs off, and the lady shakes out her hair and quickly reaches for a pack of Camels. Albert speaks in Spanish to her, indicating his chest and then pointing to Max. He hands her a five-dollar bill, and then he guides Max out of the store after opening the door for her.

"What did you say? Did you tell her he had a heart attack?"

"Something like that." He shoves his hands in his pockets and starts to walk back to his Lincoln.

"Will you come upstairs and wait while I take a shower? I won't be able to hear the buzzer. I can't remember the last time I bathed." Albert is still walking, but he has slowed down.

Max fakes a frown at him. "Oh, yeah I can! It was in freaking ice and you—"

Albert turns around shaking his head, hushing her with his finger to his lips.

"Yeah, it wasn't exactly a proper bath. A bath of ice." She opens the main door with her key. The stairway up to her apartment is dark and musty. Albert goes first. Max pulls her body up by the handrail. She has her other hand on her hip bone, which feels like it's coming through her back. She thinks it would be nice if he would carry her. At her door she looks at him. He's antsy and looks at the door, waiting for her to open it. "But, thanks," she says.

Max catches her breath and starts to slide the broken door open enough to let them go through. Albert acts like he didn't hear her, helps her, and they go inside.

twenty

MAX'S APARTMENT IS dry and stuffy and smells like vinegar. Albert opens some windows. Max lies down on the beige corduroy couch peppered with stains.

"You have any coke on you? I'm weary."

"Man, cool it."

She watches Albert tug on the fridge and take out an orange Gatorade. With his pinky pointing up, he polishes off half the bottle in two gulps. Max is content.

The wall with Grandma Grace's photo is partly painted. Haphazard red brush strokes zigzag over the hospital green. At this moment, Max decides she is never going to complete the wall because she likes the evidence of work the brushstrokes give. Some more old photographs and Max's ink drawings are thumbtacked up. One with a sepia tint is of Grace from the thirties. She sits on a park bench with her friend, whose name Max has forgotten, their legs crossed, with hats on. The friend was a journalist whose son died from a heroin overdose. Max likes that friends were very important to Grace. On the floor are a palette of coagulated oil paint and a stack of canvases. Brushes in a jar of turpentine and a bottle of linseed oil sit amid a blackened spoon, useless needles, and open tubes of paint.

"You have blood on your jeans." Albert points to Max's jeans in the area of the wound and then sets the Gatorade bottle in the sink and walks to the red wall.

Blood soaks into a circle between her coin pocket and zipper.

Max can only stare at Albert. He squats down and takes the brushes out of the turpentine. Her eyes follow him to the sink, where he finds a dish towel. He wipes out each brush one at a time. Sometimes he clucks his tongue and shakes his head.

"What?" She gets no response.

"Weren't you going to take a shower?" He says it as if she had lied to him.

Ernest used to have that same tone. Max kicks off her one Chuck, sits up, now noticing the burning where the blood is, and unlaces the shoe without the sole. It disintegrates around her foot.

Albert sits on the backs of his heels, holding a tube of paint, and picks up a cap to see if it has yellow paint inside. It doesn't, so he sets it aside and picks up another cap. When he finds the matching cap he screws it onto the tube tightly. Max watches him for about a minute. She gets herself up with the intention of walking to her bathroom, but finds herself standing behind him. Then her legs bend slowly, bringing her body to the floor. She lies on her side and curls her body around his kneeling legs, squeezing him as if he needs her to.

Albert can't find the matching red. "You can't find anything here."

"I'm not looking," Max says. She doesn't mind that her face is pressed against the bottom of his sneaker, but she gets the feeling he doesn't want her there, so she starts to get up.

"Why don't you take care of your stuff? Why do you paint?"

Max realizes he was talking about not being able to find caps to tubes of paint, and stays where she is. Her arm wraps around his waist and she sighs. "I like to paint because I don't talk so well. It's like talking to someone."

"Come on, you got to get in the shower."

"I stink."

"Yes, you stink."

Albert removes Max's hand that's been clutching his sweat-shirt at the waist and stands up. Max groans as he pulls her to her feet. She uses his shoulders to steady herself.

"Thanks." Then Max is still because she is looking up into his face. Her neck suffers under the weight of her head and for a second she imagines what she must look like. She wants to let him look at her, even though it's strange. It's a way she can be held by him. He looks at her eyes, then her forehead, her cheeks, her mouth, then her eyes again, one and then the other as if those parts of her face are telling him something. She feels invaded, but then his eyes find peace, resting in hers. Finally, he opens his mouth.

"Know what I see when I look at you?" His soft voice accuses her of hurting him somehow. It shames her.

Max tightens her grip on his black sweatshirt. "What?"

"A waste of a motherfucking life."

Albert's hands, which were holding her under her shoulders, now find her cheeks and the short hair on her head. She feels weak without the support of his hands. He presses his thumbs into the dimples where her smile would be. "You're going to die. I got to stay away from you."

Max can see that he means it in the way he recoils from her. She gives her best smile and wanders into her bedroom. "I won't be long."

As she peers under her bed at the bag of heroin, she hears Albert say, "Don't matter." It feels strange to her that her body doesn't need the heroin as much.

She turns the knob in the shower, sits on the lid of the toilet, and waits for the water to get hot. This shower sounds like cats hissing. She has never liked showers. Junk sits on your skin, like the oily coat of a snake, and when you're strung out you don't want to wash it off, you want to preserve every bit of heroin in your system. But even before she became a junky, she sometimes felt uncomfortable being naked, especially in the shower.

A long time ago, she taped brown grocery-bag paper over the mirror above the sink. It was after a night of bingeing on cocaine. First she cropped her hair and shaved her head. Then she shaved off her eyebrows. She felt like how a dog must feel after getting sheared; all that work building a scent, defining oneself, only to be clipped off. Shaving off her eyebrows was like erasing anger from her face. And the darkness was left just under her eyes in half-moons. She cut out postcards and pictures from magazines and glued them to the paper over the mirror, and now she stares at a recent one, of redwoods on a dark snowy night, a black bear, partly covered in snow, up high in one of the redwoods, hugging it. Safe. He looks sad and wild and sweet, but get him down from that tree and he could tear your guts open with one swipe of his claw.

Sitting forward hurts her wound, so she stands up and unties the long athletic sock woven into the belt loops. Her jeans drop to her bare feet. When the steam starts rising behind the moldy curtain, she pulls the tank top and sweatshirt over her head together. Then, without looking at any part of herself, she steps out of the jeans, over the lip of the tub into the spitting water. Her back is to the spray, which feels like it's removing chunks of skin. It rips at her scraped-up elbows. When she gets used to it, she withstands looking down at her body, at her infection. The gauze still covers it but is soaked with blood and now water. She tears the gauze off and drops it. It spreads into pink elephant ears and floats to the drain. Max uses a rubber stopper for baths, but she doesn't know where the stopper is now. Baths have been impossible, anyway, since an old roommate shot too much heroin and drowned in the damn tub. The gauze has been partially sucked into the drain and looks to Max like a ballerina in a pink tutu reaching up with her arms and legs stuck in the drain, just waiting for some giant finger to grab on to and pull her out. Max remembers she used to be afraid she might slip down drains. Phyllis would look at Max like she was very sad and wring out the washcloth and say, "But, honey—you're not that small!"

"Yes, I am! I am!" Max picks up the gauze and lays it on the side of the tub.

Pubic hairs have formed red bumps trying to break through her skin where the nurse shaved her, and the stitches twist out of the sides of the cut. They didn't hold.

She pulls the two sides of the incision farther apart and cranes her neck to see the white pellet. It has hardly dissolved. There is nothing in the shower to scrape it out with. A half bottle of Ivory dish soap is propped upside down in the corner. She squeezes some into the palm of her hand, rubs her palms together to get some suds going. The smells in the shower become pure and good, clearing the dank odors that come from mold and from Max. She soaps up the cut. She cups her hands and collects some of the hard water and rinses it. There it is. The pellet glistens. Then she thinks that too much hot water might help it disintegrate. The steam gathers thick and rises, and Max feels the blood drain from her head as blackness dissolves the sides of her vision. She kneels down before she falls. Sitting, the hot water beating on her head, she finishes washing her hair and her body and doesn't mind the tenderness of her skin, the sharp feeling of her bones, or her heavy arms, because she is looking around trying to find a way to scrape the pellet out. Tucked back in the soap nook is a fancy razor—fancy because it's one she stole. With the end of its metal handle, she digs the pellet out, ignoring the pinch of it, and catapults it against the slimy tile in front of her. It bounces into the soapy water and dirt and hairs. The tiny white ball follows the bubbles down to the rusty hole, and Max leans in and out of the spray listening to the high-pitched, then low-pitched sounds of the water.

When the water rushing to the drain turns clear, Max stands up and turns the hot and cold faucets toward each other. Her brain is crackling and streaks of light cross in front of her eyes like fluorescent ribbons. She holds on tight to the knobs until her head and vision adjust. The extraction was simple, she thinks, and her hands are still turning the knobs after the water has stopped. It takes her a few moments to notice. The musty odor of her towel gets patted into her skin. She dabs around the soggy empty wound, white at the edges. In her bedroom, she gets down on her hands and knees, lifts the gray sheet, and peers under her bed at the bag of heroin. The buzzer gives a series of Morse code beeps: Tutu.

Max is dizzy still, but she gets up, drops her towel, shakes out the short hair on her head, and drips to her closet.

Albert buzzes Tutu in. Max can hear him open the fridge again. She pictures him sipping more Gatorade with his pinky pointing toward the heavens, and this makes her happy.

Blood rushes to her head as she rummages through a pile of clothes. Everything is either stained with blood, or smells, or both. Finally, she looks up to the clothes on hangers. These are Grandma Grace's clothes. She picks a white polyester leisure suit with a long-stemmed sequined magenta rose climbing up the right leg and a sequined rose on each side of the big collar. Max remembers Grandma Grace swaggering around a bar, telling jokes, holding a Salty Dog with two hands; she'd crippled one hand when she walked through a window. She was very good at entertaining.

She hears Tutu roll in. "Well, who are you?" It sounds like she's doing figure eights. Then she startles herself and yelps.

Albert ignores her question. "Get those fucking Rollerblades off."

Three days should be enough time, Max thinks. Maybe even two, until the Naltrexone wears off. And, if she does lots of coke, pushes it out of her system, it will probably take even less time. But she can still try. Damn. Getting strung out again is a commitment.

Max steps back into the room. Albert lights a Camel and drags hard. He rests his elbow on top of the half-size fridge. His hips jut out and his back stretches into the lean. He picks at a spot of purple paint on his black sweatshirt.

"What the hell is that?"

Max turns around and looks behind her, then back to him. Her face turns hot.

"What is what?"

"Nothin'."

"Please don't make fun of my outfit. It's special to me," Max says.

Tutu stands at about four-and-a-half-feet tall without her Rollerblades and watches the two of them and the space between. Albert crosses his arms and laughs. Tutu walks between them directly to the red wall and has to stand on her tiptoes to look at the ink drawings.

"Hi, Tutu." Max is feeling good despite Albert's cackle because she is in her grandma's fancy suit, because she freed the pellet, because she is happy not to be alone, and because now, with Tutu here, it almost feels like a party.

"Well, look at you! You remind me of Elvis," Tutu says.

Then Tutu refers to her own outfit: zebra tights, the pink tutu, and a leopard-print leotard. "Whenever I wear an animal print, I wear the prey and the predator. My tutu represents the dance of life, and, of course, death."

"Survival," Max says.

"Yeah." Tutu hits the "yeah" like a vaudeville singer finishing up a number. Her relaxed demeanor doesn't lend to the narrow view of a desperate, dope-sick person. There is no urgency contracting her body or her brain. Tutu's attention goes back to the red wall. The paper of one of the ink drawings is curling at its corners. Tutu tries but fails to pat it flat.

"I like this one."

"Thank you."

"But you got your dukes up. You don't let us in."

Max still hasn't moved from the doorway. She doesn't quite know what to do, so she smiles and says, "Okay, that's enough," finding a sound from inside her dry throat. The polyester of the suit scrapes against her skin as she moves to the refrigerator. Albert doesn't move. Max feels as if he's measuring her. She looks at him and he looks away. He moves to the open window next to the fridge and looks out. He is so tightly coiled that without effort he could spring up onto the window's ledge, crack through the glass, leap the one story to the street, and land clean on the pads of his feet. Little tics tweak his shoulder, then his neck. A reflex stretch follows the twitches around his body. He rotates his head. His hand without the cigarette stretches and clenches. There is one Gatorade left. It's tropical punch.

"Do you want to share this, Tutu?" Max asks. The couch rises up to meet her faster than she expected. Her skin feels hot and itchy. Tutu joins her on the couch and they pass the drink back and forth. Max feels the cold liquid cooling her throat and then spreading a pleasant chill across her ribs into her belly. The Librium is helping to take the pain and paranoia away, but it may be causing her blood pressure to drop. Max passes the bottle back and appreciates the sight of the pink taffeta crunching and swallowing Tutu.

"Manna," Tutu sighs after a bountiful gulp.

"Nectar of the gods," Max says.

"Yeah."

Albert, with his back to them, tightens the belt that sits low on his hips. He jimmies the window open with one hand, taps some ash out it, and turns his head toward them. "How much do you want?" The words seem to float fragmented in the air just outside the window, then join together and shoot inside, hitting them in the face, reminding them why they are here.

Tutu lifts one zebra leg, slowly, next the other, and hugs them. "Oh, I have to think."

"Well, you better figure it out." Albert pulls from his cigarette and looks at Tutu, then to Max.

"Who is this person?" Tutu says under her breath.

Albert discards his smoke and slams the window shut. "Don't talk about me like I ain't here, bitch."

"Well, stop calling me bitch."

"Albert, relax." Max puts her hand on Tutu's shoulder and a finger to her lips: hush.

"I don't got time for a fucking tea party. I got to get this done and get you back to your car and deal with some shit." He shakes his head no as if he is trying not to listen to another conversation.

"Okay," Max says.

"This bitch needs to buy some shit now."

The suit sticks to Max's skin. Something she hasn't felt in a long time is shooting down her arms. She looks at her hands. It's like they need to connect with a surface. Like her arms need to get all this energy out because if they don't, it will go to her brain and make her crazy. She shakes them out.

"Then Tutu gets the fuck out," Albert says. "You two are going to kill each other."

"You get out," Tutu says.

"What did you say?"

"Okay, just give me, um, three. Give me five?" Tutu is perched on the back of the couch. Her flushed skin is peeking through her white pancake makeup.

Max stands up and the blurry shapes and objects around her that are supposed to mean home begin to feel unfamiliar, like this is some place she just stumbled upon. "Just calm down. Nobody is dying around here. Jesus. You know? Just watch how you talk."

"Fuck you, it's just the way I talk," Albert says.

"I'm lonely. I just want to hang out with some interesting people," Tutu says.

Albert grips the corners of the open fridge door as if he is going to throw it out the window. His back heaves with breath. He slams it shut, and the building settles. The room drops a few feet, and Max falls onto the couch, and the couch and the floor succumb to gravity. She blinks a few times to clear the spots in her eyes.

Tutu's eyes peer down at Max from high above and over her zebra knees. She says quietly, "I have a secret that no one will understand."

"Me too," Max sighs, sinking further down, holding onto the sight of Tutu like she is a hand dropping a rope for her over the top of a well.

Tutu is comforted. "We did this thing in treatment in one of the groups to check in with each other. PSME. How we feel physically, spiritually, mentally, and emotionally. One word to describe each feeling. Like this." Tutu jerks her head toward Albert, indicating his reading. "Physically: coming down, well, that's two words. Spiritually: hopeless. Mentally: enslaved. And emotionally: burdened."

Max looks at Albert, who has folded his arms over the top of the fridge and is now resting his head there. "I see," she says.

"Very sad. Your turn," Tutu says.

"Well." Max closes her eyes and tries not to fight falling.

"PSME. Physical, spiritual, mental, emotional," Tutu says.

"Invisible, scared, gone, gone."

Soft wings wrap around Max, hold her tight so she can't move, and smother her. She hears Albert's footsteps in the distance.

"Perfect. I'm scared, too. Albert?"

"Get up." Albert's words wet Max's face. Max can't move. He pulls her up.

Max's head is the last part of her to leave the couch. She falls into Albert's chest. He tries to hold her up and slap her face at the same time.

"Open your eyes!"

Her eyes crack open and she sees little smears of purple and yellow and blue glowing against his black sweatshirt.

"I see stars," she says, touching the dried paint. Her head falls into his chest again, and lights flicker behind her eyes. She smells Tide detergent and cigarettes and a little of the paint.

"You smell like the guy I lost my virginity to." Her eyes stay shut and look at the black inside, and pulsing dots of light—blue, purple, and yellow spots, like fluorescent paint.

Tutu laughs with her hands covering her mouth. "Virginity seems very funny to me." She disappears into the corner of the couch.

Albert shakes Max and her neck looks as if it will snap. "I'm not shoving ice cubes up your ass again."

"That won't work," Tutu whispers.

Max's head is dropped backward. She looks at the blur of upside-down sepia pictures on the red wall.

"Her body's giving up," she hears Tutu say.

Max wants to tell them that this has happened before. That it just lasts a few minutes and then it's over. But her mouth won't move. She can control no part of her body, but her thoughts are free. The first time it happened, at Lenny's place, she was terrified. It felt like her soul was leaving her body for good. She was resting on his couch. It wasn't after a shot or a hit of crack or anything. She was just lying there. And all of a sudden, she was paralyzed. She tried to call to Lenny in his bedroom, but she couldn't move her mouth. Her mind was lucid—the thoughts running in it were *come back, please*—but it was like the force inside her that gave her life didn't exist anymore.

Albert picks her up and carries her to her bed. He takes the towel from the floor and runs into the bathroom. He puts the cold wet towel on her face. Tutu watches from the doorway. Max watches from the ceiling.

"You're really selfish," Frances says. She sits on the dusty blade of the ceiling fan.

"I know." Max looks down at her body and at Albert panicking.

"I don't know what else I can do for you." Frances holds her nose as she sneezes. "Dust."

Suddenly, Max is feeling the bed supporting her and Albert's hands cupping her face.

Words form in her head and they manage to come out her mouth. "It's happened before like this. I need to go somewhere else or something."

Albert has put his hands in his lap. Only one knuckle cracks.

"Or maybe it's low blood pressure?" Max tries not to be embarrassed.

"It's more scary for us because it's not like an overdose," she hears Tutu say from the doorway. "There's nothing we know to do."

Albert leans over Max so his head replaces her view of the ceiling fan. He puts one fist on each side of the pillow. The pillow props Max's head up and closer to Albert's. His eyes are angry, but he speaks softly. "You're fucking miserable."

"So are you," Max whispers.

Albert hugs her to him and she sees his face behind her eyelids and she smells and feels him again. "That's what this is," Albert says. He takes a deep breath as if he were drawing it from her neck.

Albert rises off the bed and brushes past Tutu. They hear the front door close.

Tutu scuttles to the bed and puts Max's hand in hers. With her other hand, she pushes the rotten-smelling towel on Max's forehead over her scalp. The water trickles along her ear and drips onto the pillow.

"Why is he so mad at you?" Tutu says.

Max tries to find the pupils in Tutu's dark brown eyes. Because Tutu's eyes are so pinned, they hide like little fleas. Max still smells the Tide and cigarettes from Albert's sweatshirt instead of the dank towel on her forehead. Then she is upside down again, when he was holding her, and she was trying to focus, but couldn't, on the old pictures and her drawings on the red wall, and his smell like an innate memory, dirty and pure, and the last thing, before her soul left, she remembers the last things she saw were the smudges of paint on his black sweatshirt, like love, like too little time, like stars.

"Because he didn't save his sister," she says.

twenty-one

I T'S TIME FOR bed and Ernest takes one of his books about Africa off the shelf in his bedroom and lies down. Max goes into the bathroom and opens the tampon box where she hides all her stuff—perfume, needles, pipe, crack. Quietly, she takes out her needle and all the stuff. There is no lock on his bathroom door, but she couldn't lock it anyway—he would think that odd because they do pee in front of each other.

She sticks a previously prepared needle of heroin in her vein. And that should be enough, but she wants just one little hit of crack. She'll spray the bathroom first with the perfume, and if he comments, she'll say—don't embarrass me, I have an upset stomach. She sprays some toward the door, and then puts the crack on the pipe. She lights the hit and sucks in.

"Max?" She hears him outside the door.

"Yeah?" That's all she can say because she is trying to hold in a hit.

"Do you think elephants will kill people?"

Max gets off the toilet and blows her hit in it and flushes. "You mean like Babar?"

"Why the perfume?" Ernest says. She can hear him turning the pages of his book. "Not like Babar."

He doesn't like perfume because he prefers her natural scent. She can tell he wants to talk about something. This is usually how he starts, on the other side of a closed door. Max puts everything back in the tampon box, and opens the door.

"Ernest, I had to go to the bathroom, Jesus," she says and washes her hands. Ernest watches her and hugs the book to his chest. Something he read about the elephants has gotten to him. His lime-green boxers make him appear more vulnerable.

"I do think elephants will rise up and kill people," she says. "Why?"

"Because they've had it. There isn't enough food. If I was an elephant, I would smash some people." Max puts toothpaste on her toothbrush.

"Elephants learn about life through experience, not from DNA. They'll remember the abuse," Ernest says.

"Like people." She spits.

"Yeah, and they have really good memories, too. They don't forget."

"That I know."

Max walks to the bed and lies down. Ernest has a nicer bed than she does, with a down comforter, which he has threatened to give to Goodwill because he feels bad for the birds. He lies down next to her with the Africa book.

"Will you read some to me?" Max asks.

Ernest holds the book up to his face. She waits for him to start reading.

"Did you think I wouldn't be able to tell?"

She is grateful he's looking inside the book. She looks at the trees on the cover. "I'm sorry," she says.

Ernest puts the book down. There is no anger, just distress and suffering. "While I'm trying to live, you're trying to die."

"I'm trying to live." Max pulls the comforter up over her face. Ernest doesn't pull it off.

"That's why you're with me, isn't it?"

Max looks at the darkness under the covers and suffocates. "What are you talking about?"

"Because you don't care about living."

Max wakes up.

"Fuck," she says and walks to the toilet. The pee lasts for a long time. Cars breaking through the air down on the street sound like waves rolling in. This feels good, like her body is working right. She checks the incision, the skin around it. It's starting to scab. On the tub, the gauze has dried out like pink papier mâché. Someone is in the other room. Max limps over to the familiar clang of a jar and a hard object. Most of the ache that used to inhabit her entire body is now just in her foot. The rest of her discomfort is in her clear head, in the self-awareness that the good sleep gave.

"You're still here?"

Tutu is on the floor in front of a piece of cardboard box she has leaned against the wall. She sits in the center of tubes of paints, banging a brush around in a murky jar of turpentine. "Good morning," she says.

Tutu appears too content. Max walks quickly back to her room to look under her bed.

"I helped myself to the five I said I was going to buy!" Tutu shouts from the other room.

Max holds the balloons in her hand and looks at the bright rubber colors stretched over the heroin against the skin of her palms. Ernest used to say her voice sounded like helium when she was uncomfortable. "Please don't yell these things," she says more to herself than Tutu. She counts the bindles like she would actually recall the number, and puts the bag back. Then she rummages through the pockets of the jeans she was wearing before she put on Grandma Grace's suit and finds her apartment key and her wallet. There's no cash in her wallet, but if she remembers correctly, there wasn't before, either.

Max shoves her feet into her kung fu slippers and shuffles back to Tutu.

"Cash?"

"On the table," she says with her nose to the board.

Max rolls up the bills and tucks them in one of her breast pockets.

"You feel better?" Tutu asks, looking Max over. "Looking marvelous."

"I guess so."

"You got a couple days off, for sure, while you were sleeping. Just keep going! Or you could go away to a place!"

"No insurance. Got to get on a list for a bed, call every day . . ."

"Wolf is back in treatment. This time in a nice one. Arizona. Or you could go to meetings!" Tutu grabs her mouth because she hadn't wanted to be pushy.

"Thirsty," Max adds on her way out.

The air is misty, or it could be Max's brain adjusting to consciousness after a long-needed rest, and she's not sure what time it is. She steps onto the sidewalk. It's dark. The streetlights glow and blur through the gloss that is over her eyes. People zoom by and she can feel their agitation and the excitement in the air: a workday ends and the rewards of night begin. No one notices her or even bumps into her. The last time she was in the corner store she was with Albert. He has her truck and Frances; now she remembers. But right this minute, it will be okay; she is invisible.

At the store, Max picks out a large bottle of orange Gatorade, a Lil' Debbie package of two chocolate peanut-butter wafers, and a Ding Dong. With a shake of her stiff hair the lady behind the counter puts a pack of Camel Wides in front of Max without being asked. Her accusations remain only in her eyes as she bags the goods and hands the bag to Max.

"What day is it?"

The lady's chin pops into her neck and one shoulder juts toward Max. "Tuesday."

Sunday, I think I took it out on Sunday, Max thinks, scratching the incision as she crosses the street.

She sees something through the vents in her mailbox. It can't be the check from the eye commercial already. Maybe it's a residual check. Maybe unemployment caught her in not declaring her earnings. The key chomps into the mail slot and Max opens it without letting it fall off the hinges. To Maxella Gordon, typed. It's from Eddie. Eddie types everything, even his checks for bills. Max opens the dented door to her apartment building and sits against the wall on the stairs. The chill on the floor cuts through the polyester of Grandma Grace's suit. She unwraps the Lil' Debbie wafers and eats them in two bites. Then she drinks some Gatorade. Her tongue wiggles against the backs of her two bottom teeth. One tooth bends forward but she can't stop herself from pushing on it, so the tooth falls into the pocket inside her gum and lower lip. She leans forward to avoid any blood staining her suit and scoops out the tooth with her forefinger. Spitting on the step below her, she folds the Lil' Debbie wrapper around the tooth and places it inside the plastic bag with the Ding Dong and Camels. The lady included matches, so Max lights a cigarette. She holds the letter, blinks, and clears her eyes. It reads:

Dear Maxella,

I don't know what to do. I'm angry at something that has no face, but inhabits the body of the person I love more than anything.

Nobody can help you.

At least use clean needles. You know, don't share. I don't know what to say anymore. Can you believe that? I am not even going to proofread this because I am tired and I don't want to retype it. But I am sure there are no typos because I am typing at a snail's pace.

Love, Dad

P.S. Leave your mother alone. Your last visit fucked her up for days. Stop being a selfish asshole.

"This is such shit," Max thinks. She hides the letter in the bag and looks down at the stairs as she takes them on, feeling her muscles suffering the weight of her. Don't throw me away, she thinks. *I can make it*. The heroin eats the cartilage in her bones, her body moving and shaking, her reflexes adjusting to her natural state. Then, for a second, and it feels like honesty, she sees the future, where she doesn't fit. At the fucked-up door, the keys drop to her feet before, out of habit, she tries to put the right one in the lock. When she bends down to pick them up, the plastic bottle of Gatorade falls and bounces down the stairs. Max kicks the metal door three times. The sound doesn't satisfy her. She headbutts it. When Tutu appears, Max is crying.

Tutu picks up the keys and puts her arms around Max. Max lets her.

"I dropped the Gatorade," she says.

Tutu goes down the stairs to get the bottle. Max slips inside the apartment and slides the door tightly into place. Tutu flies up the stairs and pushes at the door.

"Ouch!"

Max walks away from the noise and starts for her bedroom. The door moves aside for Tutu, and then slams to the floor. Max looks at the stairwell through the open space.

"You got the letter, didn't you?" Tutu says, massaging her arm.

Tutu's bag and Rollerblades are in a pile by the kitchen sink. Max's numb cheeks tingle as she dumps out the bag. There is a little black sketchbook and lots of lipstick, her white pancake powder—no outfit. In the top kitchen drawer is a sticky spoon, but no needle. Max rips open another drawer and dumps its contents on the floor; nothing but old black cottons, ties, and unopened mail. Tutu keeps smoothing the taffeta of her tutu as if it were wrinkled silk.

"I suggested he write you a letter of encouragement. It wasn't too encouraging, it seems."

Max says, "Give me your rig."

Tutu shakes her head no. "Wait a minute!" She skips past her. "I need your help."

Max picks up Tutu's Rollerblades by the wheels, shakes them out, and drops them.

"Hey, watch it!" Tutu yells.

"Where is it?"

Tutu huffs, releases a moan, and skips over to her painting. She crosses one foot in front of the other, bends her knees, and slowly eases into a comfortable cross-legged position. She sits in the middle of scattered model horses, some rearing, one lying down, a few galloping. Her hands take a horse that would be grazing if there was grass and she puts his lips to hers. She rolls her neck and breathes deeply.

"What the hell?" Max feels her foot throb from banging it on the door.

With her eyes closed, Tutu rotates her neck one more time and then sets a fresh gaze upon her work. Then she looks up at Max with her hand in her mouth and panic in her eyes. "I'm at the crux. Do you think it's done?"

Max audibly blows out air. "God help me," she says.

She limps over to stand behind Tutu. She looks at the three-foot by four-foot piece of cardboard. The left side is blue sky with some orange clouds. The sky meets a reddish brown cliff that leads her eye to the right, where a girl similar to Max is on a horse. The girl is pulling hard at the reins because the horse is about to step off the edge of the cliff. The horse's black eyes bulge and its nostrils flare as it looks down upon probably twenty others, also mustangs, that tumble into the canyon. But if she looks closely into the swirls of sky and clouds, she can see that a few more horses are coming from the left side. The Max on the horse looks in that direction. Those horses won't fall.

"I used your model horses," Tutu says.

"I figured."

"Well?" Tutu pulls at her taffeta.

"It's sad," Max says finally.

"Depending."

"Some live," Max says.

"They saw the one horse at the edge." Tutu looks at Max like she's a small child. "Oh, Max. Well, it was a good way to stay here and make sure you were still breathing without getting totally bored. You should brush your teeth once in a while."

Max breathes into her hand. "But you were painting out here."

"I did the sketch of you while you were out cold. I had to get up real close, but the second day the color came back to your cheeks and I knew all you had needed was some time off." Tutu walks to the sink, turns on the water and opens the cabinet above her. There is a pint of Jack Daniels on the shelf. She stretches for it, twists it open, and takes a neat swig. "And, gosh, you thought I would be so rude. A loaded rig here for you, if you want it." She gestures with the pint to the shelf without turning from the sink. "I figured you'd want a wake-up."

I don't need a wake-up, Max thinks, I'm not sick.

Tutu turns off the water and the pipes creak and settle. Max stands where she is, staring at the cabinet.

Tutu shoves her scattered belongings into her bag, picks up her Rollerblades, and opens the front door. "I'm going."

"Oh, okay." Max slowly starts for the open cabinet.

"You forgot about it while you were looking at my painting."

"I guess."

"You're lucky you don't need it; you're free." Tutu winks at her and closes the door.

The rig is in Max's hand. It's full. She pumps her fist and ties off. Because her favorite old faithful vein hasn't been subjected to cocaine for a few days, she plunges the needle in fast. The tip of the needle scrapes along the callused walls of the first layers of skin, then it pops into the vein. Max pulls back and red mixes with brown, but it doesn't swirl. There's too much water, she thinks. Tutu wanted to be careful.

She pushes down on the plunger. The taste of Jack Daniels hits her tongue and the back of her mouth. Her hips spread and her spine drops, the whiskey doing its job. No heroin was in that shot. Her body swerves to the window, but Tutu has already rolled away. Max walks and doesn't run to her bed because she already knows it's not there, but she gets down on her knees and looks anyway. The grocery bag is there. Max looks inside. It's full of nothing. The girl must have stashed the bindles in her leotard under the tutu. Max stays on her knees for a while with her head and her hands resting on the mattress, too dizzy to move, until her legs fall asleep and her kneecaps begin to really hurt and the room stops moving and her breath comes slower and softer.

"Please help me," she says because she doesn't know how the needle got in her hand. Sometimes she goes dumb, deaf, and blind. What do I do with that? Fuck it. I don't have to know. Just move forward. Stretching one dead leg at a time, she stands up.

twenty-two

"I WOULD RATHER be dead than be a victim again," Phyllis tells Eddie, who is sitting very erect, with his lower back flush against the back of the chair in the adjoining dinette. He's found that if he doesn't slouch, his spinal stenosis will allow him to actually sit for up to an hour and a half. Eddie watches Phyllis chop scallions on a soggy wood cutting board.

"If you were dead, isn't that being a victim?" His hands drum on the table, but Phyllis gives him a look, and he places them in his armpits.

"No, because it would have been my choice."

"Do you even know what you're saying?"

"I was brave back then." She knows that she doesn't have to say when, because Eddie will know. Phyllis scrapes the scallions into a big yellow bowl half full of soaking bulgur wheat. Then she dashes a tomato from her fledgling plant under the water and slices into that. "Are you going to come with me to the meeting this evening?"

"No. You better stop wearing that goddamn Rolex. You're making yourself a target. Don't you watch the news? With guns, Phyllis—in broad daylight—they're stealing Rolexes." Whenever Eddie's throat tightens he gets a tickle in it. He coughs and coughs again with his mouth closed so it sounds more like a grunt.

"I like it. It's waterproof," she says, dumping the tomatoes into the bowl with the bulgur wheat, parsley, and scallions. "And besides, any fool can tell it's a fake." Phyllis has been doing things her way for a long time. After years of wanting to be taken care of (and always being disappointed), she grew into a woman who refuses to compromise her independence. No one can take care of her now but herself.

"Goddamnit, Phyllis!" Eddie's voice disappears under his phlegm and Phyllis sets a bottle of water from the fridge in front of him. "You think you can always walk through a field of cow pies and not step in shit? One day you won't be so lucky," he says after his cough stops and he sips some water. "I'd prefer Diet Coke."

Phyllis pours the olive oil and lemon juice in the bowl at the same time. She sets them down and grabs the mint and the salt, clapping their bottoms on the counter before she shakes them hard for a few seconds over the yellow bowl. She remembers she is out of treats for Zelda. She gets the freezer drawer open halfway, and then it sticks. A blow-dryer for this problem sits on the counter. Resting one hand on her hip, she waves the blow-dryer at the inside of the drawer. The ice melts. It's loud, so she talks over it. "It's my turn to bring dinner. You want some?"

Eddie stuffs his hands in his armpits again and waits for the ice to finish melting. She knows he can't talk over that racket and that he might eat some tabouli out of goodwill. He is not a fan; she puts too much lemon and not enough mint or salt.

"Well, have some leftover then. It's better the next day anyway." Phyllis cuts off the blow-dryer, retrieves a package of livers, and kicks the freezer closed. Eddie takes a clear breath and shakes his head.

After a glass of peach champagne or a vodka tonic Phyllis's movements are light, almost seductive, and she hurries through this rudimentary stuff to get to it. The livers are easier to slice into small pieces when they're still frozen. On the chopping board, the jelly insides from the chopped tomatoes mix with the raw livers.

"Do you ever wash that board?"

"Shut up, Eddie." Phyllis barely watches what she's doing. For this reason, she often cuts herself.

"I am never eating here again."

"Good." Phyllis tosses the knife into the sink, then places the bite-sized liver pieces on the wax paper that covers a plastic drawer. She slides the drawer into the dehydrator, sets it to 110 degrees, and turns it on.

"Jesus, that stinks," Eddie says.

There is Sky vodka in the cabinet. Unfortunately, Popov makes Phyllis sick; Popov is cheaper. She likes Smirnoff better than Sky, but Sky was on sale. The freezer drawer slides open this time and Phyllis fills her glass with ice. She pours equal parts diet tonic and vodka, squeezes and drops a quarter of a lemon from her tree in it, takes a Diet Coke from the fridge, and sits down at the table with Eddie. It's a few hours before her usual cocktail hour, but Eddie knows better than to mention it.

Phyllis anticipates his thoughts. "I deserve it."

Eddie cracks open his soda. He had to stop drinking when he developed an allergy to alcohol. It did something funny to his heart. This was about the same time the doctor told him if he didn't quit smoking he would have to have his legs amputated. The cigarettes had constricted his arteries. They sit in silence for a while, listening to the seeds in the birdhouse being eaten by the squirrels and to the ice clinking in Phyllis's favorite glass.

"Do you still blame me? Are you still mad at me?" Phyllis takes a sip and leaves her nose inside the glass as she swallows and takes another small sip.

The doggie door swings open and Zelda stops in the middle of the kitchen and stares at the two of them. She walks to Eddie and stands close. She doesn't look up at him as she puts her head against his lower leg. Zelda rests her gaze upon Phyllis.

"She's mad at me," Phyllis says.

Eddie pats Zelda's rump. "She wants to go to the park."

Phyllis takes another sip and watches Eddie's hand on Zelda. "I'm trying to get her pregnant."

"Really."

"I had to hold her while this horny, discomfited Wheaton tried to mount her. I all but put it in for him."

Eddie smoothes the hair back from Zelda's eyes. "Poor baby."

Phyllis's Birkenstock dangles from her toe as she swings the leg that's crossed. She takes a sip. "It was horrible."

Eddie swigs his Diet Coke and belches. An owl "whos" but it is only the four o'clock bird on Phyllis's clock.

"Then why do it?" he says.

Phyllis hasn't taken her eyes from Zelda's. Because Eddie is rubbing Zelda's fur back, she can actually see them. "Because she kisses my tears."

"Dogs like salt."

"No. She kisses my eyes before the tears come out, because she knows."

Zelda pushes her head up against Eddie's hand.

"She loves this," he says.

"Sometimes, Eddie, a girl doesn't know what she needs until she gets it. Besides, she will make a wonderful mother."

Eddie notices a spot on his pants but it doesn't matter. These are his scrounge-around pants. He knows he always looks as though he isn't listening, but it's not usually true.

Phyllis watches Zelda slump to the ground out of Eddie's reach, sufficiently relaxed by his affection, and listens to her long sighs that come before a nap. The ice has melted a bit in Phyllis's drink, cutting the vodka. She watches the ice settle in the long thin glass after she takes a sip, puts it down, and nods slowly. "She will be a good mother."

After petting Zelda it's as if Eddie's hand still needs to touch something. He brushes Phyllis's fingers, which are wrapped lightly around her glass. She lets him peel them away and lay her hand open on the table, palm up. He unclasps the Rolex and slides it off. Phyllis wipes her eyes with her other hand and then tucks her wet fingers between her crossed legs. Eddie squeezes her wrist without the watch like he is squeezing her heart.

"A great mother," he says.

twenty-three

MAX RESTS HER cheek against the old porcelain of the sink because it has always felt like the skin of someone who loves her. There is something familiar about the way she feels at the moment. It's not just the doom. Doom is always there, but it's normal. There is something right, something responsible about the feeling. Maybe it's because she has Jack Daniels in her system, like the time in high school when she pulled her passed-out, half-naked friend out from under a drunk boy in a closet at a house party. When the boy told Max to get herself and her "whore" friend out of his house, she felt this same feeling. It was peaceful. It was purposeful. When Max realized her hand was heading toward the boy's head, she made a fist. After that, seeing the distorted faces of drunken teenaged boys crazed with hormones and sexual frustration made perfect sense. And, when she felt the blow that broke her nose, it, too, just felt right.

Before Max goes downstairs, she puts on the Canadian post-woman's jacket Eddie gave her a long time ago. It wards off the harshest cold. She sits on the curb in front of her building to wait for Albert to bring her truck. They hadn't exchanged many words over the phone, she and Albert. Just the logistics. Some men are putting up lights and blinking snowflakes across the street. For a second, she imagines Albert is coming because he wants to see her. A group of Christmas carolers walks by; a Filipino man shakes a tambourine and starts them into "O Holy Night." A child with a blond Mohawk straggles behind and waves to Max. Max waves back and thinks of the episode on *I Love Lucy* when Lucy joins up with a group called the Friends of the Friendless. Cars race down the street while families stand in front of their windows and participate in the serene illusion of Christmas. She wonders what kind of Christmas Albert and Carlotta will have now that Yosakwa's gone. She gets steamed thinking about how Tutu took the bag of dope that she was supposed to sell. Then she remembers that a person who wants to live should be scared of Carlotta.

Albert pulls up to the curb, just missing Max's toes. She pulls herself up by the door handle. The bones in Albert's face stick out more than before, and the skin under his eyes is purple.

"Albert, can you wait just one second?" She almost forgot.

"Hurry up, man."

"One second." She hurries into the building.

In her closet under a pile of clothes is a cardboard box. Inside the box is a teal and yellow Chinese satin jewelry bag holding the diamond ring that was her great grandmother's, then her Grandma Grace's. Platinum, three and a half carats. It had been Grace's engagement ring. This ring was on reserve; it wasn't to be pawned for drugs. That had been a promise she had already kept for a while. Maybe she can just get a loan on it. Then she won't have to lose it. There are also some gold necklaces tucked in a zippered compartment that she forgot about the last low time.

Max shoves the jewelry bag into one of the many pockets of the postwoman's jacket. Almost out the door, she doubles back to the kitchen, opens the cabinet, and takes a swig of Jack Daniels, then puts the pint in an inside pocket. The alcohol stings the roof of her mouth but warms the ache in her belly. Outside, the cold air squeezes her forehead. Albert shuts the glove compartment as she walks up to the truck.

"Anything interesting?" Max says.

"I was just making sure I got rid of all your paraphernalia. I have a bad feeling."

Albert remains in the driver's seat, so Max gets in the passenger's.

"Thanks for bringing my truck back. We taking you home?"

"Some business to take care of."

"Could I come with you?"

"No."

Their bodies rock gently to the stop-and-go of her truck in the evening's rush hour traffic. Albert's down jacket makes him look smaller in size, rather than bigger.

"You look like your mom bundled you up for school."

"Of course you would say that. It's cold, man." He sits up a little bit.

"You're in bad shape." Max keeps her eyes on Albert's ears, which are small but have very big lobes.

"No shit."

In the distance, Max sees a row of palm trees that bend but refuse to intertwine.

"I don't know what I'm doing, Albert."

"You just keep doing it."

"Albert, I wish . . . I was . . . more . . . You have three scars?"

"Five. Five of the ones you're talking about."

"Are you going to get another one?"

"I don't know."

"Why are we like this?"

"Because there's no other way, no matter what. I don't know, man. Why are you like this?"

"My heart is perforated."

The light is only yellow but Albert stops anyway. His eyes are red. He pulls out his bandana from his back pocket, unfolds it, and blows his nose.

"She's on the decline. I don't want to take care of her anymore." Then, like an old man, he wipes his mustache, folds the cloth, and stuffs it in his pocket.

On Albert's street, no one is putting lights up. He double-parks next to his old Lincoln.

Max stays in her seat and watches Albert hustle around the front of the truck. She jumps out.

"Albert?"

He turns around. She can barely make out his eyes. They seem to have sunk into his skull. The security light for his building buzzes.

"She said she wanted me to help her get her legs back."

A look of sardonic pity changes his face, and he looks down to the ground. She realizes it's not pity. It's hopelessness.

"So get them."

Max's truck chokes down the last little bit of oil. Albert walks back to Max and stands real close. She can see the snot running down into his mustache.

Inside his jacket his collarbones are sticking out of his thermal. She lays her hands on them.

"I didn't once ask you for any stuff on the way here," she says.

"I know. But I don't care. Come upstairs. I'll give you all the shit you want. That's part of her deal, man. You're just a fucking duck." He starts to back away, watching her.

"A duck?"

"A fucking sitting duck."

He lets out a maniacal laugh, dangling his ring of keys from his fingertip, then flipping them into the palm of his hand. He starts making a noise and flapping his arms. "Quack! Quack!" He opens his eyes wide and bats his eyelashes.

"Cut it out." Max spits on the ground between them. The spit is pink. Her gums are still bleeding from where her bottom tooth was.

Albert continues to make bird noises until his hands fall to his sides. As if someone told him to be graceful and he listened, he points a finger at Max, finds his aim, and pulls the trigger. "Pow," he says.

Max watches Albert as he walks through the gate and inside the door to his building.

One window on the seventh floor is decorated with lights, but it doesn't count. It's Carlotta's. She lets them burn all year round.

twenty-four

SHE'LL HIT TOMMY Banks first. Max always goes to Tommy's first. They have a parking lot with plenty of spaces. The employees do their best to show that they don't know how fucked-up you are, but they still act like they are doing you a huge favor. Tommy is the only one who treats her like a person, so Max opens the first door and waits for someone to buzz her in the second door. It buzzes.

Tommy has gray curly hair and an eye patch, a long well-groomed beard, white at the tips, which stops just below the second button of his silk Hawaiian shirt. He glides around the cluttered room and usually chats smooth with customers, like he is hosting a party, but today the store is pretty empty. Motorcycle helmets hang from a tattered chandelier. Leather jackets and fur coats marked thirty percent off are strung on a thick cord high up out of reach. An espresso maker and an Osterizer blender are placed between 8-tracks and record players.

Everything is organized according to Tommy. People give him things they find. The hoof of a zebra's leg wears a bulbous rubber hand and sits next to an unused antique cash register. In the hand is some artificial money. A bald owl and the heads of a deer and a moose watch over the shelf of cameras. Above books of poetry, on their own shelf, sit two shiny black ravens, stuffed of course, but in better condition than the other animals. There are baskets of hard candy on the counters, most often butterscotch. Tommy offers them to his customers. "Enjoy sweets," he says. He does all the bargaining and pricing while his daughter sits on a stool behind a bulletproof glass partition, doling out or collecting money with her manicured hands and long red acrylic nails. A sheer lace blouse conceals four rolls on her belly that would surely disappear if she didn't slouch. Peeking above the last closed button is a white lace camisole that scoops her breasts snugly together. Her long, black, always freshly brushed hair provides a curtain from which she can catch a glimpse, if necessary, of what's happening. She is usually on the phone, the receiver cradled between her shoulder and ear. Max watches as she tries on a diamond ring from a pile of jewelry that she's supposed to be cleaning.

A lot of musicians use Tommy's as a place to either buy or hock and, as a result, Tommy has everything a musician would need. Gold records even line the wall. Tommy said one time he had a heavyweight championship belt, but he wouldn't tell Max who sold it to him. And most of the time the people Max sees in the store are dense, as in molecules, so dense that no light can get through. They are people on some kind of a mission; destroying themselves and, at the same time, trying to survive. But right now, Tommy helps a mother and son pick out an amp. They're the only other customers in the store. The woman keeps trying to free her hand from the boy's, but he won't let go. When he finally does for a moment, she scratches the skin underneath her wig. Tommy pats his curls down and says, "Take your time."

Max pulls the jewelry sack from her pocket and sets it on the glass countertop over a variety of microphones. She unties the satin ribbon and unrolls it like she's opening a set of knives. The necklaces are in the zipper compartment and the ring is alone on the ring holder. She puts it all on the counter.

Tommy walks over. His smile is easy.

"Hello, Max."

"Hey, Tommy."

"You are emaciated, but rosy. Death has been calling you?"

"Yeah, but thanks. You want to take a look?"

He puts a large hand smelling of soap and earth on Max's shoulder as if to calm her. "Valerie," he calls to his daughter, "bring our fighter here a big cup of miso soup." Valerie leaves the ring on. She shrugs and then rolls her head as if the momentum will propel her off the stool. Her hair follows. Tommy looks down at Max. She could rest the top of her forehead on the ends of his beard, but doesn't. "Instant okay?" he asks.

"Sure, whatever." Max watches Tommy get distracted by an itch on his nose. He scratches the rim of his nostril with his one long pointed pinky nail and resists taking it farther inside the opening. "How are your other daughters?" she says, remembering that things happen here in Tommy's time. Her jewelry will wait.

"Oh, they're doing great out there. Of course, they're not as mulish as Valerie, but she'll get it. She has her own way. There are limitless ways to help. Some people have the eyes to see who needs it, to anticipate what it is."

"Did my keyboard sell yet?"

"You're not very skilled in the art of conversation, are you?"

"Well, I—"

"Simple terms. You have a dog?"

"Uh, my mom has a dog, Zelda."

"Ah, good name. Have you ever taken Zelda to the park to let her play with the other dogs?"

Max fights the need to exhale loudly. "Mmhm."

"You need to socialize yourself, Max."

"But I don't like people."

"I think you do."

For a moment, they both watch the mother and son turn knobs on a mini amp,

"The Gorilla Amp." Max says.

"Excited for Christmas?" Tommy asks the mother. His voice commands attention with its volume and deep timbre, however hard he tries to sound gentle.

"Hanukkah," the woman says. She nudges the boy and he jumps, taking his hand away from the amp.

"It's okay," Tommy says, "turn them all you care to. Get a good feel for what you want."

The lady smiles. "Thank you." The boy stands with both hands dangling at his sides and his mouth hanging wide open like his eyes.

Valerie comes out from behind the glass carrying a steaming mug of instant miso. Max had never noticed how tall Valerie is— she must be nearly six feet tall. She has a slight mustache that is yellow from not leaving the bleach on long enough. She hands Max the soup unceremoniously.

"Thank you." Max feels very awkward.

"Enjoy soup," she says in a monotone, and sashays back to her perch.

Tommy releases a deep sigh while he observes Max.

"When I first saw you I knew you were riparian. You just don't know it. You follow the river. Sometimes it's still and deep. Sometimes it rushes, picking up stones and turning them over, setting them in a new place. A river isn't a stream, but they both end up in the same place. They both come from the same place, too. Do you know where that is?"

Max catches herself before she rolls her eyes. "The ocean."

"No, the heart. Yes, the ocean is the heart of the earth, with streams and river veins."

"Oh, yeah."

"Yes, well, it's all really beautiful and conspicuous. Quite boring, really. What I'm interested in are the discarded bits, the dregs, the things that were in the thick of it, carried along for miles or inches, and then left uncovered, on the banks."

Max takes a sip of the soup, burning her tongue.

"Test it with the tip of your upper lip next time."

Lay off, Max thinks.

"But it's the most apparent things that we overlook or forget and need to be reminded of," he says. "Now to the matter of your jewels."

Max holds her mug with both hands and dips her upper lip in the soup, then sips while she watches Tommy. She makes a loud slurping sound, but Tommy ignores it.

"Oh no, Max," he says, holding up the ring. "You should take this to a jeweler. You'll get more money. Or do you want to lend it to me?" His smile makes his cheek cut into the bottom of his eye patch. The skin crinkles into a rainbow.

She looks at her ring on the countertop. Underneath the glass, next to the microphones, is a row of eyeballs with irises in different colors. She sets her soup over them.

"Would you ever wear a fake eye instead of your patch?"

"I have an eye, my dear. I just can't let light touch it." His good eye peers at Max and starts to pull something out of her. It comes from her chest and makes her cheeks hot.

Max takes the ring from him and fits it over just the first knuckle of her ring finger because it's too small for her.

"Everybody has a place on them that will not adapt to light, mine just happens to be my poor eye." He taps on his eye patch, then takes Max's hand that has the ring and holds it up to the light. "Three karats?"

"Three and a half." Max wants to pull her hand away from his grasp, but doesn't.

"Do you know where your place is?"

She can feel it skip inside her rib cage. "It's just an organ."

"I understand," he says.

Max finally pulls her hand away from his and takes out her pint of Jack Daniels. "Do you mind?"

She whips the cap off and takes a long drink. It doesn't mix well with the miso. Tommy looks through Max's jewelry bag compartments, pulling out gold chains.

"How do you know what someone needs?" Max says, wiping her mouth.

"Practice," he says and strokes his beard. "I know that you need a cigarette."

"Well, that's obvious." Max's nose starts to run because the soup and booze have done their job of defrosting her.

"And a tissue," he says, smiling. "Valerie!"

Max cringes.

"Max needs a cigarette and some tissue!"

Max dries her nose on the sleeve of her coat, "Really, you don't have to keep bugging her."

"It's what she's supposed to do. This is where she learns."

Max gulps some more whiskey and slides the bottle into her pocket. Already Valerie has appeared with some tissue and two cigarettes and she hands them to Max. She looks up at her father from under heavy brows as she forces a curtsy, then takes the empty mug away, replacing it with an ashtray.

"Wow," Max says. Before Tommy can say anything, Max gets her lighter out of her jacket pocket. "I can light it myself." After the smoke soaks into her lungs she says, "See, I anticipated there pretty good, huh?" With one hand, Max blows her nose with a Kleenex.

"Not quite."

Max rests her elbows on the top of the glass counter, which has a sign that says "no leaning." The fake eyeballs stare up at her blankly, unlike real eyes with stories behind them, the skin holding them in place, marking time.

The mother is steering her son away from the small Gorilla

amp to the big Marshalls. Her gold anklet is pressed under her tan panty hose.

The boy and the Marshall amplifier are the same size. He sticks his fingers through the grate covering the speakers. "Someday, Fred!" She rubs his head. His shoulders tighten. Max senses that the boy already carries his mother's dreams.

Max picks a butterscotch and crunches it because it's stale. She immediately puts another one in her mouth and sucks on this one while emptying a handful of the candies into her pocket. In the case under the basket of candies are arms. On the fingers are rings. Bracelets encircle the wrists up to the elbows. Some arms wear silver and turquoise and other arms only gold. One arm wears antique jewelry.

The woman takes a green guitar down from the wall. "Play it."

The boy looks at the guitar and then at Max. Max smiles and looks away, so he isn't embarrassed, and puts the ring on her pinky. Her fingers are swollen. The ring looks out of place to her, with her dirty nails and pink chapped hands. The moons of her nails have turned gray. A man named Franklyn gave Grandma Grace the ring. He scraped up all the money he could from his friends and family, but then he spent it all on a bender, so he asked his mother for one of her rings to give to Grace. He needed to hurry up and propose because Grace was pregnant. It didn't take long for Grandma Grace to find out the real story after Franklyn cheated on her and it was over between them. Franklyn, their son, was named after him, but as soon as he was old enough, he changed his name legally, using his middle name, Edward, or Eddie, so that the only thing he would have in common with his father was blood. Clearly, Eddie had the ability to walk away from something or someone and never look back.

The boy won't play the guitar.

"Play like you play by yourself in your room." The mother raises her eyebrows and her forehead disappears under her wig.

His back is to Max, but she hears the son say, "It's not the same."

Max finishes her cigarette and sucks on her candy as she looks around for more body parts she's never seen before. On a shelf as high as the ravens are heads with painted red lips and false eyelashes. They are bald, but wear cowboy hats, berets, and old army helmets, looking strangely complete without any bodies. With her back to Max, in the display window, is a lady mannequin in a leotard that reminds Max of Jane Fonda from the exercise tape Phyllis and she watched and kind of exercised with every day when Max was a little girl. The leotard has purple and pink stripes. The mannequin has sweatbands on her slender wrists, and she leans on one narrow hip. No tights cover her scratched-up thighs with smudges of dirt and grease, but she wears purple leg warmers. Max walks closer to her. She sees that the mannequin stands easily in white Reeboks with Velcro straps next to a tall plant. Under the leg warmers are metal bones. Max holds a plastic thigh with one hand and pulls down one of the leg warmers with the other. It's a prosthetic leg. Max picks up the mannequin and carries her to the counter; she's heavier than she looks. She lays her on top of the jewelry case and looks for the lever to unclasp the leg.

Tommy stands next to Max, rubbing his back.

Max's heart beats fast. "How much?"

"Well, you wouldn't know it, but these are worth a lot."

She lodges the candy between her cheek and teeth. The corn syrup slicks her throat. She holds out her hand to him. The ring sparkles.

"A computerized leg costs sixty thousand," Tommy says, looking at the ring.

Max examines one of the legs for any sign of computer stuff. There are only shiny metal tendons, clasps, and what look like shock absorbers. She feels Tommy's unease. He puts his hand protectively on the other leg.

"These are for someone who is challenged below the knee." Tommy tries to push Max aside. "Allow me."

Max stiffens her body and stands firm. She ignores him and finds the correct clasp to unhook the leg from the thigh. She picks up one of the legs. "It's light."

"How perceptive."

Max rotates the Reebok around the shiny ankle. It hardly makes a sound. "I bet my ring is worth a lot."

She puts the leg back with the body, and starts to unfasten the other one. It's easier this time. Max places the leg next to her right leg.

Tommy lets out a long sigh and quickly picks up his exercise mannequin, leaving the other prosthetic on the counter. "I'm taking her to the back."

Max takes a red candy from the basket. It's not cinnamon, it's cherry. She watches him go and then looks over at Tommy's daughter behind the glass. Her hair covers half of her face and the phone. The girl's hand stretches and poses underneath someone else's ring. She says something into the phone and laughs while looking at Max.

Tommy returns, carrying a long narrow box. He puts it on

the counter. "There's an instruction guide." He opens the catalog and fans it slowly in front of Max's face. Max puts the legs
in their casket.

"What about money?" Max's gold necklaces fall through his
fingers. "Would you like cash? Sixty?"

"Swell."

"So who is worth your diamond ring?"

Max doesn't answer, just exhales loudly.

The boy drags his mother past them to the door. His eyes are
glazed like he's pretending he's invisible.

"You're going to have to start playing so I can hear you,
Fred." The mother notices Tommy watching them and her
patent leather purse slips off her shoulder as she waves. "Oh
well, next time!" For a moment, the mother and son are trapped
in the small space between the two doors. The mother waits for
the boy to open the door for them. Finally, she reaches over him,
opens it and nudges him out.

Max looks over at Tommy's daughter. Now she is trimming
the frayed threads along the seam of the inner thigh of her
tight jeans.

Max swallows the cherry juice from the last of her candy. She
can feel the sugar eat at a cavity on one of her molars.

Usually the smile comes first, but this time Tommy's wrinkles around his eyes and down his cheeks anticipate what's
coming. "To be of use," he says with a nod. Then the jewelry
takes his attention, and with an outstretched arm and a bend in
his knee as if he was presenting a duchess, he ushers Max to his
daughter behind the glass.

twenty-five

THE COLD NIGHT has delivered a clearness in the outlines of things. The edges of buildings and billboards are crisp against the dark sky, but it's the Christmas lights that sting the eyes. Max drives east on Melrose Avenue, a tight grip on the steering wheel. Her skin stretches white over her knuckles, cracks and bleeds some. She passes crackhead alley, the gas station, the phone booth where Wolf was beaten up, and turns right to Callocco Town. Now on residential streets, she takes long drinks from her pint of Jack Daniels. It loosens her. After a few swigs, the pain in her stomach finally grows numb. She looks in the glove compartment where she thought she left Frances and doesn't find her there. What if Albert threw her away? Max reaches under the seat and feels around. She pushes the thought out of her mind and looks at the box wrapped in gold Christmas paper and a gold bow on the seat next to her. Tommy's daughter gave her the paper and ribbon and even helped her tape up the box. Max doesn't listen to the radio. She thinks of the boy who wouldn't play the guitar in front of his mother. Probably because it's Christmas, there's nowhere to park. She circles Carlotta's block a few times, and finally brake lights appear on one of the parked cars before it bumps its way out of its space. Max is thankful she won't have far to walk.

Albert opens the apartment door. He looks through Max to the floor behind her. His eyes are glazed like the boy's were at Tommy's, as if they had been forced to stay open for a long time. His tank top is drenched and sticks to his concave stomach. Max smells burnt tortillas and roses.

"What are you doing here?" says Albert.

"I have a present for you." Max surprises herself because she's almost smiling.

He considers Max's kung fu slippers for a moment. "Shit," he sighs. He walks away from the open door.

Albert watches her as she seats herself and the box on the red couch. Max hears running water from the bathroom.

"Albert, where are you!" Carlotta whines.

"We'll be right out." Albert plunges into the dark hall with long strides.

On the altars in the corners of the room, candles are burning but the roses have lost their petals. Four Bibles are stacked on the coffee table and stickers of hearts and flowers, crosses and saints spread around them. A stove lighter and a pair of scissors are on the table, too. Sprinkled on the wood floor are shavings from a Chore Boy.

Max creeps down the steamy hall to Albert's room. She

passes the bathroom, its door open just enough so she can see in. Albert is kneeling beside the bathtub, which has support rails around it. Carlotta sits amid rose-scented bubbles. She leans slightly forward to compensate for her lack of leg weight. She lifts a droopy washcloth from the water to her face and rubs it up and down. When she takes it away her skin is red, her eyebrows are gone, and mascara sticks to the bags of skin beneath her eyes. Her hair falls in a long dark streak down the rolls of her wide back and then blends into the color of her skin. Albert pulls it over her shoulder, and then spreads the washcloth across her upper back. He holds one of Carlotta's hands above her head, at an angle, as he washes under her breast and up to her armpit. Carlotta takes deep breaths with her head back like she is trying not to be ticklish. Albert bends away from Max, across Carlotta to her other side. The thin wife beater strains against his spine, like it's the only thing protecting him from the cruel air. He grabs the razor.

Carlotta raises her right arm, resting it against the green tile, and Albert scrapes the razor against the pale skin of her armpit.

"I told you I want the deep conditioner today, not the daily," she says.

He wipes his nose with a wet hand and picks up her left arm and shaves the stubbles of hair.

"So you should have washed my hair and put the conditioner in before all this," Carlotta says in a baby voice.

Albert shakes the hairs out of the razor under the water. Soapsuds stick to his arms as he takes the Suave shampoo and squirts it directly on her head. With the tips of his fingers he lathers her head with quick short bursts.

"It's not like you couldn't do this yourself." He talks as if he is scolding a child. By the way she cried for Albert when he left her alone in the tub, Max suspects Carlotta is afraid of drowning. Albert holds a large plastic pitcher under the hot running water, and then pours it on her hair to create more suds. Carlotta's hair is piled on top of her head in a crown of bubbles. While Albert fills up the pitcher again, Max moves to Albert's room. The thought of getting high is in her head. She just has to see if it will happen.

Albert has been too busy to clean, or too sick, or too strung out. Max opens the cigar box on the shelf under the coffee table. She can't believe it—balloons and a syringe and a spoon. Q-tips. Everything she needs, of course, because Albert is strung out. Even a glass of water on the table. She reaches into the pockets of her postwoman's coat. Her lighter is still there.

With the brand new needle, Max finds a vein and shoots the heroin slow. The air becomes sweet and rich like fudge waiting for her to eat it. Faded letters surface on the wall and she squints her eyes to read them. Sounds begin to float from underground as the dirty futon swallows her in. She hears rushing water like it's a river to the ocean and wonders what did she shoot that for? She thinks about the legs.

Max drifts up and down the hall, slightly nauseated. The air is wet in the hall by the bathroom, and now it's almost too hazy to see in. Carlotta's hair is waxy with conditioner. Albert hands Carlotta the washcloth and then sits on the toilet with the lid closed and looks at the floor. Carlotta takes the cloth down to her belly and lower, under the tiny bubbles. Her sigh sounds like a growl. Max feels her stomach rise from the heroin and from witnessing this intimacy. She drifts down the hall to the living room and the red velvet couch to wait.

She focuses on objects around the room so she won't nod off. In front of one window on a small table is a white miniature Christmas tree with red lights that flash, making the room pulse in a pink glow. Other than the lights there are no ornaments and there are no gifts. In front of the other window, surrounded by more blinking red lights, is the life-size papier mâché Jesus. He looks out the window, and his head tilts slightly to the left either in inquisitiveness or sadness about the state of things. Max approaches Jesus. He is shiny and well cared for but aged. She turns him around and looks him in the face. The whites of his eyes have cracks in them like broken blood vessels. Brown painted skin is peeling off his cheekbones, and the gray papier mâché shows through like he can't hide that he is sick. His mustache and beard are made out of synthetic hair that has remained pretty clean. His eyebrows point up to his forehead as if asking, "Why am I here?" Max leans him against the window so that he looks at the room. She sinks back onto the couch. Jesus seems overwhelmed and exhausted by everything, but at least now he looks a little more involved.

Max hears wheels rolling on the wood floor, and Carlotta appears out of the vapor. Albert, glistening, pushes her into the living room while she combs out her hair. She smiles contentedly, looking like a baby because her eyebrows haven't been drawn on yet, and her cheeks are dappled pink. Albert parks her across from Max.

Just as he is about to sit down, Carlotta says, "Get us a little Christmas Eve rock, baby." Then she looks at Max and smiles, showing a gold-rimmed tooth. "I think we deserve it." Albert looks like he's holding himself up by his shoulders, like if he relaxed and dropped them even a little he would collapse. When he leaves the room, Max begins to shrink inside herself. She pets the velvet couch, making streaks that appear and disappear.

"I'm worried about Albert," Max says and scratches her nose.

"He's hitting the lick again. When that magic pellet wears off, you better hope that Jesus is willing to help keep you straight."

It's possible that Carlotta doesn't know Max is high. Albert is taking some time in his room, Max is sure, to get in a fix. She wonders how he will react to her helping herself to his stash, or if he'll even notice.

The heroin shortens time by collapsing it. It's like a divine intervention.

"You think I don't worry, too? I told you, Albert is soft. He needs drive. Everybody's got to have an enemy, sweetheart. Everybody needs to have somebody to hate. He needs that hate to survive. I give him purpose. I sacrifice. But Jesus says, 'The meek shall inherit the earth,' so maybe we should just mind our own business." Her eyes turn mean and accuse Max for a second.

"But then again, he says 'the earth.' Shall inherit the earth. Not the Kingdom of Heaven. And the earth is about ready to do us in. Stuck down here on earth with our earthly desires and problems. Oh, I am so tired, child. Worn out. I don't feel like I got much fight left in me. Our lives together are almost over. Sometimes I just don't think it's worth it. You could pick me up and throw me out the window and I would not try to resist."

Max pictures Carlotta sailing headfirst out the window.

Albert walks in with a ziplock bag full of rock cocaine and a pipe. His face has relaxed along with his shoulders. Albert sits down next to Max and loads the pipe.

"We're supposed to destroy ourselves. That's how the earth survives. We are the ashes upon which the earth will build anew. My body is not on the side of the strong. I am the meek and I am the tired. But, of course, my soul is strong because I have Jesus." She rakes the comb across her scalp more for the feeling than the result, as her hair is already slicked back and detangled. Her eyes roll up into her skull.

Max watches the pink light on Carlotta's face. She wants to reach out and wipe it off. "But Albert shouldn't have to pay anymore," Max says.

Carlotta stops her combing and looks at Max. "Pay for what?"

Albert hands Max the pipe. Except for the nausea, it's nice to feel the smoothness in her movements from the heroin again, and the feeling of invincibility.

"He shouldn't have to pay for your fears. He's got his own. And he's got an imagination. You can't see that?" Max holds the pipe up so the piece of crack won't fall off. "You take prisoners."

"Of course I do, bitch! You be a single mother of two with no legs! That's just prideful! If I had my legs I'd get up right now and smack you silly. Talking just to hear your fucking head rattle."

Max puts the pipe to her lips and Albert holds the stove lighter's flame underneath the tip and not exactly on the piece of crack so when Max slowly inhales she sucks in the heat and rich smoke and not a hot empty flame. Albert puts his hand on Max's knee and she turns her head toward him. Before she can exhale he puts his mouth on hers and takes in her crack-soaked air. As Max exhales into Albert's body, the flower in her brain opens. At the same time she feels the change happening inside her mind, she feels Albert's mustache against her lips and his hand cradling the back of her head. She opens her eyes to look at him. He keeps his gently closed. The skin on his face looks like a sheet over bones. If he were a dog he would be on his back right now. Max breathes in after all the air has left her and smells the heroin and ether escaping Albert's pores. He hands the pipe to Carlotta as he holds his breath.

"What the fuck does imagination have to do with anything?" Carlotta says.

Max is silent. She watches Carlotta glare at the flame down the end of the pipe and then take a few sharp inhales. After she exhales, the dimensions of her face change. Before, her pink round cheeks protruded the most; now her eyes are bulging. Max fixes the gold bow on the present and remembers Tommy's last words to her: "To be of use."

"You told me you wanted this," Max says.

"Who the fuck moved Jesus?" Carlotta asks.

"I did." Max places the present on Carlotta's lap and Carlotta slaps her.

"Jesus, Carlotta." Carlotta swings at her again, but misses because Max is standing up, rubbing her jaw.

Albert finally blows out his hit. "Open the fucking present, Ma."

Carlotta unties the bow and smiles sarcastically at Albert. She pops up the tape on the two paper corners at the ends of the box, and then rips the gold paper off like it's skin. She looks wide-eyed at Max as she holds the brown box up to her ear and shakes it.

Max sits back down. She wants a cigarette. She takes out her pint of Jack Daniels and finishes off the last of it in an attempt to push down the bile coming up her throat. She'll let that slap slide. Just so long as Carlotta puts on those damn legs. She reaches for the pipe from Albert. Max takes a quick hit, lighting it herself.

Carlotta lifts the top of the box off and drops it on the floor. She stares at the legs. She picks one up by its metal tendon.

"They're legs," says Max, bursting smoke.

"I know what they are," Carlotta says.

"They're adjustable." Max waits while Carlotta's cold face stares inside the box.

"You can put your favorite pair of shoes on them. There's a pamphlet in the—"

"I see it."

Carlotta won't look up from the box. Max glances at Albert, whose eyes seem to be fixated on nothing in particular, perhaps his future. He sits forward with his elbows on his thighs, clasping his hands, measuring his will. Max can feel something coming off him, something being turned loose inside him, so she watches the red lights turning the room pink and the pink has a sound like air being blown through a flute. The space of time between each beat from shadow to pink light is an abyss. Max's head is beginning to throb from the heroin and crack. The Jack Daniels was a bad idea.

"This doesn't mean shit," Carlotta says.

Albert, who hasn't blinked for the last few minutes, says, "It means something to me." Carlotta and Max watch as he gets up from the couch and walks out the front door.

"Fucking boy has no sense. He's all wet like a drowned rat. Bring him his coat there." She points to the kitchen counter, where Albert's coat sits next to a bowl of rotten bananas.

Max takes the coat.

At the door, Max turns to Carlotta. "You drew the cross on my forehead, and the wings? Remember? And you said, 'You're going to get me back my—'"

"You misunderstood."

"He's going to die, too."

"We'll see."

Carlotta holds the box to her lap as if she has a stomachache. She holds her head high.

"Get the fuck out," she says, and Max does.

twenty-six

WHEN MAX GETS outside, Albert is already across the street and almost to the end of the block. A cold wind hollows out his body but he still moves fast against it, chin first. Max does her best to run without throwing up.

"Albert!" Her voice gets lost.

Albert keeps pushing his long strides. When she catches up with him he doesn't stop; she has to jog to keep up.

"Albert, for Christ's sake, will you wait!"

Albert puts his hands in his pockets and turns to her, and the stream of energy that was chasing him circles around them. The apartment building behind him looks flat, unreal like a movie backdrop. Max stands there feeling as if she is inside a glass bubble snow scene, except there is no snow falling, just sparkling bits of her and him being born into the air. Albert's gold cross around his neck catches some light and glows.

"Here." She hands him his big green down coat. He just holds it, squeezing its feathers and looking at it.

"Well, put it on." Before he does, Max sees him try to hide a shiver while she catches her breath.

"Where're you going?" For every exhale, Max feels her heart beat a flurry. Her head still pounds.

"Here." Albert lifts his face, but his gaze travels above and past Max's head.

"Well, you are the light of the world." She doesn't know why she says it.

"You're quoting Jesus now?" Albert looks at her. He can't quite smile, but his furrowed brow relaxes some.

"Well, my world anyway . . ." Another hit of crack still pulls on her brain, and she tries to shut it out. Albert zips his jacket up to his chin. The green hue of streetlights illuminates the pink and brown tender skin under his eyes. Max fights the urge to run from words, so she focuses on Albert's big earlobes, the left and then the right. His face is changing. He looks mad, but it's not anger. It's his spirit inhabiting his defenseless face. And the face is shocked at being overtaken, at losing its rights, if only for a moment. A woman being dragged by her pit bull passes them. If she were to notice Max and Albert, she would think they were sore with one another, possibly heartbroken, the way they are glaring at each other. It's true the heart is breaking, but for its own good. Albert's expression reminds Max of when Grandpops died, how she saw his tormented self set free a second before he left.

Gloom sweeps down on Albert like he remembers who he is supposed to be, and then, as if to cover it up, he smiles. He gives all of himself in a smile to Max. Suddenly dizzy, she's gone from her body. She's got no choice. The pieces of Albert and

Max swirl, gleaming, but do not land, like the ashes of a fire caught in the place between the flames and the smoke.

"Okay," he says, like there is an ending to be had.

"Maybe we should go see the ocean." Max hangs in the darkest parts of Albert's eyes, and he looks at her with that expression of great pity she has become comfortable with.

He pulls out a pack of Camel straights from the pocket of his coat. He gives one to Max and lights it for her. The tip of her cigarette almost burns the nylon of his jacket because she has to stand close and hide from the restless air.

Max feels like she's just cracked her way out of a shell.

Albert takes Max's lit cigarette and lights his own with it. Smoke comes out of his mouth when he talks. "I had a fish once. A little angelfish I raised from a baby. And then I felt so bad for this little guy. I said, let's put you in the ocean. So I got a snorkel, put him in a baggie, and went to the beach. Do you know what the angelfish did when I let him go?"

"He died?" Max says, taking another drag.

"He swam in a rectangle over and over again, like he was still in the tank. Can you believe it? All that big ocean, and he's swimming inside an invisible fish tank. I got all pruned up watching him, and then, finally, he swims off into the rest of the ocean."

Max knows that angelfish only live in fresh water, but she doesn't tell Albert this. Maybe it was a different kind of fish. Angelfish are often misnamed.

"That was the last time I was at the ocean."

Max watches Albert. Albert watches the corner boys. The corner boys watch for customers and cops.

"It's not easy to keep certain fish alive, you know," he says as they take drags.

The breeze that was panting and whistling turns into long deep sighs of wind that push empty bottles, cans, and plastic bags. The smoke disappears in it.

"I hope she wears them," Albert says.

"Doesn't matter. You got yours."

Someone fires up a loud motorcycle. A car alarm goes off. The hourly church bell chimes. Some kids scream.

"What're you going to do with all this ocean, Albert?"

Albert tucks his chin behind the zipped turned-up collar and takes Max's hand in his. He squeezes her hand like it will tell him what to say.

Max looks at the tattoo of his sister's face on the top of his hand. Albert's thumb presses into her wrist like he's checking her pulse. Just his eyes and nose peek over the top of his collar. It muffles his voice.

"You did good. You did good by me."

Max lifts Albert's hand. Yosakwa's tiny tattooed face becomes more real as it gets closer to her mouth and Max kisses her. Albert's smooth skin still smells like Carlotta's lavender bath. She holds Yosakwa to her cheek and looks at Albert. "You did good by us, too."

Her stomach sucks in like it does right before she vomits, but she holds on to Albert's hand to make sure he gets it. She holds his hand and bends over, holding her breath until her stomach settles. She spits to the street, then looks at him and finds herself smiling. Albert slips his hand out of hers. His big eyes that always look wet blink away his difference of opinion. They squint from his smile as he backs away from her. Then he turns. Max likes how the wind is at his back as he walks away.

Dust blows in her eyes and she puts her face down and walks

headfirst, occasionally puffing from her cigarette. Her polyester pants press against her legs. Noises zip past her ears like dirty confessions. She can't look ahead, only at one kung fu slipper at a time as it appears below her until she gets to her truck.

Max is still breathing hard. It's quiet in the truck, if not warm. She starts driving. At a stoplight, she scrounges another cigarette from her coat. Something has been rattling around on the floor of the passenger side. She rolls down the window and blows the smoke out like burning ghosts and the coldness clears her head a little. At the next stoplight, as there are many along Wilshire, she brakes hard, and a round glass snow globe rolls out from under the seat. Then she hears a scraping sound. Frances crawls to the snow globe and uses it to lean against.

"Hello, again," Frances says, and shakes her wings. "Well, it's kind of pointless, isn't it?" Green bile stains cover her once-white dress, but a little of the dust falls off.

Max picks her up and sets her on the seat.

"That Albert scared the heck out of me, pounding on the dashboard and things. So I hid."

"You're not done with me?"

"I don't really have a choice!"

When Max turns right and heads to the 10 West, she doesn't think about the fact that she is high.

"Any sky dogs out tonight?" Frances asks.

"Nope, haven't seen any for a while." Max ashes out the window.

"That's good." Frances folds her hands in her lap. "When did you eat last?"

"I don't know." Miso soup at Tommy Banks, she thinks.

"You look just awful."

Max takes a drag; the smoke is hot and hits her lungs hard. She turns on the radio and then turns it off when she can't find anything but Christmas tunes. Her stomach feels like it's being shredded, and the blood vessels in her brain are constricting. Her tongue is a dry sponge sticking to all sides of her mouth.

"Say, where we goin'?" Max asks.

"Home," says Frances.

The white roses shine with the help of little white lights. All the house lights are on too. Max rings the doorbell and then puts her hands inside the huge warm coat. The smell of night-blooming jasmine makes her feel dirty. One hand rests on the globe of the snow scene, the other clutches Frances.

Phyllis opens the door. She tries not to cry and overcomes her emotions as if she were greeting an old friend. Cinnamon, nutmeg, and turkey fill Max's nose and hurt her heart. Phyllis looks smaller than she remembered. Max waits to be asked inside instead of barging past her like she usually does. Phyllis's cheeks are pink, from eggnog probably. Max hears Dolly Parton singing "I'm Dreaming of a White Christmas."

"I didn't expect to see you. Come in, come in!"

"I didn't expect to see you either," Max says, stepping into the house.

Phyllis looks at her with the kind of smile one wears instead of crying. "We were just about to have some pie."

Max walks to her mom and considers hugging her, but can't.

In the dining room sit Eddie and Tutu. The room is painted peach. The old chandelier that Phyllis picked up at a flea market and that hangs above the table is set to low. The light from the tall red candles on the table glitters in the glass beads. The flames are still and then they twitch, reaching up; then they're calm again. Phyllis has put a new lace tablecloth underneath the round glass tabletop, and is using her good china and real silverware. The table is cluttered with more food than they can eat, but Phyllis and Eddie love leftovers. Phyllis has hung some of her own paintings of still lifes on the walls, one of an orange and a pitcher and one of roses, antique white against a dark background. Every old pine piece of furniture, whether it is a shelf or an old school bench, is covered with baskets of cloth and beads or plates and hats, glue guns, and fabric paint—Phyllis's projects for Christmas presents. Eddie sits with his back to Max. He's got to know she is there; he must have heard her when she came in. He's put down his fork and his shoulders lift as he crosses his arms. He isn't ready to look at her yet.

"Oh, hi Max, I was just telling them how crazy my parents are," Tutu says. She has on a headband with stag horns attached and her tiger-striped tights. Her tutu is red tonight.

"Miss Prey and Predator," Max says.

Tutu looks happy, like she's been reunited with long lost friends. She breathes in deeply and smiles, nodding her head slowly as if a really good song just ended. "Exactly."

Eddie looks at Max for a split second and turns back to Tutu.

"It's my yin and yang. Winter solstice is a very fertile time," Tutu says, looking at Phyllis, then at Eddie, as she smoothes her tutu.

Phyllis takes Max's hand. It isn't until her hand feels the warmth in Phyllis's that she realizes how frozen hers are. "Tutu was just telling us why she isn't with her parents for Christmas." She rubs Max's hand.

"Well, they're Jewish—but, yeah, my mother changed her name from Delilah to Mona and refuses to celebrate any holidays. She never takes off her sunglasses or her mink fur scarf. She likes to pet it."

"Is that right?" Eddie is determined to keep eating. He starved himself all day for this meal. Plus, food is the perfect distraction. He cuts up the rest of the turkey on his plate.

"Oh yes, well this is all due to my father leaving her for, yes, a younger woman. I know, so typical. But she's dating a Rastafarian pot dealer now who is so dang gorgeous he gives me the creeps."

Max squeezes out of Phyllis's hands, walks over, and stands between Eddie and Tutu's chairs. She fights the urge to choke Tutu. "You stole from me. How can you be in my house?"

Eddie's eyebrows appear above his glasses. "It's not your house, Max."

Max thinks about reaching out to the chandelier, ripping it out of the ceiling, and watching it fall, spilling beads into the bourbon sweet potatoes, knocking the candles over.

"I got your letter," she says to Eddie.

Eddie salts what's left of his favorite, mashed potatoes, and takes a bite.

"Mmhmm, so what are you doing here?"

Max and Eddie both look at his plate.

"It's Christmas Eve."

He puts down his fork and picks up his glass of Diet Coke. He sits back in the chair, making sure his lower back is snug against it because of his spinal stenosis. The light from the low chandelier and candles reflects in his glasses. Max can see the room but she can't see into his eyes. As he sips his soda, Eddie lifts his head so his eyes look through the bifocal part of his glasses. Max doesn't expect to see the dread, but that's what it is in his eyes. He is shell-shocked. Next to him, Tutu eats the crumble topping off the apple pie with her fingers, crumb by crumb.

"Are you on something now?" Eddie says as if the question is written and he's reading it.

Max thinks yes, and opens her mouth to say yes, but hears the words, "No, Dad, I'm not."

Phyllis takes Max's arm and pulls her into the kitchen. The wind outside blows through her collection of chimes hanging by the window across from the sink.

"Take off your coat, honey. Stay awhile." Phyllis winks at her and gets a plate from one of her mirrored cabinets. "I can nuke you some turkey and fixings."

Max starts to remind her she doesn't like turkey, but instead she says, "Thanks, Mom." She steadies herself by leaning against the countertop.

Phyllis scoops a big pile of mashed potatoes onto a plate with a ladle that has gravy all over it. She wipes her hand on her sweats. The most apparent stains are from the cranberries. "Dark meat, white meat? How about a leg?" Phyllis is almost frantic.

Max unzips her coat. "Anything."

Grandma Grace's white polyester suit with the magenta sequined roses has stayed clean underneath the coat, except for the dirt on the pants. Max lays her coat on the chopping board and remembers to check if any blood has seeped through her sleeve. There's a dark red spot.

"I'm going to go to the bathroom, wash my hands."

Phyllis stops in front of the microwave and slams the plate down on the counter, causing the turkey leg to roll to the terra-cotta floor. "Goddamnit, Max!"

"Mom, I'm just going to go pee, you can watch me."

"I am suffocating!" Frances yells from the pocket.

Max carries her coat with Frances in it to the bathroom. She leaves the door open. She hears the door bang closed on the microwave and a few beeps, and then Tutu singing along to Dolly Parton. Max takes Frances out of the pocket and sets her on the sink. Max pulls down her pants, stretching the elastic over the incision—the scab has been ripped off—and sits on the toilet. It's a relief to sit. She doesn't have to pee because the heroin always prevents that from happening.

"They won't notice the spot. I can barely see it myself," Frances says, balancing on the drain plug.

"You obviously didn't spend much time with my dad like you were meant to do in the first place."

"Well, I'm sorry. You were the one who really needed the help!"

Phyllis stands in the doorway. "Who are you talking to?"

Max tears off some toilet paper and wipes for Phyllis's sake, "Mom, Frances. Frances, this is my mother." She pulls up her pants. The blood drains from her head.

Phyllis looks at the tattered doll. Max knows it won't seem absurd to Phyllis that Max would talk to a doll because, to her, Max is still a child. Phyllis's eyes turn inward and look at memories. "You haven't talked to dolls since you were very small. Oops, don't flush, I have to pee."

Max washes her hands, dries them, and sits on the edge of the bathtub, the bones of her ass like knuckles against the porcelain. Frances flies up and sits on the curtain rod over the window.

"I'm going to stay up here. I am so over this," she says.

"You do that." Max looks at her mom on the toilet.

Phyllis finishes peeing, unaware Max is talking to Frances. "I just did. I'm fast." She flushes, washes her hands quickly, and wipes them on her sweatshirt. "Go sit at the table."

"But Tutu—"

"She wanted to come here, and your father feels bad for her."

"What is she, some spy for him?"

"Displaced love. Go sit down." Phyllis pats her back, pushing her out of the bathroom.

"Oh my god, Mom."

"I love it when you call me that."

"Call you what?"

"Mommy."

Max doesn't correct her. She sits at the round table that seats eight. Now four chairs are being used.

Eddie salts his second plate of food. The microwave dings. Phyllis brings Max her plate, setting it in front of her with a fork and a knife, and goes back to the kitchen. Eddie and Max look at each other. She refrains from telling him to stop salting his food so much like she used to. One time she tasted his food and gagged because it was so salty. The salt is bad for his hypertension, bad for his heart.

"So, Max, what do you want for Christmas?" Tutu chews a bite of apple pie.

Max would rather have some pie. She watches Tutu press her fork through another chunk of Granny Smith apple smothered in butter, cinnamon, a little nutmeg, a little vanilla, lemon juice, and the secret ingredient—apricot preserves—inside the shell. Max used to make the pie on these kinds of occasions. Then she watches Eddie spread his mashed potatoes and gravy that he saved for last into a large circle and salt it. "I'd like to know what is real and what isn't," she says.

Phyllis comes in with a glass of peach sparkling wine on ice. She sits down next to Max and props one leg on Max's chair. Her feet are bare except for her gold toe ring. She sets her glass on top of her knee. Phyllis appears totally casual. She often does when she's nervous.

"What do you mean, sweetheart?"

"I just can't tell what is the drugs and what is me."

"Ooh, ooh! I know how to break that!" Tutu swings her legs up into a cross-legged position and pontificates with her fork. "The truth! The truth nips all that in the bud."

Max looks at Tutu and decides one day she should choke her.

Eddie salts his last bite of potatoes.

"Edward," Phyllis says, sipping from her drink.

"Leave me alone," Eddie growls and slips the fork in his mouth.

Max finds Frances in her pants pocket but doesn't know how she got there. She puts her next to the cranberries.

"You don't even know what the truth is, Max!" Frances says as some cranberry sauce seeps into her wing.

Max glares at her and imagines swatting her and how that would feel in the sweet spot of her hand or even a tennis racket and then the sound of Frances connecting with the wall or maybe a window and the glass breaking.

"I'm high!" Max slams her hands on the table. "I'm high right now. Well, I wouldn't call it high; there's stuff in my system. I'm more sick than anything, but I'm not strung out. I'm sick because I'm not strung out. I hadn't done heroin for a week, I think. When I saw you, Dad, I wasn't on heroin, I was on coke. I was selling stuff to Tutu because the building manager had a heart attack and died right in front of me, so I stole his drugs, and Carlotta, his boss, thought I killed him, and she was grateful because he had raped and given drugs to her daughter who then OD'd and died, and now that I think about it, the lady is just sad and lonely! And crazy! So she gave me a load of heroin, I mean a load, and told me to sell it. Just to keep me around, you see?" Max looks at Phyllis. "Anyway, I didn't know it at first, that she was happy I killed Grandpops, and I thought she was going to kill me. Her daughter just died a couple months ago for Christ's sake! People do strange things, but Tutu was going to buy some stuff, and then she stole it."

Max hears her stomach growl and gurgle. Eddie pours more Diet Coke. Tutu smiles at Max.

Eddie says, "I know she did."

And Max understands that Eddie told Tutu to take the bag of heroin. Eddie and Max watch Eddie's soda can as he turns it around and around.

"So what do you want? A fucking medal for your confession?" Eddie chokes a bit and drinks some soda.

"Eddie . . ." Tutu pushes her bottle of Evian toward him, and the Dolly Parton music ends. She holds her head in her hands, elbows on the table. "That was excellent, Max."

"Would you wind me up, please?" Frances says. Max, holding her too tightly, winds the metal dial between her wings. Frances yelps, and then the melody of "Amazing Grace" plays one note at a time.

"Jesus," Max mutters under her breath, feeling sick with the sentimentality of it all.

The four of them sit there in silence for a moment. Eddie folds his napkin and then puts his fork and knife on the plate. Phyllis runs her hand through her hair, moving it off her neck. Tutu picks up the crust of her piece of pie and takes small bites.

"Finally, an audience," Frances whispers to Max.

But Tutu talks over her song. "You know, the guy who wrote this was like a slave trader, but then he found God."

"Really?" Phyllis says, making do with the ice left in her glass.

"Oh yeah, he was the lowest of the low, sailor guy, drinking and cursing. I mean, this guy had been through it, publicly flogged for desertion, and then he was beaten regularly by his boss, the big slave trader, and then when he was steering his own ship full of slaves through hours of a vicious storm, he asked God for help. I forget the rest, but I know he eventually helped abolish slavery."

"Maxella." Eddie has been wiping under his glasses and down his cheeks with his napkin.

Frances stops playing her simple melody. Now it's just the chimes outside reacting to the wind with their random notes.

"Why'd you do that?" Eddie tries to find the right word as he points his finger at Frances. "Manipulative."

Max tells the truth. "She asked me to."

"Good." Eddie throws his napkin on his plate. "The fucking angel talks to her, Phyllis." He declares this as if it were a most wonderful thing.

Phyllis's toes wiggle under Max's leg. She smiles at her. "She's always talked to dolls. And part of that, the special part, is that sometimes, if you're really lucky, they talk back."

"Jesus Christ, Phyllis!"

Eddie would leave but he needs to make the point that he is not going to cosign this.

"Maxella." Eddie gathers up what he's got left. "Maxella, I think you'd better leave."

"All she really wants to know is if you love her," Tutu says.

"Of course we love her! But she has to love herself. I'm not going to be the one to kill her."

Tutu rolls her eyes and grabs her lips with her fingers, forcing them shut.

A buzzing starts inside Max's ears and the room begins to tip. She has to get out of there before she falls out.

"Your body is so done with you," says Frances, slowly walking away from the cranberries, Tutu, and Eddie, toward Max.

"I know, but it's not my body that's—"

"Oh for Christ's sake!" Eddie shouts. "If it's not your body then who the hell's is it?! Jesus!"

Max doesn't want to tell him she was talking to Frances.

"Well, some part or other is certainly dying," Frances says. "It's plain as day to me."

"Honey, eat. You've got to eat something. Low blood sugar," Phyllis says.

"It's true!" But Max meant that for Frances.

"So eat," Phyllis says.

Max looks at her plate. Everything on it is brown and gelatinous with gravy. Max thinks she can see some tiny hairs sticking out of the turkey skin. Her face gets hot, then her pores open to let out some sweat. She picks up the fork and moves it through the thick oyster stuffing.

"I think I better go," she manages to mutter.

"I am going with you." Tutu stands up so fast her chair flies backward. Tutu fixes the chair and Max pushes herself with all her might out of hers. She inhales loudly. She needs air.

"I am going to give you a piece of apple pie to take with you," Phyllis says.

"I'm just thirsty." Max pours some eggnog from the heavy pitcher into her glass and swallows it in two gulps. The rum hits her like sour milk.

"I just have to use the bathroom, then I'll go." She sees Eddie shaking his head, angry, because it's anger that keeps him together.

She closes the bathroom door. The toilet seat is oak. It knocks against the porcelain when she lifts it up. She bends over the toilet, and nothing happens. Sometimes, she would stash rigs on the top of the medicine cabinet above the sink, too high for Phyllis to reach without a step stool. Max runs her hands over the top of the cabinet and sees herself in the mirror. She starts dry heaving, falls on her knees, bows over the toilet, and thankfully vomits. Now she should feel a little better. This is what happens before a habit. The eggnog didn't help. She pictures her lies falling into the toilet and all the hurt she causes being flushed away. She splashes cold water on her face and rubs it into her hair. She turns off the water and rests her head in the sink against the cold tile, taking big breaths through her nose, which doesn't seem to give her enough oxygen, ever. She takes her jacket, which was hanging on the old-fashioned scale, and goes back into the dining room. Tutu is holding her fake fur coat and waiting for Max in the alcove.

Phyllis hands Max half of a pie with Saran Wrap covering it. She turns to Eddie, licking apple pie off her fingers. "Remember when I got arrested for shoplifting?"

"Not now, Phyllis." Eddie winces as he gets out of his chair and starts taking empty plates to the kitchen.

Phyllis holds Max's arm. "Well, they were mostly samples. How do you think I got all that Chanel makeup you stole from me!?"

"I never stole your makeup."

"You loved that makeup."

Phyllis loses it. She starts to cry and tucks her head under Max's chin and hugs her. Max's arms, which were hanging useless, now wrap around her tiny mother. But she lets Phyllis hold her up so Phyllis can feel like she is strong for this moment.

"I just miss all the parts of you you don't remember, I guess."

Max lets go of her, and Phyllis holds her face. "Just don't die, okay?"

"Oh my God, she has to die." Tutu stands next to the table, watching. "Don't look at me like that. I mean in order to live!" Tutu's beady brown eyes look at Max. "I think I better stay here with your parents."

"You should, they'd like that."

Tutu's mouth drops open and she covers it.

"I mean it," Max says. "They're really good."

Max takes a last look, quickly, before anything else happens. Phyllis waves and Eddie stands behind her, busy with a toothpick in his mouth.

twenty-seven

MAX FEELS LIKE her limbs are too heavy, while her head floats just above her body as she walks past the jasmine and out the gate. Her truck is there and it's not too inviting, seeing as it's got no heater, but she's going to get in it. She smells the roses and the jasmine and feels the eyes of Phyllis, Eddie, and Tutu watching her. She does her best not to swerve as she walks to the truck. She puts her hands in her pockets to look for her keys. In one pocket is the snow globe she forgot to give to Phyllis, and in the other is Frances. She's glad Frances is quiet for a moment. She doesn't feel like talking. She has just enough energy to drive. Max gets her keys, climbs in, starts up the engine, and turns the radio to the classical station. Beethoven's Moonlight Sonata plays.

"Fucking hell," she says, and turns it off, but it still plays in her head. She looks at the house and pulls Frances out of her pocket.

"Where now?" Frances asks.

"Back to Carlotta's." Max puts her on the seat.

"Don't you want to stop?" Frances asks.

The trees are like hooded and hunched old men. Wise keepers of secrets. She's passed out against them. They have seen her healthy, dancing in the street. And lying down in it for a kiss. She and Ernest jumped out of the truck because the Bee Gees came on the radio singing "Stayin' Alive" and it was important to dance to it. Ernest had his own way of moving his hips and giving little kicks, with his fingers pointing at trees, houses, the sky, and then to the ground. He put his finger on Max's head and she twirled around and around until she fell to the ground. When she was lying in the middle of the street, Ernest kissed her while everything was spinning, and she was happy that he could be corny like her. Max rolls forward and sees herself in the street doing these things. She drives through herself.

"I'm cold," Frances says.

Max puts Frances in her pocket to keep her warm. She pulls slowly away from the curb and rolls through the shadows and light. The street turns blank and gray.

Carlotta stands in her narrow kitchen at the counter, mashing bananas with the end of a child-sized baseball bat, a clean white pair of Keds on the metal feet of her new legs. There is something lonely about Carlotta with legs, without her chair. It's as if with the slightest push she could topple. Max is glad there's no sign of Albert.

Carlotta squeezes her nose as she sneezes.

"My friend came over and got the legs on and got me dressed."

"Good friend." Max wonders how long she's going to make her wait, or if she'll have to come right out and ask. Maybe Carlotta doesn't get high on Christmas. She looks at the altar for Yosakwa. A tiny box wrapped in aluminum foil with a ribbon sits by her picture. Other than that there are no gifts.

"Humility is a good friend, but you wouldn't know about humility." Carlotta looks at Max. "Albert thinks he's the only one. He thinks he is God, that's his problem; your problem, too."

"I'm just trying." Max cracks her knuckles against the white octagon tiles of the kitchen counter.

"Trying to what? Don't try."

Max sighs. "I'm trying to make everything all right."

"Some people are born selfish. They want what they want. They take it. Everything they do has a selfish motive. Even if you want to help someone, it's to make yourself feel good. That's just the way it is, so why in hell are you trying to be something that's not natural to who you are? I'm telling you, sweetie, if you just accept that you're a selfish sinner, you will feel a whole lot better."

Carlotta turns her attention back to smashing bananas.

"This is my banana bat, and sometimes I'll use it for a knee or two. Maybe I should give yours a good whack." She scrapes the end of the bat with her finger and flicks the sweet-smelling paste into the shallow bowl.

"Was it Yosakwa's?"

Carlotta cleans her finger on the side of the bowl as her penciled eyebrows rise. "Yes, it was." Then she snorts, "You know it wasn't Albert's!"

Max tries to ignore the pain in her head.

Still not enough banana mush, so Carlotta takes a few more rotten ones and starts peeling. She throws two to Max. Max picks the black skin off and holds them out to Carlotta.

"Oh, you're so tired," Carlotta says. She puts the bruised fruit into the bowl and picks up the bat with two hands, slightly rocking on her Keds as if she were on stilts. Max's arms have already dropped toward the floor, useless, and she sits down. She tries to take deep breaths in through her nose but that just makes her more nauseated from the heroin. Things are crackling in the corners of the ceiling. How long can Carlotta keep mashing bananas? Just one slightly yellow piece, one hit, would push the heroin right through her.

"You don't have friends, do you?" Carlotta bangs the bat into the bowl and the bowl slams onto the counter.

"Friends? No." As she looks up at Carlotta, the base of Max's head rests on the top of her back like she doesn't have a neck. "But you told me you wanted your legs back."

Carlotta tears the wrapping off a block of butter and plops it into a large mixing bowl. She holds the counter as she walks to the cupboard, opens it and pulls out vanilla, cinnamon, nutmeg, and cloves, tapping them on the counter one at a time to loosen the contents.

"Don't get up." She heaves a full bag of flour off the shelf. "I got it."

Max's temples absorb most of the shock from each erratic sound wave. She has no intention of getting up.

"Do you like poetry?"

Well, hell, Carlotta is plum full of surprises, Max thinks. Her eyes are drawn to the smudges left by fingers on the doors of the cupboard, probably Albert's, since Carlotta's hands have never been there before now. "Sometimes," Max answers.

"I memorize a poem a month. It settles my head. If you can tell me who wrote this one I won't smash your left knee. Bet that would give you some humility."

"Really? You really think you could hurt me?" Max takes her eyes from the fingerprints, finds Carlotta's right ear and focuses on its sagging lobe. She holds her knees in their cross-legged position while Carlotta pours flour into a large measuring cup. Her face is dewy. It could be kneaded like dough. The gold hoops stretch her piercings and make half-moons against the planet of her face. She is round circles except for her eyes, which are pulled into her skull. Either that or they are fighting to get out of her. She sets the bag of flour down hard and some of it spouts up and dissipates in the air around her. Her face is lost in flour smoke while her eyes disappear; then some of the flour settles on her brow bone, her nose and cheeks.

Carlotta picks up the electric beater and turns it on. She lets the metal beat against the sides of the bowl and ignores the sprays of mixture. Max wipes a chunk from her cheek. Carlotta scoops the mashed bananas into the big bowl with the whipped butter, flour, and spices.

"The secret is just how you blend the ingredients. You can't thin out the bananas too much, got to leave them thick." She rubs the remaining butter along the insides of a square pan. "He'll be back, you know. He hasn't got a good hustle besides slinging and nobody hooks up a dope-sick junky for nothing. And nothing is all he got. So, tell me, what's he going to do,

huh? Sell his ass? He'd probably like that." She remembers the
oven and tests if it's hot. Apparently it's not. She slams it shut.
"Did you give him his coat?" She crosses her arms under her
low-hanging breasts.

Max presses her temples. "Yeah."

"And what did he say?"

"He told me about the angelfish."

"Stupid kid." Carlotta shakes her head and puts the pan in
the oven. "He killed that fish. That's classic Albert. He'll be
back. You watch."

Max can't take it anymore. "Can I have my hit now?" She
stands up even though it feels like hands are pushing her down.

"You want a shot instead, Puppy? Forget about your hot
shot?" Carlotta checks the temperature.

The bat is on the countertop to her right.

"My poem first." She turns to Max.

Max's nausea starts to bring her back to her knees but instead
she takes the bat. Carlotta lunges for it. She slips and falls backward
to the floor. She looks like a repentant demon, her face spackled with
flour, her eyes bulging and her upper lip curled back.

"Ay, Mami, give me my bat." Carlotta reaches her hand up to
Max. Max leans on the bat and waits for her dizzy spell to pass.

"Come on, help me!" Carlotta's jowls and the skin on her
neck shake as she tries to push herself up.

Max holds the bat out to her to pull her up. But with her
hands around Yosakwa's bat she feels she has the right to take a
swing, not to hit, but to swing fast and hard. The bat flies above
Carlotta's face. Max tightens her grip and takes another swing,
this time from the right. The glass part of the oven door cracks.
Carlotta covers her head and screams. Max swings again and lets

242 (michele matheson

the bat fly where it wants. It rises above her head and hits the cupboard that bears Albert's fingerprints. The shock of the blow runs down her arms, stopping at her elbows. The old door drops off its hinges. Some of the spices fall out and roll off the counter on top of Carlotta. Carlotta has curled into a fetal position.

"Don't hurt me! Please!"

Max swings again, hitting the bag of flour. It bursts into clouds and then drops onto Carlotta's side, forcing a loud groan from her. The sound causes the bat to fall from Max's hands.

"You," Max catches her breath to finish, "are not a good mother." She stumbles to Albert's room to get what she came for.

Max hears Carlotta whimpering to Jesus as she looks under Albert's coffee table. Inside the cigar box is everything she needs. She begins to lay each item out, the pipe, the baggie of crack, and the syringe. She wasn't going to do any heroin, but it's there in balloons. Then, Carlotta's voice, more shrill than she has ever heard it, comes into the room.

"It's called 'This Time'! No use abusing, when we could have good loving! / I was too blind to realize, I got rights to a honey prize. / Now I got the devil in my bones, and I'm playing mean." Max strikes a match, smells the sulfur, and likes the sound of it igniting and crackling against Carlotta's voice. She lights the purple votive candle on the coffee table because it's easier to cook heroin in a spoon over a candle when your hands are shaking. "This time he's going down." Carlotta stretches out the word "down," mightily sending the Devil there. "Now, what I do ain't up to you. / I got my hands on the Devil's throat," Carlotta sings. "My grip's so tight I ain't never letting go. / And I say that this time, I'm playing for keeps. This time, it's up to me."

Max watches the flame grow. It is calm and bright white in its middle for a moment and then it stretches tall and thin, swirling, making a little tornado of smoke as if it were trying to shake itself free from the wick, from the blue part. Max wonders who the father of Albert and Yosakwa was and if Carlotta ever misses him. She sits forward and hovers above the paraphernalia on the coffee table. The flame keeps rising, flickering in no particular pattern, waving streams of black smoke like a warning signal. She feels her throat collapsing, and her heart feels like it's stuck. It's trying to rise up hot through her jugular. Her fingers touch her throat and then the big vein. It bulges but she feels no pulse. Isn't there an expression that goes, "her heart is stuck in her throat"? Max wonders, but then decides yes, there surely is. For a second, she feels like she knows answers, like maybe answers could be found where love begins. She has to blow at the candle twice before it goes out.

Max automatically puts the pipe and the syringe, the heroin, coke, and crack back into the cigar box and into the pocket of her postwoman's jacket, just because it's what she came there for. She gets up and walks to the kitchen.

It's hard for her to tell if the whiteness in the air is the flour or the thin veil that separates realities. She stops. She can barely see Carlotta, still on her back, her legs splayed. "You wrote that," Max says.

"Good guess." Carlotta's chest rises and falls.

"It made me remember."

Max kneels in front of Carlotta's legs. Carlotta tries to kick at her, but the legs are too heavy for her weak body. Max was going to take the legs back; she's going to need the money. Instead, she puts the cigar box next to Carlotta.

"Remember what?" Carlotta looks at the box.

"It's—I can't—it's an action."

Carlotta lies there like a baby bird that fell out of the nest, blinking and fuzzy. "So now you don't want any drugs?"

The flour is in piles around Carlotta like stuff.

"I can't."

"You going to leave me like this, on the floor?"

Max lies down next to Carlotta. Carlotta stiffens. It feels good to lie down, but Max has to go. She rolls to her side and uses the counter to pull herself up and then steady herself. "Here," Max says, "take my hands."

Carlotta is heavier than Max thought. She almost drops her when Carlotta's hands slip through hers. Max reaches out and catches her by the wrists, and feels something in her chest. Yosakwa's old baseball bat lies next to Albert's cigar box, some things Carlotta has left of them.

Max hugs her. Carlotta's head rests on Max's shoulder. She grunts. Max cradles Carlotta's head and wraps her other arm around her. Her hand is snug between two rolls of flesh. She hears short restless breaths from Carlotta, like a sleeping child with fever. Carlotta's rose oil smells too sweet; Max holds her breath so she can hold Carlotta a moment longer there on the other side of blame. Inside her eyes, which are squeezed shut, she sees Phyllis for a second and longs to have the same strange feeling when she hugs her again someday.

Max lets go and starts to pick up some broken glass.

"Just get out of here," Carlotta says.

Max tosses the glass in the garbage. "Sorry." She walks to the door, then turns around.

Carlotta is wiping the flour from her eyelids. She sneezes again and then she sets the timer for her bread. "The bread will be done in about an hour. Come back if you're hungry."

"Thank you." Max shuts the door behind her.

The carpet in the hall is maroon with mustard vines running through it. She waits for the elevator. She pulls the gate closed. As soon as the elevator jerks to descend, she vomits, but only a little. On the ground floor, she holds the door open for a small girl carrying a white plastic purse. The girl casually holds her nose as she steps in. Perhaps people often vomit in the elevator.

Max steps into the darkest part of night that's just before dawn and finds her truck. She thanks her heart for never stopping. It feels funny, like it's soft, she thinks. Maybe some light is hitting it.

The streets are nice when there's almost no one on them. Her eyes are slightly unfocused, so the houses and trees to the sides of her are what grab her attention. They rush past her in a blur and the road disappears beneath her. Max gets on Sunset Boulevard because it runs straight to the ocean and she wants to pretend she is gliding on a river vein. She follows the yellow lines in the middle of the road and for a long time it feels like she's surrounded by green, in a tunnel of trees. Then the world opens up and the beach is in front of her, the mountains to the right, Santa Monica Pier to the left. The new moon makes the night blacker, giving the stars a chance to really shine. Ruffles of sheer clouds slide from the sky into the gray water. She hears the waves, but they seem very far away.

Max is walking on the sand and it's like climbing up little hills. It's soft and so cold it feels wet, but the sand rubs her toes inside her kung fu slippers, so she takes them off. Max watches the ocean, trying to take her mind off her body, and listens to the seagulls chirrup. Piles of seaweed are discarded on the sand like dirty dresses. This is as good a time as any, she thinks. The ocean has always had answers. Far out there is an abyss where something is listening and even paying attention. When she says the name of someone she's mad at or worried about, or who is lost to her, the ocean takes it and pummels it and then brings it to that place. Anyway, it makes Max feel better.

Max stands at the water's edge. Some oil liners break up the horizon, and two pelicans hover above the surface, then, seeing something, plunge into the water. Her shivers are becoming annoying because she can't make them stop, so she sits down and hugs her knees. Tiny airholes appear in the sand when the ocean draws back, like she and the sand and the waves are breathing together. And bird footprints have left a pattern of lines the water hasn't washed away yet. Max sticks her fingers in the holes and wonders what happened to all the seashells. She likes how the ocean is loud, then quiet, how it breathes.

"Mom and Dad," she says. The ocean swallows her voice and crushes it under a wave.

Max feels as if she is sitting next to herself. She holds her hand open on the sand and waits for the feeling to come like Ernest is holding it.

"Now what?" she asks.

Her eyelids feel heavy, but she is not going to let them close. The ocean is like a big dark stage. Images begin to float above it so she lets them.

The seagulls circling overhead think she has something for them.

While the ocean touches her feet, she whispers, "Me." Then she says her name loudly: "Maxella Gordon." It feels like she is referring to someone else as she wiggles her sore foot in the water. The water quietly slinks away.

Fog is beginning to smear the line where the ocean meets the sky; a wave breaks, sprays and rolls in.

"Gigi and Grace."

One treatment center had a poisonous grapefruit tree in the middle of the courtyard. Tables and chairs were set up under it, but no one could eat the damn grapefruits. That tree was bountiful, and sometimes the fruit would fall on the addicts, right on their heads. Gigi had died and Max would look at the tree and feel bothered. She knew Gigi was hungry. Gigi used to eat a grapefruit every day and when Max was a little girl, when she stayed with Gigi, she would too. Max had secretly rolled a grapefruit that had fallen into her bag of books, went into the bathroom, and ate it. It wouldn't make her sick, she thought, because it was for Gigi.

She squeezes her hand into a fist because it still feels empty. But then she feels Valeria's bat again, and sees Carlotta lying dusted in flour, shaking on the floor.

Max bows her head. "Jesus, man," she says. "Carlotta, too."

Max concentrates and opens her fist. Rocks are scattered along the shoreline, and empty beer bottles, some kind of junk food wrappers. "Albert," she says and something hurts high on her chest, scaring her, as she watches Albert pick up the trash.

Ernest walks toward her from the ocean, holding his own against the waves as they push him forward. He rides one in, stands up and pushes the hair out of his eyes. He looks at her like she is an unsafe place. Max closes her eyes and they are belly dancing in her kitchen. Then he lies on top of her, securing her deeper into the sand, and holds her. "You smell like a puppy," he says and drifts off, back into the gray water.

Tutu sits next to her, a pale orphan, looking guilty about having stayed with Phyllis and Eddie. Max smiles at her. "And Tutu. Also Wolf, I guess."

Max lies back onto the sand and looks at the morning stars. She grips the sand like the earth is spinning and she has to hold on. The chill soothes her burning head, and she drags her arms in the sand above her and opens her legs, moving her limbs up and down and in and out, trying to make a sand angel. After a few seconds she stops, tired, and a little less cold on her body. She searches her pockets, takes out the snow globe, and shakes it.

"Frances." She pulls Frances out of the other pocket, having forgotten her all this time. "Check out the sky."

Max holds Frances upright on her chest by her little hands. She never noticed how perfect Frances's hands are. Frances looks at her with her head tilted and her arms outstretched as if she is going to start singing.

"Frances?"

Frances's eyes don't move. Max taps on her cheeks with her index finger, but Frances's eyes don't blink. She touches the eyes. They are hard and dry and the porcelain of her face is chipped. Underneath Frances's tattered wings, Max finds the metal dial and winds it. No music plays; there is only silence in between the breaking of waves. Max places Frances in the crook of her neck, and stares up at the stars. What can she expect from Rite Aid?

The ocean now touches Max's heels. Her stomach collapses inside her ribs as she gasps. "Banana bread," she says, smelling it. The cold water cramps her feet, and she tries to relax into the sensation. Under her postwoman's coat her upper body is warm. The misty air bites her cheeks and neck, the parts of her that are exposed.

The water soaks the back of her coat, washing some of the dirt off Grandma Grace's polyester pants. The salt will make them white again. It's quiet for a second while the ocean settles, and she thinks how there are sounds in it she will never hear. She rolls her head to the side, watching the ocean come at her, and her body stiffens for it. When the water leaves, a petal of pink sequins from the rose edging the right leg has fallen away. "I'm but a little piece of you. I'm feeling pretty small here, but I'm staying like this."

As if it heard her, the ocean pulls back, and then floods her neck and Frances there, then her ears and the back of her head. Max doesn't want to move. This way she will be clean for when the water around her body trades for air; she knows that the best of her will have been left and the bad carried out to the place, to the abyss. It will just take some time to let it work. Waiting is worse than quiet, but she is going to wait here for as long as it takes. After a while, the cold becomes part of her and she can't feel her limbs. At least the shivers are subsiding. And Max still has her eyes open when she finally falls asleep.

Acknowledgements

MY GRATITUDE AND thanks to the following people for their generous advice, guidance, and support: Jim Krusoe, Lee Montgomery, Meg Storey, and Elizabeth Winick. My friends and family. Fellow writers and specifically Susan Jonaitis, Molly Martin, Dylan Landis, John Lescroart, and Yasmin Indrizzo. Michelle Wildgen and the design team at Tin House.